A COLD DEATH
IN AMSTERDAM

A COLD DEATH IN AMSTERDAM

ANJA DE JAGER

Constable • London

CONSTABLE

First published in Great Britain in 2015 by Constable

Copyright © Anja de Jager, 2015

1 3 5 7 9 10 8 6 4 2

The moral right of the author has been asserted.

A CIP catalogue record for this book
is available from the British Library.

ISBN: 978-1-47212-059-5 (hardback)
ISBN: 978-1-47212-060-1 (trade paperback)

Typeset in Bembo by Photoprint, Torquay
Printed and bound in Great Britain by
CPI Group (UK) Ltd, Croydon, CR0 4YY

Papers used by Constable are from well-managed forests and
other responsible sources.

MIX
Paper from
responsible sources
FSC
www.fsc.org   FSC® C104740

Constable
An imprint of
Little, Brown Book Group
Carmelite House
50 Victoria Embankment
London EC4Y 0DZ

An Hachette UK Company
www.hachette.co.uk

www.littlebrown.co.uk

Voor mijn vader

Chapter One

They were strange, those minutes that ticked by slowly as I waited for the ambulance to turn up. My concentration never wandered; my focus was purely on stemming the bleeding.

I'd had no real reason to pull into the petrol station, but the streaming lights had drawn my eye from more than a kilometre away, promising company and warmth on this deadly cold night. Although I was only ten minutes away from home, I had glanced down at the petrol gauge, and the half-empty tank had given me enough of an excuse to pull in. I put my indicator light on. It was 2 a.m. and there was nobody else on the road, but it was a reflex – an action that came from muscle memory not from thought, as was grabbing my handbag when I got out, and holstering my gun.

Outside the car it was icy cold; fog flowed from my mouth with each breath. A shiver ran down my arm when my hand touched the metal cap on the petrol tank. If I had kept it there for much longer, my skin would have frozen tight to the car. I put the petrol pump in with my free hand tucked under my arm.

I didn't often get out of the car on these nightly drives that took me from one end of the country to the other. In the Netherlands that didn't take much, of course: a two-hour drive east from my home in Amsterdam got me to the German border; one hour south would make me cross into Belgium, and forty-five minutes north would land me in the sea. I tried to limit myself to one hour, with just the hum of the car's engine to keep me company along the dark roads. It was normally enough to help me get to sleep when I got back home. When it was one of those nights, I couldn't stay in my flat; I needed to get out. I'd been offered counselling, but so far I'd refused it. Counselling would mean talking about it. Telling somebody would mean reliving it. Why would I want to do that, when I was trying so hard to forget?

As I watched the counter on the petrol pump tick up, I realised I was finally feeling calm. I could face myself in the mirror without wanting to attack my own skin. Tonight had been a bad one.

Just then, another car pulled up on to the forecourt and stopped in front of the shop. A man got out but I couldn't see him properly as some of the steel construction holding the roof up blocked my view. He'd probably just run out of cigarettes, or maybe he too was just looking for someone to talk to. I turned back to watch the numbers on the display race up.

The jolt on the pump came when the meter wasn't even on 20 euros. I dribbled in a few more drops to get it to the round figure then walked over to pay. The path of lights deepened the winter darkness even further and made the ice crystals on the ground sparkle like diamonds. Now that I'd been outside for a few minutes, my toes were cold inside my boots. The weather forecasters had been predicting snow for a few days now, but none had fallen. The only thing that was falling was the temperature: with the clear skies, it was getting down to minus ten. It would grow colder still before dawn, in that lonely time before the sun came up and created a new day.

I bunched my fingers into fists inside the pockets of my jacket to keep my hands as warm as I could, grateful when the door to the shop opened automatically and I was greeted by a blast of heat and some modern rendition of 'Silent Night'.

The man behind the counter — young, a student maybe — turned to me and the warning look in his eyes made me come to a halt. I saw the other man, one hand in his pocket. He was wearing a balaclava so I could only see his eyes. I wished I could have had a better look at him when he'd arrived.

'Stop right there,' the man warned me.

I stood still. The automatic door behind me opened and closed again with a whoosh, followed by a short stream of cold air on my neck. I didn't move. It opened and closed again and I took a step forward.

'I said stop.'

I pointed behind me. 'The doors.'

He nodded, one hand still in his pocket, and addressed the

guy behind the counter. 'Give me the cash now and nobody gets hurt.'

When he said the clichéd words, I wanted to smile but kept a straight face. 'I'm a police officer,' I told him. 'You're under arrest.' I felt completely calm even when the man pulled a gun out of his pocket and pointed it at me. Out of the corner of my eye I saw the shop assistant duck behind the counter, his head now hidden by a small plastic Christmas tree.

'You don't want to do this,' I said. 'You want to put the gun away now and come with me quietly.'

The gun in his hand wobbled all over the place. He should be using his other hand to keep it steady.

'Because right now, your options are either to put the gun away or to shoot me,' I said. All the textbooks would tell me to keep talking. Instead, my hand went to my own gun and I undid the button on the holster without my eyes ever leaving his. The palm of my hand fitted around the grip of the weapon. Against my cold fingers it felt warm, heated up from sitting on my hip. I pulled it out slowly.

The CD of Christmas songs finished and the night was silent at last. I anticipated the impact of the bullet in my body, the pain that would take away all other pains, and bring the final end to everything. The events of the past six months, which had led to the discovery of Wendy Leeuwenhoek's body, ran through my mind – each incident and each mistake as clear and urgent to me as what was happening right now, in the petrol station shop. I made the movement slow, raising the gun centimetre by centimetre, inviting him to shoot and giving him time to make up his mind. Maybe I should have gone fast and drawn an automatic reaction. His eyes were locked into mine. We stood like that for a few seconds, which my total concentration turned into an eternity.

Everything I'd noticed before became insignificant: the half-price Christmas cards and reduced boxes of candles in a bin to the side, the rows of chocolate bars in front of the counter and the packs of cigarettes behind it. All I was aware of were his eyes, which seemed incredibly blue, staring at me from the black balaclava. Every thump of my heart against my ribcage felt slow even though I knew my pulse must be racing. I took a deep breath.

When the shot finally came, the sound was harsh in the silence. My ears rang with the bang. I could smell the smoke, but I couldn't feel anything. For a second I thought it was just the adrenaline that kept the pain at bay and I waited for the agony to kick in. Then I looked down and realised he'd missed. He was only a few metres away and he'd missed.

I increased the pressure on the trigger and shot his arm. It was a textbook manoeuvre: left hand under right wrist to stabilise the gun, and it wasn't hard from this distance. He dropped his gun with what seemed like relief and sagged to his knees. I took three steps towards him, bent over, put my left hand to his arm to stop the bleeding and asked the youth behind the counter to call 112. After I'd holstered my gun, one hand still applying pressure to his arm, I pulled off his balaclava and saw his blond curls. He was young, maybe a

5

teenager. I felt sick. Why hadn't I let him have another go? Had the guy behind the counter ever really been in danger?

The kid wanted to talk and I read him his rights. He told me his name: Ben van Ravensberger. I told him he should have a lawyer. I tried to keep him silent because I didn't want to hear what he had to say. But he kept repeating: 'Don't you know who I am? My uncle is famous.'

I waited for what seemed a long time, but would turn out to have been less than ten minutes, until my legs started to cramp from crouching by his side and my voice was hoarse from talking to him continuously. I'd put a tourniquet on his arm to stop the bleeding. Apart from calling the emergency services, the guy manning the shop was useless. He looked in a state of shock: his face white, his hands shaking too much to help me with Ben.

Now I heard the siren of an ambulance and the sound had never been more welcome: I could finally take my eyes from the kid. The paramedics took over, bandaged him up and took him out on a stretcher that was only a precaution. One of the paramedics told me it was just a flesh wound and that the kid should be fine. My colleagues would meet me at the hospital. It wouldn't be a problem for me: the kid had shot first, his bullet still wedged in the wall of the petrol station, and I had followed the correct procedure.

I drove behind the ambulance to Amsterdam's Slotervaart Hospital, walked beside the stretcher through the corridors and waited with Ben until the doctors could see him. It was warmer here indoors, but I didn't take my coat off: I was only wearing my pyjama top underneath.

Ben was telling me again about his famous uncle.

I didn't want to listen any more.

'I'm a law student,' he said. 'This is just a mistake.'

'You can forget all about law now.'

'But I can tell you something that—'

'What's a law student doing holding up a petrol station?' I interrupted him. He wanted to hold my hand as if I was his mother or something, and tears were rolling down his cheeks.

'Can't we make a deal? I can tell you—'

'Be quiet now. Tell my colleagues later.'

'My uncle, he's famous. But he's killed someone.' Ben's eyes drifted close. 'Or at least he said he did.' His last words sounded mumbled.

I didn't say anything but just sat there with his hand in mine until the nurse wheeled him away.

Chapter Two

The bells of the Westerkerk rang out over the streets of
Amsterdam. It was 7 a.m. and still dark outside. I'd been
home for three hours. As I reached out to switch on the light
by the side of my bed, my hand bumped against something
and I heard the rattle of the pills the doctor had prescribed
two weeks ago. He'd said that these would make me sleep
deeply and stop the dreams. He said I was suffering from
post-traumatic stress and that he'd recently seen a number of
other police officers with the same complaint, many of them
women. I'd been annoyed with the generalisation. After all,
I'd been in CID for over ten years and in uniform before
then and I'd never needed pills or anything else. I didn't take
the medication. I deserved my dreams.

I slid my legs from under the duvet. The parquet floor
sucked the warmth from my feet and the pale blue walls,
which normally reminded me of a washed-out hazy summer sky, seemed the colour of frozen limbs. I peeked around
the curtain and saw that the forecasted snow had arrived in
the night and most of Amsterdam's sins and dirt were now
hidden beneath it. The snow had come too late for a white

Christmas but just in time to swaddle the newborn year in a blanket of innocence. The wasteland of roofs before me were covered with centimetres of white that took away the edges and left everything with a smooth contour.

I dumped my clean clothes on the bed, ready to strip off one set, shower and get as quickly as possible into the other. I didn't care what I was going to wear — it didn't matter what I looked like. Thick trousers, I thought — yesterday's brown tweed ones — with an almost matching brown jacket over a cream woollen jumper. And that was just for indoors.

In the bathroom, cold air blasted through a small gap around the window that I never managed to shut completely. A thick layer of ice had flowered on the glass. I wished it was on the mirror, so I couldn't see myself. Lack of sleep was taking its toll. I scraped my hair back in a pony tail and plaited it. It made me look worse as it hid nothing. I made no attempt to put any make-up on: I deserved to look this bad.

I was forty-two but didn't look a day under fifty.

Showered and dressed, I went downstairs, opened the front door and entered the snowstorm in the dark. My feet sank into the soft powder — there had to be ten centimetres at least. The pavement was deserted, so my footprints appeared in virgin snow. It made a whispering sound, as if I was crushing something fragile underfoot with every step. I wanted to close my eyes against the wind — to close my eyes against the world. Instead I moved along mechanically, too tired to worry about slipping.

The snowflakes whirled around my face, floated in front of my eyes and danced this way and that, in time with the thoughts inside my head. I couldn't stop thinking about my dream. I had seen Wendy Leeuwenhoek's face as I knew it from her photo, seen it decay slowly, frame by frame, into the white skull I'd found. I saw the flies laying their eggs. I saw the grubs eating her flesh. I could see them now in the falling flakes.

I trudged past the bakery on the corner, the small bar where I never drank, the church that was shared by Syrian Orthodox Jews and Roman Catholics, an emblem of Amsterdam's multiculturalism, and an endless row of seventeenth-century canal houses that were now home to banks and businesses. I walked slowly until I crossed the final canal to the police station on the Marnixstraat. Stopping for a while on the bridge, I let my eyes follow the fall of snowflakes down to where they were visible in the ring of streetlights. They moved in and out of sight before they drifted to the street and had their short life reduced even further by darkness. One landed on my eyelashes and turned the world white until it melted into a tear; others floated onto the cling film of ice that had been stretched over the water in the night and was barely thick enough to carry the weight of the flakes.

Resting my hands, lukewarm inside their gloves, on the iron railing, I leaned over and stared down into the blackness. It was early, I thought, and there weren't many people around. It was cold. They'd never get me out in time. I'd only have to step off the bridge and . . .

A hand landed on my back. 'Morning, Lotte. Lost something?'

I pulled back from the edge. 'Hi, Hans. Just watching the ice.' My colleague would have placed his large hand on my arm if I hadn't moved away. Hans Kraai was descended from many generations of strong farming stock and his hefty body, made for withstanding the eternal wind of the north, was out of place in the office, where he had to duck whenever he walked through a door and had to force himself in to his chair like a spade in to the clay soil of his parents' farm. Even his dirty-blond hair was the colour of potato peelings.

We walked through the entrance to the police station together, but I stayed out of step with him so that my footsteps kept their own individual sound.

It was around lunchtime when I got the call that Ben van Ravensberger was being questioned. I immediately made my way down the stairs to the interview rooms and went inside the observation booth. A previous occupant had left a brown plastic cup behind them, as well as the faint smell of sweat. I sat down in front of the one-way mirror, clutching my mug of coffee, the fifth of the day, and thinking that I'd rather be anywhere else than here, in the dark, watching the kid I'd shot – but I felt an obligation towards him. I'd made his situation so much worse and I should at least hear the story of what his uncle had supposedly done.

In the dimness of the observation booth, I watched the interrogation room where André Kamp was interviewing the kid. The detective's dark hair was streaked through with grey, the same colour as his suit. We used to work together before I moved to another team.

'Tell me what you heard,' the detective said. The microphone on the table made his voice tinny and electronic.

'I already did that twice.' The bright light flirted with the kid's high cheekbones and flawless skin. He would look good on the tapes. He was a little older than I'd originally thought in the petrol station – in his early twenties, maybe, and those tight blond curls circled his head like bouncing question marks. He also had a heavily bandaged arm that I tried not to look at. I took another sip of coffee. Ben had told the truth about one thing: his uncle was famous. Ferdinand van Ravensberger was often on TV, famous for being rich and for mixing with movie stars and other celebrities – and now it seemed he might be guilty of murder. I hadn't thought we would take Ben's accusations seriously, but my colleagues clearly thought otherwise: that it was important enough to keep Ben here to be interviewed.

'They were shouting,' the kid said. 'She was having an affair. She said: "You're never here, you're always at work."'

'Your aunt and uncle?' The detective steepled his fingers and rested them against his bottom lip.

'Right. And then he said: "Don't blame me for this. You're the one doing it." This went on for a bit. But then he said: "If you don't stop seeing him, I'll kill him. You know I've killed someone before."'

My eyelids felt heavy. I wrote down: *Ferdinand van Ravensberger said he killed someone*, to keep myself awake. With a blue pen I drew concentric circles on my notepad then squares around them with a pencil. My watch said I'd been in the observation area for five minutes. I'd stay another five, I decided. I'd heard the main line; I could report back on the information we got from Ben and let that be it. I needed to get through the paperwork on the Wendy Leeuwenhoek case and make sure everything was in order before it went to the prosecution.

'Ferdinand van Ravensberger said that?' André Kamp tapped his fingers against his bottom lip.

'Right.'

'How long ago was this?'

'Six years.'

The detective pushed his chair back and got up. He stayed to the right, to keep my line of sight clear. 'Where were you?'

'In the hallway. I'd been to the loo.'

My colleague stepped close to the glass and looked over my head at himself. He adjusted his already straight tie and winked. I couldn't tell if it was at me or at the kid via the mirror. 'Did you flush?'

The kid screwed up his forehead in puzzlement, leaned back and folded his arms. 'Does that matter?'

'Let me put it like this: did they notice you were there?' My colleague kept looking at the kid indirectly. Without the wall between us, he would stand in my personal space. I got a close-up of his tie with a red-brown stain of spilled

13

meatballs, today's special in the canteen, surrounded by small water-damage creases, signs of futile scrubbing in the men's toilets.

The kid's face relaxed and he raked a hand through his curls, fitting them around his fingers like rings. His other arm stayed motionless by his side, strapped in large bandages. 'I don't think they did. Well, I flushed, I'm sure, but at first they didn't know I was there . . .'

The door behind me opened with the soft click of a light switch. I pretended to be concentrating on what was going on in front of me and didn't look round. Someone pulled up the chair beside mine – someone who smelled of cigarettes.

'Hi Lotte, can I join you?' Stefanie Dekkers asked.

I nodded because I didn't know how to refuse. I wasn't surprised that someone from the Financial Fraud department was interested in Ben's uncle. She sat down and moved her chair forward. Her high-heeled shoe kicked my foot. 'Sorry.'

My sturdy boot, fit for the weather, came off better than her black leather shoe, the type you wore if you didn't walk anywhere. I was sure her husband drove her to work. I glanced at her sideways but didn't meet her eyes. She kept her knees together and to one side to accommodate her tight pencil skirt. The waistband vanished between rolls of flesh and the swell of her hip was cut in two by the line of underwear digging in.

'Congratulations on closing the Wendy Leeuwenhoek case.' Her voice was like a mobile phone going off in the theatre. We hadn't exchanged more than a hello in the last ten years. I shifted my coffee mug out of her way.

Stefanie moved her chair closer to mine and confided, 'I knew you'd be great at looking at some of these old cases. Even at university you had that eye for detail, getting stuck into the nitty-gritty . . .'

I kept staring at the window. I didn't move, didn't give her a centimetre of space. 'You used to call me anal.' I locked the grooves of my molars together.

She made a gesture with a manicured hand, her wedding ring locked safely in place by protruding flesh. 'I want my photo on the front page. Like the Wendy Leeuwenhoek case did for you.'

Why on earth would she want that? For me, that photo and that front page stood for all the mistakes I'd made. I shook my head and switched my eyes from the interview room to my notepad. I filled in another circle. My long plait dangled like a length of dead rope over my shoulder. I pushed it back with my pencil and then rubbed my hands clean and dry on my tweed trousers.

Stefanie picked up my pen from my notepad and turned it over and over between her fingers. 'I want you to get Ferdinand van Ravensberger for me,' she said. 'I don't care what on.'

I used my pencil to draw a square around the circle. I wanted to get out of the observation area but I couldn't leave as Stefanie's chair blocked the exit.

She pointed at the observation window with my pen. 'He was holding up a petrol station and got unlucky when a police officer walked in. But then you know that,' she laughed, 'because you shot him.'

The coffee did somersaults in my stomach.

Behind the window, the interrogation continued. 'So your uncle said he'd killed someone. You remember this exactly?' André Kamp pulled back the chair. 'You were pretty young at the time.' He sat down.

The kid's eyes followed the detective. He didn't break eye-contact. 'It was a traumatic experience for me. Especially when my aunt noticed me over my uncle's shoulder. He turned round and looked this pale green colour, as if he was about to be sick or something.'

I tried to ignore Stefanie's close proximity by picturing Ferdinand van Ravensberger with a face the colour of the interrogation-room walls. It was hard. I'd only seen him tanned on TV or in the serious black-and-white of the financial pages.

'So I didn't say anything. I just walked away,' the kid said.

'Did he ever mention it again?'

'My aunt did, the next day at breakfast. My uncle wasn't there, probably sleeping through his hangover, and she said: "You know he was just joking, don't you?" And I said: "Didn't look like a joke to me." So she said: "Maybe joke is the wrong word. It was just a threat. He'll never kill me and he's never killed anyone else."'

Stefanie rested her left elbow on the shelf and pivoted her body towards me. 'We've been trying to get Ferdinand van Ravensberger on tax evasion and money laundering for ages. When we found out the kid was his nephew we put the screws on a bit. After all, he took a shot at you.' She tapped with my pen on the edge of my notepad. The smell of stale tobacco was oppressive. 'You get all the excitement. I'm surprised you're here, watching your handiwork.'

I wanted to snatch my pen back but instead I extracted my paper and pretended to take notes, writing random words with my pencil. The tip snapped. 'So why didn't you ask the kid about Van Ravensberger's financial setup? Much more your thing,' I said.

'That's what we wanted. But he kept talking about this murder.'

I had to stretch to peer over Stefanie's shoulder in order to keep watching the interview.

In the room, André Kamp was saying, 'Your aunt tells you he's kidding, but you don't believe her.'

'He's killed someone,' the youth insisted.

The detective tipped his head back and looked at the ceiling. Then he faced Ferdinand van Ravensberger's nephew again and scratched his greying head. 'Problem is, you don't believe your aunt and I don't believe you.'

I positioned the pointless pencil on the notepad, parallel to the lines, and muttered, 'The kid already told me that in the hospital. It's nothing.'

'Ferdinand van Ravensberger killed someone, for Christ's sake.' Stefanie threw my pen down. It collided with the pencil and dropped onto the floor.

Now I removed my eyes from the window and turned to her. 'His nephew *says* he killed someone. Different thing.'

Stefanie pushed her chair back. 'He shot at you. You're angry – I understand that. But we're working on this for the next two weeks. Didn't your boss tell you?' I watched her get up. At the door she turned and added, 'Oh, and Happy New Year,' before snapping it closed. I tore off the page of circles and squares and threw it in the bin.

The office was still empty when I got back upstairs to my desk. I picked up a file from the stack on the floor, my fingers caressing the dark green cardboard before I flipped it open. When I heard Hans Kraai's heavy footsteps come down the corridor, I took a long last look at my favourite photo and said goodbye to the little girl before I closed my file and put it back on the floor. I then logged on to the police computer to see if Ben's Uncle Ferdinand had any prior form.

Two hours later, having drawn a blank with Van Ravensberger, I was working on the Wendy Leeuwenhoek report.

'I've got you one,' Stefanie said from right behind me.

I jumped in shock. I hated having my back towards the door. People could sneak up on you. Hans Kraai, who was lucky enough to have the window seat, sniggered.

Stefanie stood too close to me. She tipped my chair by resting her weight on the back of it. 'Coffee?' she asked.

'I'm rather busy.' I gestured with my hand at the papers.

She looked over my shoulder. 'Wendy Leeuwenhoek. I see.'

I shuffled the papers together in a single pile and started reading the top one, pencil in hand, to check for any spelling mistakes, typos or inconsistencies.

Stefanie threw a pink folder on my desk. 'Here's one that's possibly linked to Van Ravensberger.'

The folder landed against my papers and knocked them sideways, causing my pencil to make a long scratch. I gave the folder back to her and used my eraser to remove the line. Taking her file, she planted herself opposite me at the empty desk belonging to the third member of our team, Thomas Jansen, who was still on his Christmas break.

She started talking but I turned the page over and the rustling drowned out the sound of her voice. As soon as I read about Wendy that voice was no competition anyway. I tuned it out until it was no more than the whining drone of a mosquito, annoying but unimportant. I went through three more pages of my report.

Then she said the word 'Alkmaar' and I looked up from my papers.

'Ah,' she said, 'I knew *that* would interest you – Moerdijk's old murder case, before his promotion, before he became your boss.'

I didn't correct her.

'Don't look at his stuff,' Hans Kraai put in. 'That's a mine-field. Do you want to be the one to prove him wrong? Career-ending move.'

'But you get to work closely together with him,' Stefanie turned to Hans and lectured him with a pointing finger, 'so he notices how good you really are.'

Hans shook his large head. 'No way. Not worth the risk.'

'A murder in Alkmaar? When was this?' I asked.

'More than ten years ago.' She riffled through the pages. 'Twelve years – 2002.'

I held out a hand for the thin pink folder on Otto Petersen's death and quickly flipped through it. 'He was shot?' I asked.

Stefanie pulled her hair behind her head with both hands. 'Yes. Just one hour after he was released from prison.'

'Where? Outside the prison?'

'No. Outside his house.'

I grinned at Hans. 'Must have been the wife then, nothing to do with your Ferdinand.'

'She had a perfect alibi,' Stefanie said, unsmiling.

I was reading and talking at the same time, trying to see what would get me the information I needed first. 'What was he in for?'

She lifted her eyebrows. 'You don't remember him?'

'Should I?'

'He was the head of Petersen Capital. We busted them for fraud.'

I shrugged; finance never was my area of interest.

'They were the darlings of the financial industry for years, a high-flying investment fund putting up all these wonderful returns, but it turned out it was all bogus. Millions of euros disappeared. They never found the money . . .'

'And Van Ravensberger?'

'One of the investors Petersen embezzled.'

I nodded. 'Get me the rest of the files on this.'

'They're in my office. You can fetch them yourself.'

'You want this done, right? So bring me what you've got. I'm going to talk to the boss.'

Chief Inspector Moerdijk was writing with his head bent low over his desk. I stood in the doorway for a second before knocking on the doorframe to get his attention.

'Hi, Lotte,' he said pleasantly. 'Not too annoyed about having to work with our friends from the Financial Fraud department, I hope.'

I took a seat. I wouldn't describe Stefanie Dekkers as a friend. 'It's fine.'

CI Moerdijk was an efficient man. Even his body didn't have a gram of redundant fat, not one extra layer where none was needed. His white hair and thin frame gave him the look of a zealot, the type who would, centuries ago, have been a firebrand preacher, but who in today's society worshipped at the temple of athletics. He was a serious marathon runner and triathlete. He claimed running gave him time to think, but I suspected that running allowed him to forget.

'You're done with the Wendy Leeuwenhoek files? You haven't forgotten you're taking the evidence to the prosecution office tomorrow, I hope.'

I imagined giving my files and report to the prosecutor, chatting about the murder and talking about the upcoming trial – and it made me feel as if a rat was gnawing at my stomach. I knew then that I wouldn't be able to talk about it, not even about the parts I'd put in the report. I couldn't go through with it – couldn't face going to the prosecution office tomorrow. I was too tired; it would be too hard. I was in no fit state to lie.

'Yes, it's done,' I said. Maybe when my report had left my desk, I would finally stop thinking about that little girl and about the errors of judgement that had brought me such unwanted recognition.

'Good, good. You've made sure it's watertight?' the CI asked.

'It is.'

'So you can start on Van Ravensberger?'

'I don't think there's much in it, but Stefanie Dekkers has come up with something.'

'Anything promising?'

'Otto Petersen . . .'

'One of my old cases?' His voice rose in the middle of the sentence, turning it into a surprised half-question. 'One of my early ones.' He screwed the top on his fountain pen and put it down. 'Think it's got legs?'

'I'm pretty sure it hasn't. But if you want me to work with Stefanie for two weeks, I might as well have a look at some of the things she suggests.'

'Sure. I don't think I looked at Van Ravensberger for that at all.' He took his glasses off and dangled them from one hand. 'I can't remember all of it, but I would have remembered him.'

'He was an investor.'

'In Petersen Capital?'

'That's right.'

22

The chief inspector pursed his lips. 'OK, why not. We looked at some of the other investors, especially after the Alkmaar police made such a mess of it. You don't expect these local forces to be up to much, but . . .'

'Who worked on it?' I managed to keep my voice neutral as if I wasn't that interested in finding out the answer.

'Can't remember. Anyway, read what's in there. Petersen has been dead for over ten years. He can wait,' he pointed at his paperwork. 'This can't.' He unscrewed the top of his fountain pen again. 'Thanks, Lotte.' He gave me a quick look. 'Are you OK with this? Working on this, I mean?'

'I'm fine.'

'The shooting—'

'I had no choice.'

'I know, I know.' He looked at his screen again.

'There won't be a problem – he shot at me first.'

'Yes, good for the case review but . . . Anyway. As long as you're OK with it.' His eyes went back to his paperwork and I was dismissed. I knew what he was thinking: that I was angry and upset with being shot at. But I knew I'd made the kid do it. I didn't feel angry or upset. I felt guilty.

Her years in the Financial Fraud department had made Stefanie more efficient than I remembered. She'd left a stack of files by the side of my desk. I started to go through them. She was right: Otto was killed just one hour after he'd been paroled. I flicked through the papers until I found the photos. I liked starting with the photos. The body had been

23

found on the path two metres from his own front door. There was no weapon. The crime scene was clean of foot-prints or any debris. The CI's report contained the statement from Karin Petersen, Otto's wife. She'd claimed to have been waiting outside the prison when her husband was shot. I turned over the pages until I found the text of the interview with the prison guard. He'd remembered Karin and con-firmed her story: she was there at Otto's time of death. I made some notes with my pencil. I wanted to double-check this. Why was she at the prison when her husband had already been released and was on his way home in Alkmaar?

Hans passed by the back of my chair on his way out. He said goodbye and gave the threatening weather as an excuse for leaving early. I nodded, only raising my eyes from the reports to check my watch. It was just after half past four. When he'd gone, I stared out of the window and watched the clouds hang over the canal. They were so heavy they barely floated. Gravity would pull more snow out of them before the day was over.

I searched for the report from Alkmaar. It didn't seem to be there. I turned page after page in the files. Finally I found it somewhere in the middle: six pages stapled together in the top left-hand corner. An insult to the dead man, this staple. Was this not important enough to warrant a proper cover? I scanned the pages: a technical report, one page describing who called in the murder, some photos – and that was that. This was first-day stuff. The CI must have taken the investigation over quickly. I went back to the CI's papers and checked the date he made the first notes. Otto Petersen was killed on 17 April 2002. The CI's first report was dated 3 August 2002. Almost four months. What had happened in between? I found official requests for more information from the CI. No response from Alkmaar. In total there were five attempts by the CI to get additional files from them, but no sign that anybody ever replied.

And then I saw his name on one of the forms in the back of the file: *Original Investigative Officer for the Alkmaar police: DI Piet Huizen*. I weighed the six pages with the staple in my hand, then rolled them up and tapped them on my palm.

When I'd joined the police, I hadn't told anybody about my father. It was none of their business. Not talking about him had become a habit.

I didn't want to meet the prosecutor tomorrow. I didn't want to meet him at all. I would at least postpone that encounter if I went to Alkmaar to see my father. With a bit of luck, someone from the prosecution office would collect the reports while I was away. Afterwards, I could use the clear conflict of interest as the reason to hand the Petersen case straight back to Stefanie.

Chapter Three

I rearranged the cards in my hand and took the five of hearts. It went at the end of a run, leaving me with just three to get rid of. We sat at our usual places at the table, my mother at the head and me to her left, and played our Wednesday evening game of cards.

I sat back in my chair and almost brushed against the Christmas tree in the corner. With the addition of the tree, all the furniture was in intimate contact, the leg of an oak chair touching the arm of the sofa, and there was hardly room to move around. Two strings of Christmas cards dangled down either side of the door, most of them from people who went to my mother's church.

'Lotte, you don't look at all well,' my mother said as she added a six to my five. She reached out and tucked a strand of hair behind my ear.

I pulled back. 'I'm fine.' Through the gaps in the table-cloth, I could see the large dent in the wood. In an old gesture I rubbed my thumb over the mark in the table, where I had once tried to carve my initials with my knife. It hadn't been sharp enough to let me succeed but a thick line in the light oak showed the start of a capital L. I was eight or nine. I couldn't remember why I did it, but I could clearly remember my mother's anger and the punishment that followed.

'I'm worried about you,' she went. 'I saw the photos – you looked so tired.'

'Which ones?' Cards in one hand, I wrapped the other around my mug of tea for warmth. My mother kept her small flat a couple of degrees colder than was comfortable, saving money on the heating. The mug with the smiling clown was the same one I'd had when I was five. My mug, my plate, the cutlery with my initials on it – they all came out as soon as I was here. Even the smell of boiled kale, which my mother had had for her early dinner, mashed together with some potatoes and probably with a sausage or some diced bacon, reminded me of childhood.

'The ones in the paper,' she said, and picked up her mug in a gesture mirroring mine, her other hand shielding her cards close to her chest. I hoped the heat warmed up her ringless fingers with their swollen knuckles. 'In the *Telegraaf*. I threw it away. You looked just awful.'

'Thanks, Mum.' I rearranged the run and slid my four of hearts in between. Two to go. I knew the one she meant. I'd cut it out of the paper and put it in the black ring-binder with my press cuttings, a history of all the cases I'd worked on in my eighteen-year career. They had taken the photo just after the team had carried off Wendy's skeleton. My head was bowed low, and you could only see one side of me, but the streaks of tears down my cheeks were clear; my plait had come partially undone and strands of hair streamed down. I remembered the flash of the photographer, the annoyance of being caught and eternalised like this.

'You have to look after yourself. You're getting too thin.'

I laughed. Who was she to talk? You could see every bone in her skull. Her cheekbones looked so sharp, they might cut through the wrinkled skin that hung off them. At seventy-three she should carry a bit more weight or the first bout of flu would take her away. Her hair, short and curly, was as white as the home-knitted jumper she was wearing. She looked as if she'd melt away against the snow outside.

'You didn't like having your picture taken, did you?' She picked up a new card from the stack, grimaced and slid the card with its red back between two blue ones. The backs of both packs were equally faded, the red cards now the colour of my mother's cracked lips, the others the shade of her eyes, bleached by age from sky to duck-egg blue. We always used this double set; not a single card had been lost in over twenty years of playing.

'No, I hated every second of it. All those photographers looking at me, clicking away, lights going off in my face.'

'Even as a child.' She smiled at the memory. 'You'd scream as soon as I got the camera out.'

'I loathe being the centre of attention.'

'So much fuss over this one case.'

I couldn't get rid of either one of my cards and had to pick up a new one – a three of clubs, its corner battered and tattered from over-use. 'The papers had been writing about it for years. There'd been so much speculation,' I explained.

'There's plenty of other things to write about. Proper news. There's no need to put *you* on the front page.'

'It's what sells, I suppose.'

'You sell?' Her eyes scanned the cards on the table. She took three runs, clubs, spades and diamonds, and rearranged them into three sets of the same numbers. The cards moved over the table with the sound of dead autumn leaves falling to the ground. She added a fourth card. Her smile bunched up the skin on her cheekbones.

'Well no, not me specifically. But Wendy Leeuwenhoek. Her disappearance had been selling papers for years.' I picked up another new card, hardly having looked at my old ones.

'But it's not front-page news.'

'Neither is a footballer's wedding, but that gets on there too. It was more important than a footballer's wedding, don't you think?'

My mother put an eight of diamonds on the table. I added a card to my hand.

'I suppose so,' she said. 'You're right. But it's horrible how they make money out of people's grief.' Her eyes were glued to the table.

'At least we found a body to bury.' I reshuffled the cards in my hands, breaking up sets and creating new ones. We would never know what had happened. I would never know why Wendy had been killed. Just another thing to keep me awake at night.

'But at what cost to you? This job isn't good for you.' She held her last card between her fingers and checked the ones on the table. She put it back face down on the table and took a sip of tea.

I tried to guess what she had left based on the sets she was examining. It was probably a low number – they were the hardest to get rid of. 'It's my job. It's what I do.'

She sighed and picked a new card from the stack. 'You went to university. You had so many choices, great opportunities. You still do. Now you see bad things all the time, suspect everybody you meet, nothing good ever happens. It's hard on you. I can see it in your face.'

'I just haven't been sleeping well.' I had a run of low clubs and could put them on the table, but then she could use my cards to get rid of her last two. Instead I picked a new one and hoped she'd have to do the same. Her eyes met mine. She looked at the number of cards I had left and could probably guess my tactics.

'I had hoped this new team would be better, because you were looking at older cases. You seemed happy. Much happier than you'd been for a while.'

'It's like that. When you first start a case there's excitement. Something new. A new puzzle. A new challenge.'

She was silent for a bit, then reached over and picked some fluff off the sleeve of my jumper. 'I'm worried about you,' she repeated. 'I've never seen you like this. It's because it was a little girl, isn't it?'

Amongst other things. *His hands on my body, his fingers in my hair.*

'Have you spoken to Arjen lately?' she asked.

I had no reason to talk to my ex-husband. 'No, not in

months.' I rubbed my thumb over the tattered corner of the three of clubs.

'I saw him and his new wife in the Kalverstraat yesterday.'

I took a gulp of my tea without waiting for it to cool down and let the hot liquid burn the roof of my mouth and the back of my throat.

'He looked very well,' she said.

'Good for him,' I said. Then: 'Come on, make a move, you've been thinking for long enough. Pick a new card – you know you're stuck.'

She added a card to her hand. 'You should stay in touch. You never know.'

I heaved a sigh. 'You're crazy.' I wanted to give her hand a soft squeeze, careful not to squash the swollen knuckles together. Instead I put out my set of low-numbered clubs. Only two more cards to go – a ten and the queen of spades.

'No, no, I read a book where exactly that happened.'

'I wouldn't take him back.'

'Why not? There's hardly a queue of men outside your door. You're forty-two. It'll take you a while to find some-one else.'

'So you keep telling me.'

She picked up a new card. She had four left; she had finally fallen behind. 'But there's a chance, isn't there? That you might get back together?'

I moved the dead weight of my plait over my shoulder. 'No.'

'Why not?'

'Well, they've got a child now.'

31

'Oh yes. The child . . .'

I slotted the ten in the middle of a run. We were both silent for a bit. The queen of spades, all alone in my hand, looked at me with her one eye, as if urging me not to say anything. I knew what my mother was thinking anyway, but she didn't mention it. Kept quiet about my own little lost daughter. 'You didn't stay friends with Dad either,' I said.

'That was different.'

'How?'

She put out the four cards in one set; it was a run of diamonds from seven to ten. So much for my theory that she had low numbers.

'Different how?' I persisted.

'It's time for *Lingo*,' she said. 'I don't want to miss that.' She got up, picked up the remote control and switched on the television.

I threw my leftover card on the table. Yes, she couldn't possibly miss her television programme, apparently the most popular programme amongst the over-sixties, so popular that a previous prime minister had once mentioned his displeasure when it was moved to an earlier hour in the schedule. And in this case, it was the perfect excuse to avoid talking. She'd never told me why she left my father.

Even though the flat was so small that we could see the television perfectly well from where we sat, we moved to the sofa. There were some rules: the table was for eating and playing cards, the sofa for watching the television.

The game show ate up the time until I had to go. I put all my layers back on, my thick coat, gloves, scarf and hat, and made my goodbyes. I descended the concrete steps of the communal staircase, my hand on the red plastic banister. Downstairs, I unchained my bicycle from its attachment to my mother's fence and pushed the pedals as hard as I could as I cycled through the cold darkness. January was a depressing month at the best of times.

Chapter Four

After another sleepless night, this trip north up the A9 from Amsterdam to Alkmaar didn't seem like such a good idea any more. The road ahead of me glistened in the morning light and stretched through the snow-covered white flatness of the landscape like a charcoal-grey pencil line on a blank page. Scattered villages broke the monotony of the never-ending fields. Churches pointed their steeples to the sky like warning fingers. 'Be careful,' they said. 'You can see a long way – but that doesn't mean things are out in the open.'

My car still smelled new, leather mixed with that odour of burnt dust you get when you first turn on the heating in late October. Its paintwork was poison green, and I imagined my ex-husband, Arjen, naming my car The Frog and joking about hopping to the shops or hopping into town. The car dealer hadn't understood. 'Stupid woman,' his eyes said. 'Fancy choosing a car just for its colour.' Maybe he hadn't known green was the colour of envy.

A long left-hand curve, which pressed me closer into my seatbelt, led to the roundabout on the ring road approaching Alkmaar. The lights were in my favour, no wished-for delay, no other cars. I changed gears. The engine hummed louder, as if I'd disturbed a nest of wasps with the gear-stick. I moved my foot off the accelerator and it quietened down. The thin pink folder lay on the passenger seat, the only evidence that this solitary trip was a flagrant breach of police procedures.

I consulted the map that I'd printed out last night – second right, first left – and parked my car behind a dark blue BMW that had the understated look of money. I double-checked the address but found I was in the right place. When I opened the car door, cold air rushed in. It hurt to breathe. I grabbed the folder and my bag and swung my legs out. Someone had sown salt on the path and the snow had turned to mush.

The white triangle of the house would have blended in with the snow, had it not been for the cedar guardians on either side of the path and the No Entry-sign red front door. I rang the doorbell, which sounded oddly non-electric, like a bicycle bell. Footsteps were approaching – I wished they weren't. I wished I couldn't see the door swing inwards. But I did.

He had changed since the last time I'd seen him, at my wedding fourteen years ago. His short-cropped hair still resembled a newly harvested field, but it had gone from steel to ice. His face was now a roadmap with lines showing which route laughter took and where frowns turned up.

'Hi, Dad,' I said.

★　★　★

My father took my coat and put it on the same hanger as a short scarlet jacket that had to belong to his new wife. My coat embraced hers and my first instinct was to grab it back. Instead I wrapped my hands around my folder. I did my best to stamp the snow off my boots on the rubber mat. I didn't want to leave traces of myself behind on their sterile off-white ice rink of a carpet. A clump of snow remained stuck in the sole and I gave up, took my boots off and left them by the door.

My father pointed me to the large L-shaped rat-fur-brown leather sofa. I made sure to sit in the middle of the long leg of the L, leaving him no room to sit next to me. I wanted to see his face as I talked to him.

'Can I get you anything? Tea? Coffee?'

'Coffee would be nice.' My hands felt numb and cold.

He walked away, showing me the slope in his back, the upper half rounded and hunched.

The loud whine of grinding beans travelled from the kitchen, followed by a hiss and the smell of coffee. It mingled with the hint of lemon that came from fresh cleaning. The place was pristine.

After a bit, he returned with the coffee.

'Do you take sugar?' he asked, handing me my cup. He surely must remember I never took sugar. I shook my head. With a click he added sweeteners to his. The cups were from the police station. I recognised the flame, the symbol of the police force, in relief on the white porcelain. The police was the only thing we had in common.

He sat down.

36

'You look well,' he said.

'Thanks.'

'How's Arjen?' His eyes moved to my right hand, which for over a year had been ringless.

'Fine.'

'Good, good.'

I returned the cup to the table and picked up the pink folder. I opened it and took out the first piece of paper.

'Not a social call, then,' he said.

'We're re-investigating Otto Petersen's murder.'

'My last case.' He smiled and showed perfect white teeth. I was sure they used to be yellow and stained. 'I read about Wendy Leeuwenhoek. Saw your name. Saw you on the front page of the *Telegraaf.*' He picked up his cup and took a sip. 'Almost called to congratulate you.'

'But you didn't.'

He rubbed his hand through his white hair a couple of times. It was so short, it didn't make a difference. 'I didn't think you'd want me to.'

I flicked the page as if I needed to read it. 'We were disappointed by the work of the Alkmaar police.'

'Sorry?' The line between his eyebrows deepened from a gully to a full-blown ravine.

'You had the Petersen case for four months and all you did was this.' I got the six pages out of the folder and waved them at him like a fan. The one with the photos was thicker and snapped against the other sheets with each forward and back motion.

'We worked hard.'

37

'And only wrote six pages?'

'We nearly closed it.'

'On which page does it say that?' I made a show of studying each one.

'That can't be all,' he said. 'There was more. Boxes more.'

He leaned further forward to get at the papers. I snatched them back towards me and put them in the folder. Then I handed him the whole thing abruptly before I could change my mind. He picked out one page after the other and turned them over. When he'd run out of pages, he pushed his glasses higher up his nose and faced me. 'What have you done with the rest?' he asked me softly.

'What have *I* done with the rest? There *is* no rest! That's what I'm telling you. This is all I got from the archives.'

'They must have misfiled it.'

'The CI noted that there wasn't much from Alkmaar.' I took the papers back. 'Here,' I pressed my finger on the page. '*12/09/02 request for more information from DI Huizen*. And here,' my finger found another place, '*09/11/02 follow-up request*. This wasn't misfiled – it was never there.'

'OK. OK.' His face had turned the colour of the salty snow outside, white mixed with dirt from the path. 'Maybe it got lost on the way.'

'Half a file? I don't think so.'

'Not just half a file. There were boxes full.'

'So you say. Even less likely they got lost.' My heart beat fast; my face felt flushed. 'They were never there, were they, Dad?'

He got up and walked away. The sound of running water

trickled down from the kitchen. He came back with a glass, put a pill in his mouth and swallowed.

'We had a witness,' he said, eyes on the window. 'He saw Anton Lantinga's gold-metallic Porsche in front of Petersen's house an hour or so before the murder.'

'Lantinga?' I took the file and looked through the CI's notes. In the margins of the white pages, the CI's spidery handwriting spelled out his thoughts. There had been three partners in Petersen Capital: Otto Petersen, Anton Lantinga and Geert-Jan Goosens. The latter was the CI's main suspect, called in for interviews twice as often as the others – including the wife. 'Lantinga was a director of Petersen Capital, wasn't he? The CI interviewed him briefly, but he was never the main suspect.'

My father raised his eyebrows. 'No? So who was?'

'We're looking at the Petersen case because we had a tip-off about Van Ravensberger. Something a few years back.'

'Ferdinand van Ravensberger? That rich TV guy who owns that football club? What does *he* have to do with any of this?'

I sat back on the sofa and pulled my legs underneath me to get comfortable. Then I remembered where I was and put my feet back on the floor. 'He was an investor in Petersen Capital.'

'Interesting. We never looked at him – but this was done by Anton Lantinga.' My father's face had returned to the colour it had been when he opened the door to me. 'And it's still worth investigating.'

I shrugged. 'Maybe. Tell me what Lantinga had to do with it.'

'It was clear from the beginning. Lantinga had been fooling around with Petersen's wife, Karin, in the . . . seven?' He picked up the file. 'Yes, seven years that Petersen was locked up. Also, he'd been running the firm or a spin-off firm, I'm not sure which, but he took all the clients. He clearly wasn't keen on seeing Petersen come back and neither was Karin. So Karin drove to the prison . . . Look, stay for lunch and I'll tell you the rest.'

I looked at my watch. Yes, it was midday, but if I had lunch, I couldn't leave whenever I wanted to. I would be trapped by food, sat at his large table and obliged to hang around until we'd finished eating, maybe help clear up as well – and I wasn't hungry anyway. I felt the urge to get up and drive off in my green car, back to Amsterdam. The impulse to make the visit as short as I could was still with me after all these years.

'I'm rather busy, Dad.'

His shoulders sagged and he looked disappointed.

'Of course, of course, I understand.' Then he rallied. 'Why don't you talk to Ronald de Boer? He worked with me on this. He can take you to the murder scene and maybe you can interview the witness as well. Better you go with him than with me.'

'Thanks, Dad. But I'm not sure how much we'll do on this, if it isn't Van Ravensberger.'

'Just meet Ronald, have a chat and then decide.'

'OK, why not.' As long as I got back to Amsterdam before dark.

'If you're not staying for lunch, can I make you another coffee?'

I shook my head.

'Cup of tea?'

'No thanks, Dad.'

'Right. Let me give Ronald a call, see if he's around.'

He walked off. There was a phone right beside the sofa so he must have a reason to use the other one. He didn't want me to hear what he was saying. What did they have to talk about in private? Was he warning him? Telling this Ronald de Boer what to say to me?

I looked at the photographs of the crime scene again. There was a close-up of Otto Petersen's face. He was lying on his back. He had been forty-eight when he'd been shot. He looked older. He also looked quite different from the financial high-flyer Stefanie had described. I'd expected an expensive suit, a costly watch, someone who looked rich.

I lifted the picture into the light that crawled through the window. The dead man's hair was cropped to coarse grey stubble, several folds of flesh coated his neck, and a roll of fat over his cheekbones had reduced his eyes to slits. The shortness of his hair made the small hole in his left temple perfectly visible. The concentric circle of the abrasion wound marked this as the entry. The next picture revealed the star-shaped serrated exit of the bullet. The forensic report said the shooting had been done from close range, as the shape of the wounds would suggest. The full-body photos,

41

presenting the dead man from multiple angles, showed a bulky carcass, dressed in white clothes. The photos of the surroundings were of an ordinary house with a sheltered path coming from the side.

I put the photos away, then looked around at the room.

A photo of my father and his new wife stood on a shelf in the display cabinet, above a line of cut-crystal goblets and below a row of paperbacks. I got up to have a closer look. They were all travel guides: *Lonely Planet Thailand*, *Lonely Planet Greece*. All places my mother and I hadn't been able to afford to go to. 'I never took a cent of his money,' she had told me, time and time again. From what I could see, there'd been plenty.

The photo in its black frame showed the retired couple on an exotic holiday. Maaike, the new wife, leaned in towards him, her arms circling his waist. She seemed round and too warm, and a broad smile lit up her face. There was a slightly smaller one on his. My father held his arms by his side, a backpack dangling from one hand.

I checked my watch. He'd been gone a while. I nearly called out to him, but sat back on the sofa instead. A pain was pushing between my eyebrows. I got a couple of Paracetamol from my bag and swallowed them with the dregs of my coffee. I wanted to close my eyes, wished I was back home and could just roll up in a ball and try to sleep. Where was he? Finally I heard his slippered footsteps come from the kitchen.

'Ronald has just gone out, but he'll be back in half an

hour,' he said. 'Come on, eat something with me. You'll be starving otherwise.'

'No, Dad, I'm fine.'

Silence dropped between us and hung there, heavy and unavoidable like the snow clouds outside.

'You've been to Thailand then?' I finally offered.

'No, not yet. Maaike would like to go, but it's a bit hot for me.'

'You could go in the rainy season.'

It wasn't really a joke, but he laughed, a little too much. There was silence again. He stared out of the window.

'Is that a new car?' he asked.

'Yeah, I bought it a few weeks ago.'

'Nice. What make is it?'

'Peugeot.'

He nodded. 'Nice,' he said again. 'Can I have a look?'

'Of course.' Relieved, I got up. He slid his feet into a thick pair of shoes and opened the door.

'You'll need a coat,' I said. 'It's cold out there.'

The skin around his eyes creased. 'Thanks, Lotte.'

He put on a grey coat and helped me in to mine. I put my boots back on and my feet welcomed being returned to their protective casing.

'Nice colour car,' my father said. 'Green like grass.'

'Green like snakes,' I responded.

He stopped smiling and looked in front of him. After a loop around the car, we got in and talked about technical details for five minutes. Then the silence returned.

'I'd better go,' I said.

'Ronald won't be back yet.'

'Need to get some petrol.'

'OK.' He looked at me and I broke eye-contact. I pulled the seatbelt towards me and clicked it in place between us.

'Your folder,' my father remembered. 'I'll get it for you.'

I stayed in the car while he went to the house to get it. My hands started to shake and I put them on the steering wheel. When I saw him return, I rolled the window down and he handed me the file.

'Thanks, Dad,' was all I said and he gave me a small wave. I closed the window and put the car in reverse, directing my gaze towards the end of the drive and away from him and his house. I backed into the quiet road and raised my hand to my father. I could see he was saying something, but I couldn't hear him. I opened the window again.

'What?' I shouted.

'Come and visit again. Let me know how you're getting on.'

I nodded and waved back. Just before the window fully closed, he added, 'It was good to see you.'

Instantly, my eyes burned and the inside of my throat swelled up until there was no opening left. I couldn't respond even if I wanted to. He looked old and small. I raised my hand again then put the car into gear.

Chapter Five

I parked in front of the white cruise ship that was the Alkmaar police station. It seemed as if it was ready for an ocean journey and was surprised to find itself moored at the edge of a canal. To the left of the police station, a yellow double-decker train crossed the bridge over the canal, continuing its journey north from Amsterdam, the route used by thousands of commuters every day, the workers going south for jobs, the students going to the universities. Tourists came the other way in spring, to admire the fields of tulip bulbs and hyacinths that did so well on the sandy soil, and they arrived in droves in summer with buckets and spades to make the short hop from Alkmaar to the beach, to bake in the sunshine. But not many people came north in winter, finding precious little reason to visit this town in January. It was the largest city north of Amsterdam and the capital of this West Frisian farming region – but that wasn't saying much.

Inside, groups of people chatted and walked about, probably going to and from the canteen. I was aware of eyes on me and whispers. They must have read about me. Read the piece where I'd explained how I'd solved the Wendy Leeuwenhoek case. Those words had now burned a path in my brain, so I could repeat them without hesitation, without breaking eye-contact or touching my nose in the telltale body language of liars. When you tell the same lies over and over again, they form an alternative truth.

I walked up to the receptionist. 'Lotte Meerman. I'm here to see Ronald de Boer.'

'Very well.' Her fingers dialled a number without checking the screen. 'Hi, Ronald, it's me,' she said. Her skin was creamy and her hair was blonde as if she was a milkmaid who'd never eaten anything other than cheese or drunk anything other than milk. Her blue eyes had left mine and she tipped her head sideways so that her hair covered the earpiece she was wearing. She smiled a small private smile. 'I've got Lotte Meerman here. Shall I send her up?' Her smile widened. 'OK, I'll see you in a couple of minutes then.' There was pleasure in her expression, which made her look younger than the late thirties I guessed she was.

He'd come down to fetch me. That was OK – I'd never been here before. It was a courtesy, not an attempt to watch me. The receptionist put the phone down and met my gaze. 'He'll be with you shortly.' She straightened the front of her shirt and tucked it more tightly in her skirt. A silver cross glistened in the V of the shirt. 'Lotte Meerman. That name sounds familiar.' She looked at me. 'Are you the woman who solved the Wendy Leeuwenhoek case?'

'That's me,' I said. Everybody in the Netherlands had been obsessed with Wendy Leeuwenhoek. In every office they'd talked about her around the water cooler. I still couldn't open a newspaper without seeing a photo of her or of me. Callers on phone-ins were demanding a reinstatement of the death penalty and people were wondering what we could have done – as a nation, that was – to have prevented this killing. It was only two weeks since I'd found her body, but unfortunately for the journalists, unlike the rest of the country, I wasn't interested in discussing the minute details of her case over and over again. I seemed to be the only one who didn't want to talk about her in every conversation. Actually, I preferred not to talk about her at all.

'You've got such a great job. I'd love to do what you're doing,' she said.

No, you wouldn't, I thought. You should be happy you're sitting here behind your desk, protected from mental harm. Out loud I said, 'You must have seen all sorts come through here.'

She giggled. 'I wanted to join the police first, but then I saw the kind of people you have to deal with. I think I prefer to stay on this side.'

'Very wise.'

People kept passing behind me in an almost continuous stream but I hadn't turned around. Now the milkmaid's face showed me that Ronald de Boer had arrived: her eyes lit up and she tucked her hair behind her ear.

Ronald was older than I'd expected from her behaviour. His dark greying hair was bleached to white at the temples and slicked back without a single errant hair. He wore a thundercloud-grey suit, white shirt and a royal blue tie. His black shoes had a military shine to them.

'Hi, Ronald. This is Lotte.'

His jacket was undone and he had his left hand in his trouser pocket. He didn't take it out as we shook hands. This was the man who had all the information I would love to have. He had worked with my father, knew what kind of person he was. He was the owner of knowledge that should by right be mine. He was the person my father spent time with instead.

'Hi, Lotte. Nice to meet you.' He smiled easily – but how sincere was it? Did the smile reach his eyes, which were a touch lighter grey than his suit?

'Nice to meet you too,' I said.

'Piet was pleased to see you again.'

Was he? And when did my father tell you that? He said you were out when he called you. So either he lied when he said that, or he'd called you again when I was on my way. Are you my enemy, Ronald, my father's friend? I held my pink folder against my body and wrapped both my arms around it.

Ronald winked at the milkmaid before walking off at a fast pace, leaving me momentarily behind. I matched his large steps, my boots squeaking on the marble floor.

'So you're reopening the Petersen case,' he said without turning his head.

'Don't know. We're looking for something to do with Van Ravensberger.'

'This isn't it.' He pushed the glass door open and went through without holding it for me.

I had to take a few quick steps to catch it before it closed. 'When our CI investigated the case, he had never heard about your witness,' I said breathlessly. 'None of Alkmaar's papers ever reached him.'

'Wonder how that happened.' Ronald fished a piece of chewing gum out of the depth of his trouser pocket, undid the silver wrapper and put it in his mouth. He didn't offer me one. My fingers itched around the folder I was holding, to check if he was the person the CI had asked for more information from but never received it. It would have to wait until I was back in the car.

'Yes, so do I,' I said. 'Could it have got lost in the post?'

'Two people came to collect it.'

'Do you know their names?'

'No, but they were from Amsterdam. Your father might know.'

'I'll ask.'

We got in Ronald's car to go to the original crime scene, Otto Petersen's house, and crossed Alkmaar in a silence broken only by the sound of Ronald chewing his gum and the noise of the engine. I could chit-chat or ask questions about Karin Petersen and Anton Lantinga, but these were not the questions I wanted to ask. I sat as far to the right as the car would allow, as near to the door as possible without actually leaving. Nervously, I ran my fingers through my hair and crossed and re-crossed my feet at the ankles.

49

Ronald turned right over a speed bump into a quiet street that wasn't wide enough for two cars to pass without one pulling into the parking spaces at the side.

'We're here,' he said, stopping. 'This is the house, number twenty-one.'

I pushed the car door open and took a few deep breaths of the freezing air. The clouds were a yellow-tinged deep grey, the colour of dirty pigeons, and were hanging so low I felt I could stretch my hand out and touch them. It seemed as if only the fingers of the treetops kept them in the air, which made the sky come closer and left me less oxygen to breathe.

This area was not what I'd expected, even though I'd seen the photos. We were in an ordinary suburb. This was not the house of a financial high-flyer, but a normal, average home. High shrubs formed a silent windbreak. Their two-toned solidity, deadly white at the top but vibrant green underneath, kept the world away from the front door. I walked a few steps along the leafy corridor until I could see the door. I hardly recognised the place from the photos. It had been repainted and, of course, the white outline around the body had long since been washed away. A green door with stained-glass windows was now protecting the house's inhabitants. The path hadn't been swept and was still covered with a layer of snow. The black parallel lines were the tracks of parents with a child on a sleigh enjoying the winter. In the garden at the back there'd be a snowman. It was that kind of house, that kind of area.

'This is a nice place, isn't it?' Ronald said. His words floated past me in a cloud of breath.

This was the type of house I had dreamed of as a child, when my mother and I had been living in our two-bedroom flat in Amsterdam. It was not nearly as big as my father's home, but everything about it spoke of safety and security. Not a car had passed since we arrived. The only sounds were my breath and the voices of children in the distance. This was the kind of place where you'd let your kids play out in the street. 'Has this garden changed much?' I asked.

'The shrubs were a little smaller then, but still too high to look over. Anybody could have stood by the front door and the neighbours would never know.'

'Any signs of a break-in?'

'No, none at all. Everything seemed in perfect order. Apart from the dead body.'

'And the neighbours called the police?'

'They thought it was a car backfiring at first. But they didn't quite trust it, so they came out to have a look.'

The net curtains twitched as the current inhabitants of the house noticed our attention.

'We can go in if you like, but there's nothing left of the way it was,' Ronald said.

I shook my head and walked off down the side passage. It led to a small square where garages came together with paths to back gardens. The gardens were all fenced in with separate entry doors. It would be just as easy to enter unseen from the front as from the back. Easy for someone to hide in either place and wait for Otto Petersen to come

51

home. I took notes and signalled to Ronald that I was done. We got back in the car.

'What next?' he enquired. 'We could meet up with Wouter Vos if he's in and if you have time. He's the guy who saw Anton. He can tell you what he witnessed.'

It was still early. 'That's a good idea,' I said. Now that I was here I might as well get all the information Alkmaar had. I clicked the seatbelt tight. 'Before we see your witness,' I went on, 'what happened to those files? We asked for more information, but you never responded.'

Ronald acted as if I hadn't spoken. He started the car and, as before, drove in silence through the centre of Alkmaar, to Wouter Vos's apartment in an area where modern flats stood side by side with eighteenth-century gabled houses. The apartment block where Wouter Vos lived was built out of a yellow brick, the colour of the cheeses that got carried around Alkmaar's cheese market on Fridays in summer, the market of which my father was so proud. It was the market Alkmaar got in the seventeenth century as a thank you for being the first town to come out in favour of William of Orange and against the Spaniards. My father would tell me these facts most weekend visits, whenever I said that Alkmaar didn't have anything Amsterdam didn't have, but we had never actually gone to this fabled market.

The balconies were painted sky-blue, giving the block the appearance of a faded Swedish flag. These were the types of flats appreciated by retired people who wanted to live close to the shops, cinemas and the theatre, and single men who liked the clean lines and modern look.

52

When he opened the door, I saw that Wouter was in his early fifties, not at retirement age yet. The first few centimetres of his grey-blond hair, from centre-parting to ear, were so heavy with gel that grooves showed where his fingers had combed it through, and he had shaved his stubble to create the impression of a straight jawline where his jowls became his neck.

He stuck out a hand and shook Ronald's, saying, 'What brings you here?'

'This is Lotte Meerman, a colleague from Amsterdam police.'

'Hi, nice to meet you.' He shook my hand too. It was a firm grip, which didn't crush my fingers but enclosed them in a comfortable warmth. He invited us in. 'Can I get you anything? Tea? Coffee?' Walking behind him down the hallway, I could see that at the back of his head the skin of his scalp showed through the hair.

Spotlights on metal wires highlighted pictures on the walls. I didn't know much about modern art, but these weren't prints; they looked like originals. A small painting, about sixty centimetres wide and forty high, of a man asleep under a tree, an entire world growing out of his head, stopped me in my tracks. The vibrant colours of his dreams were completely unlike the white and black of mine: red parrots flew through a verdant green forest, a deep-blue city floated above the trees. My fingers itched with the desire to own it.

'I was just getting ready to go to a meeting,' Wouter said

53

to Ronald before turning to me. 'You like it? It's one of my favourites too.'

'Are your dreams like that?' I asked before I could stop myself.

'I wish.' He looked serious for a second, then smiled again. 'Sorry, let me get these papers out of the way.' He picked up a number of magazines from the sofa. They looked technical. Then he put his hand on Ronald's back. 'Good to see you. It's been a while.' He looked at his watch. 'I'm really sorry. I have to go in half an hour.' He laughed and pulled at the crease in his trousers. 'That's why I'm dressed like this.'

'What do you do?' I tore myself away from the art on the wall and sat down on the sofa. Wouter sat in a large leather chair opposite.

'I'm an IT consultant and do all sorts of things – IT instal-lations for small firms and home networks for individuals. I've got this great partnership going with a local design firm.' He took his gold-rimmed glasses off and polished the lenses with a handkerchief. 'Halstra. Do you know them?'

'Heard of them.' Ronald sat down next to me. I moved further into the corner.

'They do the interior design and decoration and get me in to work out the Wi-Fi and stuff. I build some PCs from scratch as well, on spec, for the lazy enthusiast.' He gestured to a corner of the room, next to a large modern desk, where a dismantled PC showed its innards. 'They want to choose every part but can't be bothered to put it together.' These were the things the layman preferred hidden away in the casing: yellow and green plastic intestines, thick and shiny

54

like rain worms fresh out of the soil, attached frightening-looking electronic parts to one another.

'Lotte is Amsterdam CID,' Ronald said, 'so I'm sure you can guess why we're here. We're having another look at Otto Petersen's murder.'

I kept my eyes on Wouter's face. His eyes moved from Ronald to me and back again.

Ronald said, 'Just tell Lotte what you saw that evening.'

'Very well.' Wouter rested his arms on his thighs, his hands dangling between his knees. 'I saw Anton Lantinga's car on the street outside Petersen's house that afternoon. Around five o'clock. But I didn't think anything of it. He was there a lot, you know.' He picked up a packet of cigarettes. 'You don't mind if I smoke, do you?' I shook my head. It was hard to refuse a man permission to smoke in his own house. He put a cigarette in his mouth. 'So, yes, Anton was there.' Wouter offered the pack round but got no takers and lit up. 'You couldn't miss that car. It was a gold metallic Porsche.' He inhaled then blew a smoke ring at the ceiling, his cigarette held loosely between his long fingers.

'Did you see Lantinga himself?' I asked.

'Well, I saw his car. Someone was driving it but I couldn't really see who it was.'

I nodded. It reminded me of the small blue car outside the petrol station and the difficulties I'd had in seeing the driver.

'But when I heard on the news that Petersen had been shot, I immediately called Ronald and Piet — Piet Huizen — and told them what I'd seen.'

'And you're sure it was his car?'

'Well, I wasn't, but Piet was as soon as I described it. It was quite distinctive.' He looked at Ronald with a smile and took another drag of his cigarette. 'It's good you're reopening the case. I always wondered why Lantinga wasn't arrested. What do you think?' He turned his head to me.

I shrugged. At the moment I didn't know what to think.

Ronald put his hands on his upper legs and pushed himself out of the sofa. 'Thanks, Wouter,' he said. 'We won't take any more of your time today.'

Wouter got up too. 'It's always good to see you, Ronald. Are we still on for Wednesday?'

'Yes, we'll see you then.' Ronald put one hand on Wouter's arm and gave it a squeeze. He gestured at me with the other. 'Let's go.'

As we walked down the stairs, he said, 'You want to talk? Let's talk.' It sounded like a threat.

Chapter Six

In the car, Ronald briefly looked over at me before focusing on the traffic. 'You wanted to know why I never replied to the Amsterdam police,' he said. It wasn't a question.

'My father seemed—'

'Your father said you didn't get on.' Not taking his eyes off the road, he fished another piece of chewing gum out of his jacket pocket and stuck it in his mouth. He chewed noisily.

We drove along the Singel, the waterway that was the remnant of the old moat around Alkmaar's town centre. It wasn't even four o'clock yet, but the last drop of daylight had already drained from the sky. The large wings of the windmill on the corner were like ghosts, their white sails barely visible as they churned the air. I wasn't sure if the mill was still functioning, milling something or pumping water, or just for show. This was the kind of thing I'd asked my father when I'd come to see him on one of the rare weekend visits. The way I remembered it, he'd never known the answers and we'd walked together in an uncomfortable silence along the defence walls. He hadn't known what to talk to a teenager about.

There had been an eight-year gap after my parents' divorce during which I hadn't seen him, hadn't heard from him and hadn't received any birthday cards or telephone calls from him. Those eight years had made it perfectly clear that he didn't love me and had little interest in me. When it was arranged that I should see him again, I was thirteen and had no great desire for a reunion. They didn't last long, those visits, only continued for about six months, as my mother had never been happy about the idea from the beginning and I had been messed-up and angry enough to agree with her, hurt that it had taken my father all those years to contact me.

'Not getting on is too strong,' I told Ronald. The traffic light ahead of us was red and we waited. No cars came out of the crossroad. 'You seemed to know him well,' I said. At Ronald's silence I continued, 'Wouter Vos?'

Ronald turned the car into a parking bay, pulled the hand-brake on and switched the engine off. The headlights died; the car was engulfed in falling darkness. He unbuckled his seatbelt. 'OK, let's talk.'

I undid my own and reached for the door handle, but Ronald said, 'Stay in the car. I don't want anybody to over-hear us.' I turned towards him. He was staring straight ahead. He didn't click the inside light on and the dark gave a sense of isolation and anonymity. He kept his hands on the steering wheel and I could see him chewing his bottom lip. I stayed silent to give him time to gather his thoughts.

After a few moments, he looked over at me with his grey eyes as if to weigh me up. 'You look a lot like him, you know that?' he said. 'It reminds me of working with him, talking to you, sitting together in the car like this.'

I gazed out of the window. Snow was starting to fall again – fat drifting flakes. They got stuck on the windscreen and slid their way down. The streetlights revealed the poplars behind the parking bay, swaying in the wind. Pearls of snow rained on the ground at the end of each pendulum movement. The drive home would be a nightmare. With the engine off, the car was getting cold and I hugged my coat around me.

'That last day,' Ronald was saying, 'I don't think he meant to do it. He just . . .' He sighed and ran both hands through his hair. 'That Thursday, the commander called your father into his office. Told him he was taking him off the Petersen case as his retirement was only two weeks away. Piet would have understood if I'd taken over, I'm sure of it, as we'd worked on it together, but instead the commander gave the case to Amsterdam. Probably agreed to it with his Amsterdam buddy over a drink on the golf course.' He gave a bark of laughter, loosened his tie and undid the top button of his shirt. 'Anyway,' he went on, lowering his voice, 'when Piet got back to his desk, he was livid. I could see that his hands were shaking with rage. He was rifling through his desk, piling all these papers, all our files and reports, into a few large yellow crates. You know the kind I mean. "I've only got one hour," he said. "I need to get this all together." His voice was hoarse. When we had it all

59

packed, he wanted to carry it down himself. I offered to
help, but he wouldn't hear of it. "Better if you stay here," he
said. I think he wanted me to keep out of it – you know,
not get involved.' Ronald drummed his fingers on the back
of my seat. They tapped out a rhythm against my spine,
which resonated through to my stomach.

'Anyway, that's the last I saw of those files. I don't know
what he did with them. I'm sure he just wanted to delay
Amsterdam a bit, the big-town boys, but of course that night
he collapsed. Had his heart attack.'

My breath stopped in my throat and I raised my hand to
my mouth.

Ronald stopped tapping. 'You didn't know?'

I wanted to say that of course I'd known, that I had visited
him every day in hospital, but Ronald would be able to read
the truth from the tears that were forming in my eyes. I
shook my head. 'Nobody . . .' My voice broke and I coughed
before trying again. 'Nobody told me. I hadn't seen him
for a while.' I wiped the tears away. I didn't know why I was
so upset.

'I'm sorry.' He lifted his arm from behind my seat and put
out a hand. It never reached me, for he retracted it almost
immediately and put it back on the steering wheel. 'I had
no idea.' He coughed. 'He looked so vulnerable, so small.
He had these two circles', he indicated a distance between
finger and thumb, 'shaved in his chest hair where they'd
attached the electrodes.' He was breathing faster and the
sound filled the car. 'And then these letters started to come',
his voice got louder, 'from the Amsterdam investigator. That's

when I understood what he'd done. Before then, you know, I was telling myself he'd just taken the crates down, left them at Reception or waited for Amsterdam to pick them up. I never asked him; we never talked about it. But when these Requests For Information came,' his voice lingered heavily on the capital letters, 'I knew there was something wrong. But what could I do?' He gave a lengthy sigh. 'I just ignored it. And it went away.'

Ronald turned the key in the ignition; the engine started and the lights came back on. As he forced the gear into reverse he turned to me. 'So Lantinga still walks free,' he said. 'So what. He shot a criminal. I've kept an eye on him – he's done nothing since. It's a small price to pay.'

My world had shrunk to the inside of my car and the triangle of light in front of me. It was five o'clock, just before rush hour, the snow was falling heavily and I was following a snowplough south. My windscreen wipers were creating piles of snow in the corners of the window. Their back-and-forth motion had a hypnotic quality and I found myself looking at them rather than the road. I needed to focus fifty metres further ahead, at the red tail-lights of the truck in front of me. My rearview mirror was full of the cordon of cars following. I'd been driving for almost half an hour and fatigue was building up behind my eyes from the strain of staring through the thick curtain of snow.

I was torn in two directions, just like those wipers. I knew I couldn't tell anybody that Piet Huizen was my father and still expect to stay on the case. They would automatically take me off it, for obvious reasons. I'd known that this morning, when I was going the other way along the A9 all by myself. But now things were different. Should I protect him, just as Ronald had done, or should I tell the chief inspector that the Alkmaar Police had a witness and we should definitely reopen the case? My hands were clenched on the steering wheel. To tell or not to tell, that was the question. Could I mention the witness but leave my father out of it – talk and protect at the same time? But if that were possible, wouldn't Ronald de Boer have already done exactly that?

Our cordon reached the tunnel under the Noordzee-kanaal and I sat back in relief at the short interlude of respite from the snow. A car overtook me, speeding up in the improved visibility, but I stayed behind the snow truck and even fell back a bit more, hoping another car would slot in between, sheltering me from some of the truck's spray. But apart from that one car, everybody else stayed in the chain we'd formed several kilometres ago.

I peeled off on the ring road around Amsterdam. When I finally parked along the canal, the new-fallen snow was almost twenty centimetres deep. It was a miracle that a spot outside the house was free – a black rectangle of road where another car had just left. I parked slowly and carefully.

I dragged my body up the almost vertical stairs. Once inside, I didn't stop to take off my coat or boots before dialling my father's number – only to get an answering machine.

My mother had been certain I'd chosen to join the police

to be like my father, but until now I had never felt any connection with him. Knowing what he had done, however, created an unexpected bond.

For a brief moment I thought he might be able to understand my own problems, but that feeling quickly faded. I went into the bathroom and forced myself to look at my face in the mirror. I was much worse than him. He had just swiped some files. I had slept with a murderer. I brought my head forward, fast and hard. The sound of the shattering glass was followed by the comforting pain of cut skin.

I held my hands away from me, the fingers spread out so that I didn't have to feel my own skin. Blood ran down my forehead, pooling in the corner of my left eye. Revulsion coursed through every pore of my body.

The first week after I'd found Wendy Leeuwenhoek's body, I'd expected everybody to see through my lies, and I died a little every time someone believed me. I'd wanted to scream out the truth whenever they nodded gravely at my preposterous falsehoods. Now that impulse to loudly confess had ebbed away; what was left was fear of exposure and an ever-growing self-disgust. I went to work every day, as there I was doing something good, whereas here in my flat, in the dark, alone, all I could think of were my sins.

My hands started to tremble. My father must have felt like this for over a decade. He'd kept those crates behind to delay his colleagues, as a protest to his boss who clearly thought he wasn't competent any more, just because he was old. It had been a prank, a minor misdemeanour that had gone wrong when he'd had his heart attack. The thought of my father's protest action made me smile. My hands stopped shaking. I'd keep my father out of trouble, I promised myself. I pressed my hands against my face and felt the wetness of tears on my cheeks. I opened the tap, scooped handfuls of ice-cold water up and rinsed the blood from my forehead and out of my eyes.

Chapter Seven

The next morning in the office, my words of greeting to Hans stuck in my throat. My desk was a picture of emptiness, naked and exposed like never before. The grain in the wood was visible for the first time in a while. Lines came together and veered apart as if they were attracted and repelled at irregular intervals by magnets at either side of the desk. My papers and files had disappeared. Where yesterday my reports on the Wendy Leeuwenhoek case and my photos had marked out part of our shared office as mine, today my space looked as if it was ready for somebody new to move in. Could they have found out about my father so quickly? Or had they finally found out the truth about Wendy?

I traced the lines of the wood grain with a finger and wondered if I was touching my desk for the last time. I hugged my pink folder to my chest with the other hand, afraid to put it down and have it swallowed up as seemed to have happened with everything else I owned. In the shadow of my PC monitor, my pen holder with seven blue biros and a pencil stood alone on the desk like a solitary scarecrow in a field. I found my phone on the floor. I picked it up and put it back where it belonged.

'Where's my stuff?' I asked the room in general. I tried to sound calm.

'Oh, the boss took it,' Hans said, his eyes not leaving his PC screen.

'Chief Inspector Moerdijk?' I was working hard to control my voice.

Hans nodded but didn't say anything.

I walked over to his chair and looked at his screen over his shoulder. He didn't even try to hide the fact that he was looking at Facebook. 'Everything?'

He turned round. 'As you can see,' and pointed out the emptiness of our office with a sweep of his large hand as if he was sowing grains on barren ground.

'And you let him?' My hands started to tremble. 'You let him take my files? Why? Am I sacked?'

'Sacked? Why would you be?' He swivelled back to his screen. 'He was really angry with you though. Muttered about some meeting with the prosecution. You weren't here. Where were you anyway?'

Relief that I hadn't been fired, that the CI hadn't found out why I had gone to Alkmaar, battled with sudden anger. 'He's taken all of it to the prosecution? I didn't want to give them everything, just my report.' I picked up yesterday's newspaper to look underneath. 'Did he leave anything behind?' I didn't bother putting it back, but let it fall on the floor, discarding it like a pair of laddered tights. He might have missed some photos, some scraps of paper.

Hans stared at me as I opened the drawers to the left and right of him. I knelt down and looked past his legs and his feet in black leather shoes with the worn-down heels to check in his bin. He reached out a hand to place on my shoulder. I got up quickly and avoided the contact. I paced through the office, looking under desks even though in some cells of my now fevered brain I knew it was pointless. In the corner, the boxes of files in the Petersen case stood as a reminder that I should have been here rather than in Alkmaar. I took my frustration out on each of them as I dug through the papers. Photos, reports and forms in duplicate floated through the air, creating a white snowstorm inside our four walls.

'Lotte,' Hans said, 'he took everything away. You can stop looking. Talk to the CI. He was rather meticulous. There's nothing left here.'

'How could he take it without telling me?' By now I was panicking, taking shallow breaths. Oxygen only filled the top layer of my lungs. I tried to calm down, tried to focus on the modern art on the wall, a still-life of blue and red intestines combined in a frame, oddly reminiscent of the open PC in Wouter Vos's apartment, but I couldn't get myself under control.

I walked back to my desk, thinking feverishly. He had touched my photos. They were *my* photos! I should have kept them at home. If only I hadn't been in Alkmaar, I could have given them my reports and kept all my photos. The pink folder lay on my desk in silent condemnation. Someone else would be looking at those photos now. Someone else would be holding the photo I'd touched every day: Wendy Leeuwenhoek as everybody in the country knew her, the photo her parents, Paul and Monique, had given to the press and to us fifteen years ago, when Wendy had disappeared, the one they had thought best represented their daughter. It had been taken when Wendy was six years old, five months before she'd gone missing. In the photo, her hair was tied in short blonde pigtails, one either side of her head, which dangled down in corkscrews onto her shoulders. She wore a pair of jeans, white trainers and a pink T-shirt decorated with splatters of mud. She held a small plastic watering can, white with yellow daisies, with both hands crammed together side by side in the handle, straining to carry the weight. She stood in the vegetable garden at the back of her grandparents' house, smiling widely at whoever was taking the photo. One of her front teeth was missing.

I knew all these details without having to look at the photo. I also knew that she would never get her grown-up teeth. Today she should have been twenty-one, going to university maybe. Instead she'd never changed from this picture that was now part of the nation's memory.

'I can't let it go like this. I didn't get a chance to say . . .' I raised my hand to my forehead, trying to stop the pain exploding from my mind.

Hans got up from his chair. 'Calm down, Lotte.' The sound of his voice was as about soothing as sandpaper.

My heart punched the inside of my ribcage at small intervals. 'Fuck you – you let him take her.' Forcing the words out made my throat hurt. Two of my colleagues stopped and stared in the hallway. 'Fuck you too!' I screamed. Hans put a hand on my arm. I shook it off.

'He should have told me! Why didn't he call me?' The pressure behind my eyes was growing; my tongue blocked the back of my throat. 'Fuck him,' I whispered. The office started to swirl; the world went black. I gripped the back of my chair and blinked hard. My surroundings returned in a grey-red colour.

'Lotte.' Hans put his hand on my arm again, with more strength than before, getting a solid grip. It hurt. I forced my breathing to slow. Breathed in 1-2-3. Breathed out 1-2-3.

'Sorry,' I said. 'Sorry, Hans.' I peeled his hand off my arm and stormed away to the last place of privacy: the toilets.

Hans was gone when I got back but he'd left a yellow stickie on my phone with a message in his square hand-writing: *the boss wants to talk to you.*

I picked up the phone, but not to call the boss. I dialled the number of a psychiatrist. I could no longer deny that I needed help. Her first free appointment was the next morn-ing. I had to try to hold it together for one more day.

Chapter Eight

My footsteps dragged as I slowly made my way down the corridor to Chief Inspector Moerdijk's office. The door was closed. I knocked, balancing a plastic cup of water on a new notepad.

'Lotte? Yes, come in.' The CI's face was drawn into lines of disapproval. Like a sheet of origami paper that had been previously used for another pattern, laughter lines were still visible, but faint. 'Take a seat.'

I sat down opposite his desk, on the edge of my chair. I refused the temptation to slump and stayed upright, my spine long, my back straight, the majority of my weight carried by my own muscles in a display of total control. I put the plastic cup on my side of his desk, opened my notepad and waited for him to start the conversation.

'Where were you yesterday?' The chief inspector folded his arms together.

On the wall, the books lined up together on their shelves gave me strength. They kept their knowledge hidden inside until someone pulled the covers apart. 'In Alkmaar.'

70

The frown between his eyebrows deepened. 'You were supposed to take the evidence to the prosecutor's office.'

I looked at my notepad for inspiration but found none. The circles of the ring binding were almost parallel, apart from the third, which sloped down and encroached on the next spiral's space. I bent it into place with the back of my pencil. 'I know. But the Petersen case—'

'That's no excuse. I had to cover for you.' His PC emitted a beep and the chief inspector's close scrutiny travelled from me to his screen. He double-clicked with the mouse then rolled its scrolling wheel with a rapid whirr. 'Did you at least find anything interesting?'

'There might be something,' I said.

He kept his eyes on the screen, typed some text with two fingers and hit Enter with a distinct movement. Then he looked back at me. 'Like what? Come on, Lotte, don't make me drag this out of you.'

I sat still, didn't move my hands or my feet and looked the CI straight in the eye. 'Give me a couple of days. I need to check it further.'

He watched me over the edge of his reading glasses. It was a long, deep stare – as if the pale blue eyes under the white hair were attempting to look through my eyeballs and straight into my mind. Then he pushed his glasses higher up his nose and said, 'I'm sure you noticed that I took the files to the prosecution yesterday.' He opened a drawer and rummaged through some papers. His head was still bent over the open drawer as he went on: 'I gave them all the files on

Wendy Leeuwenhoek, just to be on the safe side, and all the tapes.'

'Yes, the office has lost half its contents.' Someone else was looking at those photos. It made my eyes sting. I rubbed the palm of my hand over the far corner of my eye but hid the gesture by smoothing my hair. I ran my hand all the way over my head, then reached for my plait.

'The prosecutor should see everything before the trial,' he said. 'They still haven't set a date.' He got a new diary out of the drawer, and when he flipped the thin pages, it sounded like someone thumbing through a Bible or a hymn book. 'Probably next month.'

I nodded.

'You have to testify,' he told me. 'Your statement will make all the difference. It's a shame the last meeting isn't on the tapes. A recorded confession would have made it watertight—'

The faintness I had felt in the office came crawling back from my toes, via my legs, to my stomach. Its content, mainly black coffee, rushed to my mouth. I kept my teeth locked together, waited, then took a few more deeps breaths until the blackness subsided. As I reached for my water, my hand trembled but didn't visibly shake. I lifted the plastic cup.

A picture of Wendy as I had found her jumped into my mind. The ground around her showed marks where my hands had been digging. The earth had given way easily under my fingers as if it had been ready to return her. At first my fingers had only found earthworms and woodlice amongst the soil as the earth buried itself under my nails.

Then I touched the smooth bone of her skull. That's when I stopped and called in the rest of the team. That's when I knew what I'd found. This was the first time I had allowed myself to realise the truth.

I waited by her side, crouched down but not touching her until the technical team and the police photographer turned up. I wanted to scrub my hands free of the feeling of her corpse but instead I'd waited and watched and stood guard as the photographer took shots of her skeleton partially liberated from the dark soil. Her skull looked like a delicate egg tapped open with a teaspoon. It must have taken more force to fracture her bones. By the time the team turned up, I'd stopped crying and managed to wipe the tears off my face.

I remembered how my skin had been streaked with mud from my hands. But I had been holding up; I had been keeping it together.

'You're not worried about your statement, I hope,' the boss said. 'They will question your methods.'

I wasn't sure I could keep it together for much longer. The thought of being on the stand and answering the questions of the judge and the lawyers filled me with dread.

'And I don't understand why you went to the Alkmaar police in the first place,' he continued. 'They were completely incompetent in the original investigation. It was a good thing I took over.'

'They had a witness,' I said. As soon as the words left my mouth I wished I could take them back.

CI Moerdijk tore his glasses off his nose. 'A witness? Who? In the Leeuwenhoek case?' He smacked the glasses on top of the diary. The pages flipped over and hid what was underneath, not used enough in this first week of the year to stay open.

'No, in Alkmaar. The police there had a witness who saw the suspected killer arrive at Petersen's house just before he was shot.'

The CI pushed back on his chair and stood up. He turned towards the window so that the creases in the back of his jacket faced me. 'For a second I thought . . . Never mind.' He looked at me over his shoulder. 'Are you sure?'

'They told me so themselves.'

He turned away again. It had started to snow, a white background for the CI's lean frame in its charcoal-grey suit. 'Who did this witness see?'

'Anton Lantinga. Or at least his car.'

'I never heard of this witness.' He placed his hands in the small of his back and massaged his spine, then swayed his hips from right to left to give a further stretch. 'Reliable?'

'The Alkmaar detective seemed to know him very well,' I said. 'But personally, not from police business.'

He went back to his desk and sat down. 'You met him?'

'Yes, the Alkmaar police took me.'

'It was strange how little paperwork came from them.' He pinched the bridge of his small nose.

'They told me they had boxes full of information – stacks of files.'

The PC beeped again. The CI narrowed his eyes to slits

74

and moved his face closer to the screen. He felt with his hand over the surface of his desk. 'Why didn't that get to me?'

'I don't know.'

He searched through the contents of his desk. 'And yet I asked for more information. Three times, I think.' He patted the sides of his jacket and checked inside his pockets. 'No reply.'

I pointed. 'Under the diary.'

He lifted it and retrieved his glasses. 'Anton Lantinga – that's a surprise. We talked to him, but found nothing. I'm sure I've met him at some charity event since. Well, finding a witness after all this time – it's a reason to officially reopen the case.' He read what was on the screen and started typing again. 'You, Hans and Stefanie can work on it, see where it goes.' His fingers tap-tap-tapped on the keyboard. This was the time to mention that DI Piet Huizen was my father, to say that I wouldn't – couldn't – be impartial, that there was a clear conflict of interest and that my involvement would be against all the regulations. Instead I drew circles on my notepad.

'Financial Fraud will be pleased with that one, another big fish,' he went on. 'I remember Lantinga set up his own firm after Petersen Capital went belly-up. Very successful they've been too. Let me know if I can help.' Tap-tap-tap and Enter. 'Always thought it was Geert-Jan Goosens, Petersen's other business partner. Not that he killed him, but that he hired someone. The money was never found, you know – the money they embezzled from their investors.'

'How much was it?'

'Ninety million guilders . . . just over forty million euros. No need to write it down, it's all in the notes. Check out Lantinga, and Petersen's widow. She had a watertight alibi if I remember correctly. Bit too watertight if you ask me.'

I nodded and got up out of my chair. Only last night I'd decided that I'd keep my father out of trouble, and now I'd put him directly in the firing line. And for what? To defend him against the boss's remarks? I felt like a traitor because deep down I knew I'd done it to distract the boss from the missing recorded confession and my use of violence.

I had to protect my father. I had to keep working the case to keep him in the clear. Oh my God, what if they found out? My job was all I had. My legs wobbled and I held on to the armrests. I pushed to get myself upright.

The CI was too engrossed in what was on his screen to notice. 'Talk to me on Monday,' he said.

In the canteen I had the third of my morning coffees. I held my mug tight and thought of the coffee cups in my father's house, the white flame cold on the porcelain. Was this some deep-seated revenge, getting even for being abandoned as a child? I took a gulp of coffee. The bitterness in my mouth and the scalding of my tongue was what I sought, the surge of caffeine in my blood only of secondary importance.

The canteen felt different without people. The chairs waited for lunchtime; only a few clumps of policemen in uniform were talking in hushed voices about something that couldn't be discussed at their desks. The room was poised before the rush like a church on Sunday morning before the service started. My scalp hurt as if my hair was tied back too tightly. I undid my plait and watched the different groups of people scattered around the tables. I didn't want to see the snowy world outside the window. It was too white, too pure for me to look at. My eyes hurt, as if someone was pushing a screwdriver into my brain through one of my eye-sockets. I closed them in an attempt to make it go away. I put my mug down on the table and rested my head in my hands. My hair fell forwards and covered my face.

'When are we arresting him?' Stefanie's voice shredded my thoughts like an alarm clock destroyed sleep. She pulled up the chair opposite mine, scraping it along the ground.

'We can't arrest him—' I hid my hands under the table to hide their trembling.

'But there's a witness, right? Moerdijk told me there was a witness.'

I slumped against the chair, its hard-edged back digging uncomfortably into my spine. 'When did you talk to him? I only left the boss five minutes ago.'

'He called me.'

'I've got to go.' I stood up. I needed to be alone.

'Fine – I'll come with you.' She walked beside me as we left the canteen.

I tried to shake her off. There was only just enough space to walk two abreast down the hall. On my right, the drop to the atrium beckoned as we followed the walkway that connected the old part of the building to the new. I stared down over the wooden banister and trailed my hand over the smooth iron verticals that held it up.

'Anton Lantinga – who'd have thought it? Let's pick him up now.' She needed to take two steps for every one of mine. Even in her high-heeled shoes she was almost a head shorter than me. 'That would be a front-page story right there.'

'You're insane.' I lengthened my steps further. It had been my tiredness that had made me jump to the wrong conclusion: that she had suggested arresting my father. Now I could breathe again. Still, every centimetre I put between the two of us felt like a blessing.

'Shall I get him in for questioning?' Stefanie's voice was breathless, either from trying to keep up with me or from excitement at the thought of arresting Lantinga.

I didn't respond. My office was two floors up from the canteen. We passed by the lifts but I ignored them and moved to the stairs.

'So how come the CI didn't know about this witness?' Stefanie had stopped at the lift button and now had to run to catch up with me.

'I suppose the files got lost.' I took the stairs two at a time as I always did.

'They couldn't have done,' she puffed. 'It doesn't make sense.'

'In transit?' The sound of my boots echoed through the stairwell, the concrete steps amplifying the noise.

'Didn't someone pick them up?' Somehow she was managing to keep up with my pace.

'They lost the paperwork then.' One floor up.

'But he asked for more information,' Stefanie said. I wasn't going fast enough to lose her or even to stop her talking. 'It's strange, isn't it?'

I pushed open the door at the end of the stairwell. 'No, not really.'

'Of course it is: a witness after all these years . . .'

We arrived at my office. 'It isn't "after all these years": the guy came forward immediately.'

'What's he like?' She was breathing hard and fanned herself with the front of her fitted jacket.

'Who?' I glanced over at my empty desk and the reports from the Petersen file that I'd strewn all over the floor.

'The witness, of course.' A flush moved from the top button of her white blouse up the sides of her neck and covered her cheeks, the red blotches clashing with the fuchsia pink of her suit. She wiped a few drops of sweat off her forehead, which was fleshed out and therefore unlined, unlike mine.

'I don't know – geek done good, I'd say.'

'Perfect. They make excellent witnesses. The judge will love that.'

'Stefanie, there isn't enough—'

'Not yet, but we have some time. What about the detective?'

'What about him?' I bent to pick the papers up and put them back in their cardboard box.

'What's *he* like?'

From my position on the floor I saw the ladder in her

79

tights – she'd be horrified when she noticed. 'In his fifties, seemed professional enough. Bit over-controlled.'

'I thought he was older, this – what's his name . . . Piet Huizen?'

I turned back to the floor and my tidying. 'Oh, him – yes, he's retired.'

'Interesting . . .'

'Why?'

'Well, retired guy, missing witnesses, missing records – it's worth investigating, that's all. We should look into that.'

I made a show of checking my watch. 'I thought you wanted to interview Lantinga. We've got some time – he'll still be at work.'

A smile bloomed on Stefanie's face and I sighed with relief, hoping I'd managed to drive any thoughts that linked my father to missing records from her mind.

Chapter Nine

The shiny copper plaque by the door read simply: *Omega*.
The seventeenth-century houses on the Herengracht did
their best to bend themselves around the semi-circle of the
canal. Their facades leaned forward and back as the sub-
sidence of Amsterdam's peat and sand foundations had tipped
them centimetres this way and that. Shops, businesses and
living accommodation stood in non-uniform individuality
side by side along the wide water, each house slightly different from its neighbour: some had three storeys, some four;
a different style of gable, a different colour paintwork; some
with steps leading up from the lower-ground floor, others
with ground-floor entrances. Despite the variations, they still
formed a coherent row.

We went up the flight of stone stairs above the basement
entry – ten steps that probably took us over the partners'
bicycle storage. The steps had been swept clear of snow.
When the receptionist buzzed us in, I pushed open the
door, which had been painted the green of old 1,000-
guilder notes.

A model of a sailing ship, its white sails stained nicotine-yellow by age, sat in a glass display cabinet to the left of the reception area. The wallpaper was of a pale green fleur-de-lis pattern. The girl behind Reception and her desk with the computer on it seemed to have landed by mistake in a period drama.

'Police, Financial Fraud department,' Stefanie announced, showing her badge. 'We're here to see Anton Lantinga.'

'Mr Lantinga? I'm afraid he's in New York this week. Did you have an appointment?' The dark-haired, latte-skinned girl checked her screen and typed something. 'Yes, he's back on Wednesday.'

'What about Karin Petersen?'

'I don't think we have someone of that name . . . Ah, you mean Karin Lantinga, of course.'

Stefanie and I exchanged a glance. So Karin had married Anton. How soon after Otto's death?

The receptionist dialled a number and looked at us. 'What may I say is it regarding?'

'I'll have to tell her that in person,' Stefanie said.

The young woman shrugged. 'Mrs Lantinga,' she said to the phone, 'I've got two police officers here for you . . . I don't know, they wouldn't say . . . OK . . . OK, I'll ask them to wait.' She put the phone down. 'She's in a meeting right now and will see you as soon as she's free. Please take a seat.'

I turned and sat down gingerly on a vulnerable-looking green and white striped settee. I didn't dare rest against it. Stefanie stayed standing, admired the ship and then went back to the receptionist.

'Do you have any brochures on Omega? For investors,' she said.

The receptionist moved a sheath of straightened black hair from her shoulder to her back with an imperious gesture. 'Omega is closed for new investors,' she said, 'and even before that there was a ten-million euro minimum investment. I can take your name and have our Investor Relations department contact you if and when we do accept new investors.'

'Any material on fund performance?'

'Karin Lantinga will give you everything you need. She'll be with you shortly. Please take a seat.'

Stefanie didn't. She walked up and down, picked up a copy of *Het Financieele Dagblad* and looked at the front page, then turned to page two at a speed that made it clear that she'd read no more than the headlines. How long would Karin Petersen, now Lantinga, make us wait?

Just then, a door opened and two men, both in suits, probably in their late forties, walked through accompanied by a slim woman who looked of similar age. She shook their hands, and I heard her say, 'Thank you so much for your time. Sonja will get your coats.' Sonja the receptionist opened a hidden panel to a closet and handed the men their overcoats. Throughout, we were ignored.

The woman opened the front door, shook their hands again and closed it before turning to us. 'You're the police, I suppose.' Her smile had disappeared and she looked older, but still younger than the fifty-three I knew her to be.

Stefanie introduced herself and showed her badge. Karin was a little taller than Stefanie but needed ten-centimetre heels to help her. Her hair was golden-blonde with streaks of silver grey. It was tied in a bun at the nape of her neck, the weight of it tipping her head slightly back, removing any slackness under the chin and giving her a Grace Kelly-like poise and elegance. She faced me and said, 'And you are . . .'

I got up from the sofa and said my name.

Karin threw one look at the receptionist and led us through the door. 'We won't go to my office,' she said, walking down the corridor lined with Dutch Golden Age oil paintings on either side. I didn't recognise the artists – we were moving too quickly to have a good look – but they seemed to be originals. I was reminded of Wouter Vos's apartment, where modern works decorated the hallway. 'We'll use the boardroom instead.' Karin opened a door and over her shoulder I got my first glimpse of true opulence. The ceiling was painted to show a sea battle in which large ships, one identical to the model downstairs, sailed at full mast in the kind of sea that got surfers excited. Grey thunder clouds looked even darker in contrast with the red, white and blue of the triumphant Dutch flag.

'Admiral Michiel de Ruyter,' Karin said. 'The ceiling shows his famous victory over the English at Medway. We based the decorating scheme for the entire office on this room.' She sat down at the head of the cherrywood table, looking regal, powerful and in absolute control.

Stefanie pulled out a chair to the right of Karin. I would

have liked to remain standing, preferably in a corner where I'd have a perfect view, but Stefanie pointed at the chair next to hers and gestured for me to sit down. At least I didn't have to sit between the two of them; I could watch both women at the same time. I stroked my fingers over the wood, which was glossed like a new conker. Between the painted ceiling and the green and white striped wallpaper, there were signs of the modern era in the room as well: the star phone in the middle for conference calls, microphones sunk in the table and a projector at the far end. A small stand in the corner carried a tray with bottles of Spa water and a teapot as well as a selection of chocolate biscuits. We, however, were not offered anything.

'What can I help you with?' Karin said. As she spoke, she took her BlackBerry out of her bag. Its red light flashed and she scrolled through the emails with a French-manicured finger, her eyes glued to the little screen.

I couldn't place her accent. It sounded flat, studied, as if she'd had a regional accent that she'd worked hard to get rid of. I tried to imagine her speaking in the softer tones of a southern accent or the farm-like cadences of the north – but neither suited her. A delicate perfume, with notes of apple and jasmine, floated over the table.

'We're re-investigating the murder of your husband, Otto Petersen,' Stefanie said, unsmiling and professional.

Karin put the BlackBerry on the table, sat back and folded her hands. The right was only adorned with a plain golden wedding band, but on the left the entire bottom segment of her ring finger was covered by a square-cut blue stone in a golden setting. 'Has any . . . new evidence come to light?' she asked.

'Yes,' Stefanie said. 'We've had some new information. It's too early to disclose what it is.'

Karin's face turned itself into a mask. Nothing moved, not a muscle around her lips, not a blink of an eye. Even the lines on her forehead smoothed themselves out. She looked at me. Her eyes, deep blue as the sapphire on her finger, narrowed between the crow's feet. 'Sorry, but I thought you were from the Financial Fraud department.'

'I am,' Stefanie said. 'Detective Meerman is from CID.'

'I see.' Her eyes slid from me to Stefanie.

'Could you please tell us your version of events on the evening your husband died,' Stefanie said.

'Anything in particular? Or would you like me to tell you all the minutiae?' Karin raised an eyebrow.

'Your movements in the afternoon.'

'I can't remember all of them.' She tipped her head sideways a little at the end of the sentence.

'You drove to the prison . . .' Stefanie prompted. She moved forward and I had to stretch my upper body to its full length to keep Karin in view.

'Otto had asked me to pick him up at five o'clock in front of the prison.'

'He called you?'

'As soon as his release date was decided.' She scrolled the trackball on the front of her BlackBerry again, clicked on an email and read it.

'You expected that?'

86

'Yes. I always thought he'd want me to drive him home.' Her eyes hadn't left the device.

'OK. So you drove to the prison,' Stefanie said.

Karin was silent. She let it last.

Stefanie was the first to fill the gap. 'What time did you get there?'

Karin smiled at her BlackBerry and put it back on the table. 'I got there before five – a quarter to, ten to, something like that – and waited for him. I sat there for half an hour and still he wasn't out. So I went up to the prison, to talk to the warden. Still no sign of Otto. Then the warden spoke to one of his colleagues, who told us my husband had been released just after four. He had apparently got in a cab and left.'

'Were you angry? Annoyed?'

Karin unfolded her hands and used the right one to tuck some strands of blonde hair behind her ear. 'No, I wasn't angry.' She looked Stefanie straight in the eye. 'I thought something had come up and he hadn't been able to contact me.'

Stefanie nodded. 'A change of plan.'

'Exactly.'

'He could have called?'

'I assumed he'd phoned the house.'

'And had he?'

'Sorry?'

'Was there a message on your answerphone when you got home?'

'Otto was dead when I got home.' Her voice purely stated the facts. She might as well have told us it was raining. She caressed the double string of pearls that fitted closely around her neck, probably to hide some slackness in the skin.

'But was there a message on the answerphone?'

I watched this game between Stefanie and Karin. What was truth after all this time? Could anybody still remember exactly what they'd done, felt or seen after ten years?

'No, there was no message.'

Had she been angry then? Unless she had changed a lot in the ten years since his death, this wasn't a woman to keep waiting. Had she been glad of the delay, perhaps? Glad for the extra time it gave her, to consider how she was going to tell him she was leaving him? Postponing the moment she had to tell him of her affair? In my mind I pictured her inside that car, waiting outside the prison. Nervous but controlled. He'd asked her to be there, so she was there, doing her duty. It rained – drops like tears falling on the car and streaming down the windows. She didn't want to be there: surely she was wishing she was somewhere else, anywhere else.

'So now, knowing there wasn't a message, why do you think Otto asked you to pick him up?'

Karin let her eyes rest on the table in front of her. She took a deep breath and replied, 'I think he wanted me out of the way. Whatever he had planned, whomever he was meeting, he wanted to make sure I wasn't at home.'

I wrote *what had he planned? – who was he meeting?* on my notepad.

Karin laughed, a sound like breaking glass. 'Your colleague clearly likes my explanation,' she told Stephanie. 'Hadn't you figured that out for yourself yet?'

'You had an affair with Anton Lantinga, whom you've now married.' Stefanie paused for Karin's confirming nod, then said: 'Someone saw him at the scene of the crime.'

I kicked Stefanie on her shoe, hard enough to shut her up but soft enough not to make her cry out.

'Who saw him?'

'We can't disclose that.'

'He wasn't there. He went home that morning.'

'But—' Stefanie began.

'Where's Anton now?' I interrupted her.

'New York, meeting new investors.'

'You didn't keep the Petersen Capital name,' I said.

'No, of course not. This is an entirely different firm.'

'When did you found it?' Stefanie said.

'We had to close Petersen Capital after the inquest and Otto's conviction. We worked with investors to see if they wanted to transfer their money to our new company, Omega.'

'And did they?'

'Many of them did. They realised that Otto was the rogue element. The firm was otherwise run on sound principles.'

'And you didn't know anything about what he did?'

'He was the only one of us to go to prison. The court decided we were innocent. Many of our investors agreed with the judge. And we've made them enough money to repay their trust.'

'When is Anton due back?'

'The middle of next week. I'll ask him to contact you. If you could give me your card . . .' Stefanie handed hers over. 'Is that all?' It was a graceful dismissal.

'Yes, thank you.' We left. Karin didn't show us out – we were not important investors.

We walked along the next canal over, back to the office. On a map, Amsterdam's canals looked like the concentric circles I drew on my notepad, like the year rings of a tree but cut in half, with other canals connecting them like the spokes in a bicycle wheel. Ducks slipped and slid over the ice until they found a hole and joined their friends. All skaters would hate them for keeping the gaps open. The ice was white, water mixed with snow. On this canal, where the tour boats didn't break through it once an hour, it would be thick enough to hold a person's weight in another day or two, and the frozen water would form a temporary pavement for the two houseboats more permanently moored with the ice as an extra anchor.

'I bet he was meeting Anton Lantinga,' Stefanie said, her words accompanied by a white cloud of breath. She walked with her hands deep in her pockets, a scarf wrapped around her neck, and turned to look at her reflection in a shop window. She didn't wear a hat, probably too afraid it would mess up her perfect shoulder-length cut.

'Not if it's about Anton and Karin.'

'No?'

'Would he have known about them? Who'd have told him?'

'Maybe Karin herself did.'

'And it festered in him while he was locked up, until it boiled over on his first hour out.' I said the words to check if they felt true coming out of my mouth. I couldn't tell. I didn't know Otto Petersen yet – I didn't know what he was like. I needed to get a better idea of his personality. Had he been a calculated risktaker: *I get forty million euros, that's worth seven years in jail*, or a megalomaniac: *I'm so clever, they'll never catch me*, or just someone who got sucked into circumstances, started small and watched it snowball into something huge he couldn't control, possibly egged on by his wife. 'You worked on the first Petersen case, didn't you?'

'I only helped out, mainly in clearing their office.'

'Did you meet Otto?'

'No, he had already been arrested. I only met Anton. I remember he put up quite a fight when we confiscated his PC. Wasn't having any of it. Quite funny. He gave me all this *who do you think you are* stuff. I told him: *police*, and just took it. He was livid. Hopping up and down. He told me that unplugging that PC had just cost him more money than I'd make in my entire career. He was probably right.' Karin sighed.

So I needed to find someone else who could tell me. 'Who else might have met Otto?'

'Not sure. Wasn't Freek Veenstra the main guy working on it? He died last year, remember.'

'Veenstra? God, I keep forgetting the Petersen Capital fraud was that long ago.' I wondered if my father had known

Otto. No reason he should have. He hadn't called me back after my message.

'Yes, it does seem a long time ago. That PC we took from Anton, officially it was probably portable but it was twice the size of the laptops we use now. It weighed a ton. That was state-of-the-art back then. They had all this advanced kit. Everybody ran round like headless chickens, trying to do their jobs and we were taking all their equipment away. I loved it. My best day at work *ever*. I can't wait to see the look on his face when we arrest him again.'

I didn't know what to say to that and Stefanie and I finished our walk in silence, the only sound that of our boots tramping through the snow.

'Geert-Jan Goosens on Monday?' I said as we walked past the gates of the police station. The curved modern statues in the garden, which would be partially covered by plants come spring, were now the only shapes that broke the square monotony of building and windows.

'Good idea. I'll call ahead and make an appointment. No point in trying to surprise him. I'm sure Karin has already let him know we're looking at this.'

'You think so?' I wasn't so sure. Karin Petersen, now Lantinga, had every reason not to help Goosens.

Chapter Ten

Outside the Cyber Salon hairdressers, I had the last appointment of the day at 5.45 p.m. My hands had difficulty in fastening the lock on my bike; they were as clumsy as the rest of me. I didn't normally come here – all these trendy people, hairdressers with cuts you wouldn't want to be seen dead with – but this time I mistakenly thought it would be a treat.

'Hi, I'm here for a colour and just a trim. My name is Lotte,' I hesitated, 'Meerman.' Even after more than a year, using my old name was an uncomfortable verbal admission of failure.

The man behind the counter pressed his finger along the names in the appointment book. It was hard not to stare at the orange triangle that studded his left eyebrow.

'So, yes,' his eyes took in my hair, 'cut and colour. OK, come on through. Take your coat off and slip this on. Trudelies can see you now.'

Trudelies, young enough to be my daughter, had cherry-red hair, which was probably originally blonde, built up in

93

spikes like skewers on her head. She combed through my hair with hands to appraise it.

I stared at my mirror image. The skin under my eyes was the deep purple of aubergines from lack of sleep and flecked with red where the skin had been inflamed from too much crying. My bedraggled hair hung limp around my shoulders. I looked as if I'd drowned a week ago; my face even had the waterlogged puffiness of the dead bodies we fished out of the canals. My hair disgusted me. I remembered how he'd touched it, how beautiful he'd said it was. He had played with it when we'd still been in bed. He'd said it was just like hers.

'Just shave it all off,' I whispered.

'Pardon?'

'I've changed my mind.' I lifted my head and met Trudelies's eyes in the mirror. 'I want it all shaven off.'

Trudelies laughed nervously.

'I'm serious. Just shave it. A number two all over, isn't that what you call it?'

'I – I can't do that.'

'Why not? I'm the customer.'

'That's not a Cyber Salon approved haircut.'

'Sod that. Just do it.'

She picked up the scissors and held them behind her back. 'No.'

'Cut it.'

'No.'

I started to undo the plastic coat.

'Wait, wait.' She rested a hand on my arm and put slight pressure on. 'I'll cut it short. If you don't like it, come back in a week and I'll shave it. Free of charge.'

I was too tired to fight. I sat back and grabbed my hair in one hand, saying, 'Make this go away.'

'And colour?'

'No.'

'Maybe back to your original colour?'

Whatever was that? I had dyed it as soon as my mother had let me, from mousy to sun-kissed. Mousy sounded appropriate: grey, matted – the colour of mourning.

I nodded. 'This colour.' I pressed my finger to my roots. 'This colour all over.'

A smile crept onto the stylist's face. The scissors made a snapping noise.

'I'll cut off the length, do the colour and shape it afterwards.'

I didn't respond.

'Can I get you anything? Tea? Coffee?'

'Just cut.'

I kept my eyes on the mirror, so they wouldn't drift to the growing pile of hair on the floor. It was only hair; it didn't hurt. In fact, the more she cut off, the lighter my head felt. A weight was removed from my scalp. I closed my eyes as she mixed the new colour and spread it all over my head. It burned my scalp and the ammoniac smell burned my nose.

Cutting and burning. Burning and cutting.

Trudelies had warmed to her task and brought photos of example cuts for me to see. 'How about this? It's quite striking. Or this one, a bit softer.'

I didn't even look at the book. 'Do as you please. I wanted it shaved, you wouldn't do that, now you make the decision.'

Her eyes met mine in the mirror. She tilted her head in a question. Her spiky hair never moved. I finally said to her, 'Short, then. I want it really short.'

She took me to have my hair washed by some trainee. The young girl's fingers found the bumps and hollows in my skull with a professionalism that made the intimacy bearable. The washing, conditioning and rinsing took exactly the same amount of time as number nineteen in the chart of the year, which was playing on the radio, most likely meant as a background sound but so deafening that it could not be contained there. When the trainee had finished, Trudelies squeezed the excess water from my hair and walked over to the cutting chair, expecting me to follow her. And of course I did.

She ruffled her hand through my hair, now dark, not mousy, then took up the scissors and began to clip the back of my hair until it just touched the base of my skull. I could feel air nip the nape of my neck, the top of my spine. She shaped it around my face, then blowdried it until the ends were as sharp as razors. When she had finished, she smoothed the top of my head with a gentle hand and said, 'That's great. It really suits you.'

I didn't reply. I no longer looked like myself, but then I no longer felt like myself either.

★   ★   ★

There was something about the evening that unsettled me. The Christmas tree with its bowed branches that dripped their needles on the wooden floor seemed to mock me: it was time to undress it, I decided, and remove the ten baubles and the lights.

I uncorked a bottle of wine, filled a glass and put it on the table, then collected the plastic bag for the Christmas decorations from the cupboard in the hallway. Slowly, I removed the tree's jewellery, each fragile golden globe easily crushable between my clumsy fingers, and rolled up its glossy tinsel. The smell of pine glued itself to my skin, sticky as sap, and the lights burned despondently amidst the green until I switched them off. The tree had gone back to its natural state, a mixture of green and brown mottled needles, sharp enough to sew with, and small brown nodules showing where new leaves would have grown if the tree had not been severed from its roots. No longer heavily made-up for the festive season, it looked surprisingly ugly. I laid it flat on the floor. Somewhere I had the rope I had used to get it up here. I tied it with seven loops to the wooden cross that was nailed to the trunk and opened the curtains and then the window – only to be assaulted by the blast of freezing air.

The phone rang. I let the answermachine reply.

'Hi, Lotte, it's Stefanie. Sorry to disturb you so late, but I have been thinking . . . Are you at home?'

I didn't step away from the window.

'I'm outside your door, your light's on. Is your window open? Pick up the phone.'

I sighed, closed the window and walked over to the table.

'I know you're there, Lotte. I saw you move – you live where the window was open, don't you? Come on, pick up the phone.'

I reached a finger to the button on the machine but was not sure which one to press. Should I pick up or cut her off?

'I've got some ideas about Piet Huizen.'

The decision was made. 'Hi, Stefanie.'

'Can I come in?'

'I'll buzz you up.' I opened the door and waited until I saw her climb the stairs. Once inside, she peeled off her coat like the skin of an onion. 'That's a severe haircut.'

I ignored her comment and walked ahead of her to the front room. 'Take a seat.'

She dropped the coat beside her on the sofa. My fingers ached to pick it up and put it on a hanger, but I left it where it was and sat down on the chair.

'You shouldn't be drinking by yourself,' she said, pointing at my glass. 'You'd better get me some too.'

I got a glass from the mahogany sideboard and poured a small amount, maybe two fingers high.

She took a large glug and emptied a fair amount of the wine in one go. 'What's with that tree? Why is it on the floor? Is this a bad time?'

Clearly it was. It would have been, regardless of what time it was.

'This is a lovely flat,' she said. 'You've done well. I know divorced women who are much worse off.' She raised her glass at me and rubbed her hand over the dark blue velvet of the sofa. 'Bit stark for me, you know – no scatter cushions, no rugs. Bit empty, bit cold. Suits you though.'

I didn't understand how she could think my pale-blue walls and dark wooden furniture cold. For me, the scarcity of fittings created a sense of space. Cushions and carpets would only break the lines that connected the windows to the table, the beautiful parallels of sideboard and picture rails. I had bought my flat from an interior decorator in financial difficulties. I was a cash-buyer and she needed the money. The deal, which included most of the furnishings, was done quickly. Where she kept some pieces for herself, I moved other things around to fill the gaps. She said I should come to her shop on the PC Hooftstraat, Amsterdam's most prestigious shopping area, where it had been flanked by designer clothes shops. With the proceeds of our transaction, she could keep open a bit longer and she said that she would give me a discount. I hadn't felt like buying anything, however. It had been one decision too many. Refusing her offer probably insulted her or maybe she had hoped to make more money out of me. I liked living in surroundings that somebody else had chosen.

Stefanie reached over and helped herself to a couple of mint chocolates out of a box I'd had open on the table for weeks, from before Christmas, as I liked the way the smell of chocolate and mint mingled with that of pine. I didn't stop her from eating them.

'Anyway, Piet Huizen. Did you meet him?' She put a chocolate in her mouth in its entirety, almost pushing her fingers in after.

I imagined dust flying from between her teeth when she chewed. 'I saw him before I met Ronald de Boer.'

'Right, so you went to his house. Was it big?'

'Comfortable.'

'But big? Big like this flat?' She laughed and washed the coating of chocolate from her tongue with another glug of wine. 'Too big?'

'Too big for what?'

'Well, not too big for a woman who took half her ex-husband's company just because she gave him the start-up capital.'

I clenched my fists between my knees to make sure I didn't slap her. I should throw her out; she was poisoning my home. What did she know?

The evening he told me, I had come home early and opened the door to silence. I had stepped over the threshold, unzipped my coat and hung it up. My shoes echoed over the wooden floor – I wasn't sure what to do. I sat down and switched on the TV, but as soon as a picture appeared on the screen, I pressed the remote control to go to the next channel and the next and the next, until I'd exhausted my options and switched it off. The room filled with the ticking of the clock his grandparents had given us for our wedding.

Eventually I heard keys in the door. Footsteps moved from the front door to the kitchen. They went up the stairs. I switched the TV on again. This time I left it on Nederland 1. A talking face, discussing something, hid the sound of the clock. The steps were above my head now.

I got up and walked around the table, pulled the curtains closed to ensure the neighbours couldn't look in and sat down again, waiting for the next creak, which would tell me he was ready to talk. I heard him move down the stairs and across the wooden sea of the parquet floor until he stood beside me. He switched off the TV. I watched my mug of tea and listened as the leather sofa announced his weight. The clock measured out each second of our marriage. I waited as I didn't wish to interrupt the loud ticking. I was not the one who wanted to talk.

'I'm sorry,' he said.

'If you're sorry, don't do it.'

'No, sorry. I . . .' The clock had ticked like a metronome, counting out a requiem. 'I've been stupid,' he said. 'I've been', *tick tick tick*, 'seeing someone.'

I put my mug on the table with a loud bang, unable to control my hand. The glass coffee table held. 'Stop seeing her.'

'I can't.'

My eyes closed. I leaned back against the sofa. Its leather sighed and cried for me. I shielded my face with my hand and pressed it hard against my eyes. Then I made myself face him. His eyes seemed like little blue pebbles in a stream. I looked around me, at our room, and battled with my tears. I swallowed them with the bitter last dregs of my tea. I watched his face in the glass of the table. It had that strange unfamiliarity that mirrors give. I held my tea mug close to my chest. This wasn't supposed to happen to me.

'Please,' I said.

'She's pregnant.'

I could no longer hear the clock over the beat of my heart as I stared at him. I was frozen, robbed of ways to react.

Then I raised my tea mug and smashed it with force into the table's reflection of his face. The glass cracked. The mug split down the middle and landed on the wooden floor in two halves.

'You bastard, you fucking bastard,' I whispered. I got up and felt with my hand on the back of my right hip. My husband backed away. 'Get out of here. Get the fuck out of here.' It was fortunate my fingers hadn't found my gun.

The ticking of the clock reverberated through the room. I took one step over to the mantelpiece, grabbed the bloody clock and hurled it on the floor. When the screws, wheels and glass splinters stopped trying to get away from me, there was finally silence . . .

Stefanie's voice dragged me back to the here and now. 'Is his house too big for a retired policeman?' she said. She helped herself to another couple of chocolates without taking her eyes off me. 'He could have taken a backhander.'

I'd missed what she was talking about.

'I read the files,' she went on. 'It was his last case before retirement. His last case, a witness statement disappears, a rich guy gets off the hook.'

'And?'

'Don't you see? Anton Lantinga is a multi-millionaire. He'd pay a lot to see this go away.' She took another big gulp of wine and topped her glass up from my bottle.

'I don't think so.' I brought my glass to my lips to give

102

my hands something to do and to hide my mouth. I swallowed the tiniest amount.

'But was there money? Did he have money?'

'Are you driving? Because if you are—'

'I'm fine. Nowhere near the limit. So was there money?'

'Not that I could tell,' I lied. I could check what her
numberplate was and tip-off Traffic Control.

'Shame. Still, that doesn't mean he didn't do something
else with it. We should question him.'

'We'll question Goosens on Monday morning. That's
much higher profile.'

'First thing?' She sounded like a child demanding her St
Nicolaas presents right on time.

'First thing.' I smiled a fake smile and pushed the box of
chocolates closer. It would be good if she ate them all, saved
me throwing them out.

But she refused them with a quick wave of her hand,
knocked back her wine and picked up her coat. 'Gotta rush.
Patrick's waiting with dinner.' I followed her to the door.

She turned. 'Let me help you with that tree,' she said. 'We
can carry it down the stairs together.'

I hesitated.

'How are you going to do it otherwise?'

Getting it through the window would be do-able – after
all, that's how I got it up here – but it would be difficult. I
nodded and we went back to the tree.

I slid the key ring around the thumb of my right hand
and got a firm grip on the base of the trunk. As Stefanie
stabilised the top, I lifted the bottom. I let the weight extend

my left arm as far as the socket would allow. Tied together by the tree, we walked down the stairs. As I was three steps lower than her, her head was finally higher than mine. My hand hurt, but she was not stopping so neither would I. Even on the landing, where I would have put it down normally, I kept it lifted as I opened the door. My fingers had difficulty holding the weight even though the needles were like anchors in my flesh and the sap stuck tree and skin together like superglue. I didn't look round, but kept going down, careful step by careful step, my eyes on the floor, measuring the width of each step and counting each wooden block down, twenty-two steps in total. She took a step whenever I did, our feet making twin noises on the floor.

Only when we got to the downstairs hallway did I acknowledge the existence of my colleague. 'Finally there.'

She put the tree upright and I rested it against my shoulder. I passed her the keys, she opened the front door and I dragged the Christmas tree out of the house onto the pavement. The council would pick it up tomorrow and chip it into little pieces.

'Thanks for your help,' I said. It wasn't even that hard.

She smiled. 'Thanks for the wine and chocolates. I'll see you Monday.' She waved and walked to her car. I went back upstairs, got a broom out, and removed all the needles from the steps and the marble floor in the hallway. The festive season was over for this year.

Stefanie could well be right. My father's house was bigger than it should be for a retired policeman, especially in the high-priced commuter belt of Alkmaar. Just over half an hour by train to Amsterdam, house prices had sky-rocketed there in the last ten years. In my study, which used to be the interior designer's studio, I opened my laptop and googled the address. It didn't take long to find out that he lived next door to Alkmaar's mayor and opposite two company directors. Even when he'd still been working he shouldn't have been able to afford a house in the Oranjepark.

I picked up a pen and walked over to the architect's table that dominated the study. It was perfect as a horizontal version of our office whiteboard. I paused with the pen above the virginally white sheet of paper, hesitant to spoil its pure beauty with my bad thoughts. In the centre of the white page I wrote *Otto Petersen*. I drew a careful square around the name of the dead man. Two lines went from the bottom corners of the square to new boxes with the names of the two other directors in Petersen Capital: Anton Lantinga and Geert-Jan Goosens, my father's and my boss's main suspects respectively. With a see-through green plastic ruler, I measured the distance between those two names, and drew a vertical line from the middle. At the bottom of that line I hung the amount of money missing: forty million euros. I picked up a red pen, put the witness's name to the left of Anton Lantinga and drew a dotted arrow along my ruler. I left it dotted, because Wouter Vos's evidence wasn't enough. He'd seen Anton's car; that didn't mean Anton was driving it.

At the top of the page, exactly above the box containing Otto's name, I drew a box for his wife. I put a curved line between her and Anton Lantinga and wrote *affair* above it. With a pencil I wrote *Piet Huizen* below Anton's name, inside a thin pencil square. I made it as faint as I could, hesitant to believe Stefanie's slander of my father. Ronald had told me that my father had never passed the files on to the team from Amsterdam – but he'd said it was just out of spite. *Did he pay him?* I questioned above the line. Six boxes around six names, six people linked, five alive, one dead.

Chapter Eleven

The next morning, when I opened the curtains, I revealed a world slowly turning from night to day. Children ran to wherever it was they went on Saturday morning, slid on the snow-covered pavement and threw snowballs. Their laughter sounded like the peal of church bells between the canal houses. A council truck drove along, scraping up mounds of snow, which ran off the sides of the shovel like water off the bow of a ship, heaping up in piles of ammunition for the kids. In its wake the truck left a trail of salt on the road. Soon only the gables of the houses would be white.

The thin winter light struggled through the window and barely reached the floor. I sat at my table and let the morning sun touch my face. The light made a small angle with the floor and intruded less than it did in summer.

I started my laptop to see if I had new mail, but there was nothing. I got up and went out looking for human contact. I closed my apartment door and climbed down the stairs. Now that I'd lived here for over a year, I was getting used to the extreme steepness of them, each step barely deep enough to take the length of a foot.

It wasn't far to the baker on the corner but the cold was biting my cheeks and nose even on this short stretch. I greeted the girl behind the counter. This was normality; this is what everybody did every day: talking, smiling and buying bread. But I differed from the other people in the shop with their uncomplicated dreams and concerns. I bet none of them had dreamed of dead girls or hugging skulls last night. I walked home, dropped my bread off, and cycled to my psychiatrist appointment.

I'd chosen her at random. I didn't want people to know that I was seeking help so I couldn't ask anybody to recommend one. Even if I could have asked, I didn't know if any of my friends or colleagues had ever been to counselling and I would be embarrassed to bring it up. So instead I'd picked someone whose name I liked and who was within cycling distance of my flat.

Maria Kerkstra held her practice in a flat in the Jordaan. She was young. Probably recently graduated, probably still building up her group of clients. As soon as I walked through the door and shook her limp hand, I knew I wouldn't come back. She had a couch, a long leather affair, a desk and an office chair. It all looked correct; only the flowered wallpaper was different from what I'd expected a psychiatrist's place of work to be like and it jarred.

I sat on the sofa, faced the table and was given a glass of water.

'What do you want to talk about?' Her voice was soft and probably meant to be soothing, but I had to strain to hear what she was saying. 'When you called me yesterday, it sounded like an emergency. Sounded urgent.'

'I'm having problems at work.'

'What kind of work do you do?'

'I'm a police officer.' I didn't want to talk about this but what was the point in coming here if I didn't at least try. I buried my head in my hands. I was falling over the edge of the cliff and knew I needed help. 'I worked on this case that really shook me up. I can't get over it. I . . . It's haunting me.' I took a sip of water.

'Have you been offered counselling at work?'

'Yes, but it would go on my record. Plus I don't trust them to keep their mouth shut.'

'Everything you say here is completely confidential.'

'Nor do I want somebody I see on a daily basis to know this stuff about me.' You, I don't ever have to see again, I thought.

Maria Kerkstra nodded. 'So tell me about this case.'

'It was a little girl. Wendy Leeuwenhoek.' I picked my glass up again. 'You've probably read about her. She disappeared fifteen years ago. Because the anniversary of her disappearance was coming up, our boss wanted us to go through the files again, make an appeal on television. You've probably seen it . . .'

Maria's face didn't change. She scribbled something but didn't give a sign that she knew anything about Wendy. She must do. Everybody did. Everybody thought they knew exactly what happened. Nobody did.

'Was this any different from other cases?'

'It was tough but I guess not that different.'

'But it was different for you. This is a new reaction for you. Or do you think it's just the build-up of stress over the years?'

'No, it was this one case.'

'What was it about this one?'

I couldn't talk any more. I shook my head and got up. 'This has been a mistake. I shouldn't have come.'

'You've paid. Let's at least talk for the hour. Talk about something else if you like. Anything you want.'

'The weather? Sports?' But I sat back down.

'Whatever you like.'

'It was because it was a little girl.' I repeated my mother's words. I was here because I needed help with this and I summoned all my courage to at least try.

'Do you have children?'

'I had a daughter. She died. Cot death.' I whispered the answer. Poppy, who had finally arrived after I'd already had two miscarriages and was almost ready to give up on motherhood. Poppy, who'd cried most nights. Then came the morning when I'd woken refreshed after a good night's sleep, the first in months. Arjen had gone to work after sticking his head in to say that she was still fast asleep, but when I saw her, I knew she wasn't asleep. I touched her and she was cold. 'These things happen,' the doctor had said. 'Nobody knows why.' It was something I never talked about. When I'd come back from maternity leave early, because what else was I possibly going to do other than work and the walls seemed to have collapsed on me after the death of

110

my baby, nobody asked, nobody said much. My boss at the time had tried but I'd cut him short. If I didn't speak of it, it had never happened. But I had been sick, nauseous, all day, every day, from the tears that I had locked inside. It had felt as if I had a rock in my stomach, which was heavy with sharp edges like my grief. By the time we looked into Wendy Leeuwenhoek's disappearance, I'd been back at work for years and the rock had become small and almost smooth like a pebble in a river – but it hadn't disappeared.

'So here was this other little girl,' I said. 'And her mother refused to believe she'd died.'

My role in the investigation had been to get close to the parents. They had been critical of the original investigation and the CI had wanted to make amends. The parents had divorced six months after Wendy disappeared. I met Monique, Wendy's mother, often. Not because I'd suspected her of killing her daughter but because it had been what the boss had asked me to do. Monique had kept her distance, kept herself closed to me. She probably would have been like that with everybody, with every policeman or policewoman.

She gave restrained consent when I asked her if I could record our conversations. Her pale face and long blonde hair, so devoid of colour it was almost white, gave the impression of fragility. She looked as if she was made of glass, as if any intrusion in her personal life would fracture and destroy her. I didn't want to break her, I understood her sorrow, but I just didn't have the will to treat her as kindly as she needed me to. There was never any proof of neglect or evidence that she'd abandoned her daughter in the park where the little blue shoe was found, but I had to ask her why she had let her little girl out to play that late in the evening. She told me she had been preparing dinner and could see Wendy from their kitchen window. Then she looked again and her daughter was gone. She still wasn't worried; it was a game Wendy played. Paul went to get her but came back an hour later, upset because he couldn't find her.

I hadn't expected Monique to cry. She'd answered this same question so often. The tears came as if they'd been inside for the last fifteen years and were only now allowed out. I offered her my handkerchief but she used her own tissues instead. Her house was immaculately clean and she looked ready to fluff up the cushions on the sofa as soon as I left. There was a large photo of Wendy on the mantelpiece but no others. No sign of other children, a new husband, a lover or even a pet. Only her in perfect isolation.

'She made a painting every month of what Wendy would have looked like,' I told the psychiatrist. 'She studied girls on the street to get the fashion right: the right haircut, the right clothes. She had a room full of these paintings, almost two hundred of them. It was spooky. I asked her if she got pleasure out of them. She looked at me as if I was crazy and said, "No, I don't get pleasure out of anything any more. My only pleasure is the absence of pain."' I took a sip of my water. The words had so exactly described how I felt that I had listened to Wendy's mother say them a number of times on the tape, listening, rewinding, listening, rewinding.

'When Wendy went missing, she'd just lost her first milk tooth, so there were all these photos with a smile with a single gap, but in the paintings more teeth went and later new teeth came. It made me think of what my daughter would have looked like. It was more than four years since she'd died and here I was, looking at this photo of six-year-old Wendy with a tooth missing, holding a watering can in her hands, wearing a pink dress and pink wellington boots, and I thought: This is what she would have looked like. This is how big my Poppy would have been.' I covered my eyes with my hands and took a few deep breaths. 'I kept those photos. It was as if my little girl, my Poppy, had grown, hadn't died, but was there in those photos.' Those first days after I'd held the photos, collected them and had taken them home, I'd even thought that this could be my new family, that this could be my new daughter. Of course Wendy wouldn't be six, she would be twenty-one, a student maybe or working, but she could be mine. She could be my girl. A replacement for Poppy.

'And now . . .'

'Now even Wendy's photos are gone.' And with the loss of the photos, Poppy seemed dead all over again.

'I understand why this case has been so hard for you. How is your husband coping? Do you talk about this?'

'We're not together any more.'

I took my gloves off and stuffed them in the pockets of my jacket. Even protected, the tips of my fingers had turned white and cold. I pressed the buzzer of Flat 6. It was 11 a.m.

She would be surprised I was here, but she would definitely be home.

'Hello?'

'Hi, it's me.'

Without a comment the door clicked open and I went in. I took the concrete steps two at a time. If I looked closely at them, I could see traces of the thousands of times I had walked up here. It was no warmer in the cavernous communal hallway than it had been outside.

The door to my mother's flat was slightly ajar. I pushed it fully open, went through and hung my coat on its usual hook. My mother sat at the table, reading the newspaper and drinking a cup of tea. My visit didn't mean she'd break with her morning routine of scanning every page of the *Telegraaf*.

She looked up over the edge of the paper. 'Oh no,' she said, reaching out with her hand to touch my hair. 'What's happened to my lovely blonde daughter?'

'I only had it cut.' I pulled out a chair and sat down.

'Never mind, it'll grow back. You must be regretting it.'

I tucked a strand of my newly dark hair behind my ear. 'I like it actually.'

'Much more practical, I suppose.'

'I like the way it looks.'

'Really? Had you been to this hairdresser before?' She peered at me, her head at a slight angle like a robin looking at a worm on the grass, ready to pounce.

'First time.'

'That figures. It's not quite even, not symmetrical.'

'It's not supposed to be.'

114

She nodded. 'You did it because you were angry. It's some form of self-harm – I read about that in the paper.'

'I wasn't angry. I'm not self-harming. Want to see my arms?' I pulled at the sleeves of my jumper to stop my hand touching the red cut I had inflicted on my forehead.

'Don't be stupid.' She put the paper up again and made the pages rustle. 'You must be very lonely,' she said from behind the *Telegraaf*.

'I'm fine.'

She lowered it again and looked at me. 'So why are you here on a Saturday morning?'

I avoided her question. 'You haven't taken your Christmas tree down yet?' I asked.

'Oh, we can do it now if you like.' She opened a cupboard and got the cardboard box for the baubles out. Sellotape held the corners together. I picked a silver bauble from the tree. Its skin was dulled by age.

'I remember when we bought these,' I said.

'Was it ninety or ninety-one?'

'Must have been ninety-one.'

'Yes, you were already going to university.'

We had bought them to replace the ones I'd broken the year before, when I'd come home drunk from a Christmas party at one of my few friends' places and had forgotten the tree was there.

'I want to talk about you and Dad,' I said.

She had never been willing to tell me what had happened between them. Even now she was silent. I could hear the traffic outside the flat. I plucked the silver bird with its glass-fibre tail from the tree. The texture of the tail was like metallic satin under my fingers. I remembered the first year I had been allowed to hold it. I must have been eight or nine. A few strands affixed themselves to my fingers, staying behind when I put the bird down. It was getting old, just like me, just like my mother.

'Mum, it's important,' I said.

'It wasn't the same.' We took off the lights together. I picked one from the tree like a small ripe fruit from the closest branch and handed it to my mother. 'We weren't like you and Arjen,' she said. 'Knowing about us won't help.'

I couldn't tell if I was getting angry or irate. It was probably a mixture of both. 'Mum, please tell me. You need to tell me at some point.'

'You made your own mistakes. This was different.' I passed a second light to her and she wrapped them around her hand, tying her fingers together with the green plastic wire. 'It won't help you, Lotte.'

She'd always said the same thing. We had been in the kitchen, doing the dishes, when I'd told her about my marriage breakdown. I had been nervous. My hands were sweating and I'd wiped them on the dishcloth. I had difficulties forming the words that admitted to my mother that Arjen had left me.

She'd said, 'What did you do?'

The first words out of her mouth: *what did you do?* I told her I hadn't done anything. She said that I must have done or he wouldn't have left me. In her eyes, the injured party walked, as she had done. I said that it wasn't anything that I

116

did, that it was more what he had done. With somebody else. She shrugged and returned to her scrubbing. The back of my throat felt like sandpaper.

'Mum, what am I going to do now?' I asked.

'I don't know,' she said. 'Don't look at me for help.'

It made my heart ache.

She said, 'You'll sort it out yourself. You never listened to any of my advice before.' She was going to say: *I told you so*, but managed to swallow the words. She would have been justified – she *had* told me a hundred times. She had told me to put my husband before my career, to have another child before it was too late, that work wouldn't make me happy in the long run, that I'd be more fulfilled if I stayed at home, cooked dinner and washed nappies. I never told her that after losing one child I was afraid – terrified, in fact – that the same thing would happen again. I stood there, dishcloth hanging down to the floor, and my body ached from the need of a hug that wasn't going to come.

Now we finished taking the lights off the Christmas tree, leaving it bare. I collapsed it, folded up its metal stand and put it back in its cardboard tube, all ready for next year. It was much easier than my real one. It never lost its needles but it also never smelled of pine.

After putting the Christmas things in the cupboard, I fingered a plain wineglass in the cabinet. The cheap glass was in stark contrast to the cut-crystal ones at my father's place. 'Why didn't you take his money?' I said without taking my eyes off the cabinet.

'You look cold. I'll make you a cup of tea.' She didn't ask me if I wanted one. She got up and walked out of the room. I followed her to the kitchen and stood between her and the door. She turned on the tap and filled the metal kettle. We both stared at it and said nothing, waiting for the water to boil. The gas flame danced orange. A bank of appliances behind cupboard doors with chipped paintwork led from the door that I was guarding to a small window at the other end. A washing machine with a soap dispenser that had cracked when I still lived here doubled as a windowsill and let a set of old tin cans filled with herbs catch any light that entered the small space.

The whistle of the kettle tore through the silence. My mother reached in the cupboard and got my old mug out, a large white porcelain one with the ketchup-red and mayonnaise-yellow face of a smiling clown. I caressed my mug by its often held ear, took it from the kitchen and we both sat back down at the table.

'When did you get me this?' I said.

She smiled. 'It was your first real one, after the plastic drinking cup you had. You must have been three or four.'

Warmth flowed through my body with the hot tea. It was touching that she still gave me tea in this mug. The clown smiled his wide grin at me. 'I saw Dad last week,' I said.

'Really? Where?'

'Alkmaar. I went to see him.'

'After all these years, you turn to him.'

'I didn't turn to him.'

'You should come to me for advice.'

'I didn't go to him for advice. It was only work.'

'So that's where all these questions come from.'

'Yes.' I was pleased she understood. 'I'm reopening this case he worked on—'

'What lies did he tell you about me? What did he say about me?'

'We didn't talk about you.' I immediately realised it was the wrong thing to say.

She raised her eyebrows. 'You were sitting in his house and he let the chance to blacken me go by?' Her voice sounded harsh and disappointed.

'We talked about work.'

'He still lies.'

'And we talked about cars.' I couldn't stop the small smile at the memory.

'Cars? Since when are you interested in cars?'

'I have bought a new car . . .'

'You didn't tell me. Where is it?' She went to the window.

'I came by bike.'

'But you showed him your new car?'

'I could hardly go to Alkmaar by bike,' I said, trying to be reasonable and joke about it.

'You could have shown me your car.'

'Next time I'll drive.'

'It doesn't matter.' She sat back down and opened the paper again, turned a page and pretended to read. Then she said, 'So what were your father's wise words on your lonely life?'

'I didn't talk to him about that. As I said, it was work.'

119

'You're saying that a bit too often.'

I raised my hands. 'But you're not listening.'

'And he was?'

'We're reopening a case he used to work on. I had to find out what he knew.'

'And he lied.'

I shrugged. 'Maybe.'

'Is he still married to that woman?'

'Maaike? I suppose so. There were photos of the two of them together.'

'So you're blaming me,' she said in a fake-resigned tone of voice.

'For what?'

'For your marriage breaking up. Clearly your father can manage to stay married all these years, whereas all I've done was look after you.'

'I'm not blaming you.' But I did know I didn't want to end up like her, still bitter and angry forty years later. What was the point? 'Tell me about the money.'

She pulled her grey eyebrows together. 'What money?'

'I've been to his house—'

'You've been there before.'

'I know, but it's never struck me this clearly before', I played with the edge of the tattered tablecloth, rolled it up and down, and rubbed my finger over the mark in the wood, 'that he has a lot of money. That we used to have none. That you still have none.'

She turned a page of the newspaper with an annoyed rustle. 'Not none.'

'OK, little.' What was the last piece of furniture my mother had bought? Everything in this flat had already been here when I left home after university. And that was almost twenty years ago. The sofa's grey leather had cracked and roughened up where she sat most evenings; pieces of the faded flower-patterned beige wallpaper had peeled down from the edge closest to the ceiling.

'Do you wish I'd left you with him? Look at this!' She turned the paper round and pointed to a photo of some C celebrity with hardly any clothes on. 'What is she wearing?'

'No, of course not.' I pushed the paper back towards her.

'Are you saying I didn't take good care of you?' She angrily turned another page over.

'I'm not saying that at all.' I wanted to grab hold of her chin and lift her head until she had to meet my eyes.

'I worked two jobs to raise you and bring you up.'

'And I appreciate that. I just want to know why you didn't take any of his cash.'

When I was about twelve, my mother had bought a pair of trousers for me at C&A. They had been the coolest I'd ever had, purple-blue cords with a white stripe sewn into the seam. Mum had told me to be careful with them, but I was playing after school and I fell. It was the tear in the trousers more than the pain that made me cry. I didn't go home and roller-bladed endless circles on the school playground long after all the other children had left. A teacher stopped me and asked what was wrong. 'I can come with you,' he said after I'd told him what had happened. 'I can explain to your mother that it was just an accident.'

But it hadn't been fear that stopped me from going home: it was embarrassment and shame. I knew how long she'd saved to get the money for those trousers. I should have made them last for a couple of years at least and now there was a huge rip right over my knee. My skin underneath the cloth was torn and grazed, but the pain was from letting my mother down. When I got home, she didn't say anything, simply gestured for me to take the trousers off, got her sewing machine out and stitched both frayed edges together in silence. I'd worn those trousers for another year or so, the left trouser leg always slightly shorter than the right. And even now she had little spare money even though I gave her a hundred euros a week. She wouldn't accept more.

'I didn't take any of his money because I didn't want to.' She closed the paper, folded it in two and got up. 'We should move this table back to where it was. Before the Christmas tree.'

'But it must have been tempting.' I got up as well. 'You were working so hard all the time – why not let him pay something for my upbringing?'

'You were my daughter. You were my responsibility.'

'I'm his daughter too, aren't I?'

She looked round the room, which had a hole like a scar where the Christmas tree used to be. She pulled an oak chair out towards its gap. 'Of course you are.'

'So why not make him pay alimony? Child support? If he didn't want to pay, you could have forced him.'

'You won't understand.'

'Try me.'

'It was pride, OK? My silly pride. It was probably wrong of me to leave him – we had you together.' She went to one end of the table and signalled to me to go to the other. 'My parents were very angry and upset. They wanted me to stay with him. Marriage was supposed to be forever, through thick and thin, through sickness and health, sanctified by God, but I just couldn't stay, not after I'd found out . . . OK, one – two – *lift*.'

We picked up the table and shuffled it back to its pre-Christmas place, the legs fitting into the original holes in the carpet. 'Right, that'll do.' She rested against a chair. 'And when I left, my guilt for leaving told me that if I had wanted his money, I should have stayed with him and shared my life with him. Give him something back in return. That probably doesn't make any sense to you.'

'As a matter of fact it does.' Avoiding her eyes, I pushed the other chairs back around the table. Each slotted in where it used to be.

'I couldn't take any of his money,' she said quietly. 'Not even when there was plenty.'

'Did you leave him because of the money?'

'Because of where it came from.' She visibly braced herself. 'What he got paid *for*.'

As my mother confirmed what Stefanie had thought and what I'd already suspected last night, a mixture of feelings invaded me. It was hard to unravel and make sense of them all. Part of it was shock, the jump of my stomach, similar to when Ronald had told me about my father's heart attack. But it was mainly anger. My heart raced and I would have loved to kick something. Why hadn't my father told me this when I saw him? Why had he asked me to reopen the Otto Petersen case? Why had he wanted me to talk to Ronald? It didn't make sense. Did he want to be found out? In my abdomen, the nerve endings tied themselves in knots as if somebody was knitting my intestines together. Did he want me to expose him? I wasn't sure that I could. I would be exposing myself too. No way would I jeopardise my job just to help his absolution! I gripped the back of the last chair I was putting in its pre-Christmas spot and shoved it under the table. Why did he have to make things difficult for me yet again?

'What did he get paid for?' I asked tersely.

'I can't talk about that. It's too . . .'

I waited, but she didn't complete her sentence. 'Too what?'

'I can't tell you, Lotte. Please don't force me. I don't want to tell you these things about your father.'

I gave my mother a quick hug, grateful that she had tried to protect me from this.

'You're going now? I told you what you needed to hear, now you're off?'

'Yes, Mum, I'm going back to work.' I said it loudly.

She nodded. 'On a Saturday? Right. I'll see you Wednesday.' She kissed me on my cheek.

'If I have time.'

'If you have time? I've got nothing left of importance to tell you, so now you might not even come on Wednesday?'

I gave her arm a rub. 'That's not what I said.'

124

'That's what it sounded like to me.'

'Mum, I'm sorry, that's *not* how I meant it. You know what it's like when I'm in the middle of a case.'

'That's what *he* used to say.' She sat back at the table and started reading the paper again.

'Thanks for your help, Mum. I know this is hard for you.'

She didn't reply but kept reading. I got up, touched her head with a light caress, freed my coat and left, almost running down the concrete steps.

My feet pushed against the pedals of my bicycle and I moved back in time from the new-build area where my mother lived to my home in the belt of old canal houses. My back felt as if boiling water was running down my spinal cord. It was from being pulled in so many different directions, by a kaleidoscope of feelings from sadness to anger.

Snow was falling again. Without the wind, the snowflakes brushed softly against my cheeks and eyelashes. I took one hand off the handlebar and put it in my pocket for an extra layer of cover. The snow was getting heavier as I arrived at the first canal ring. A car overtook me on the narrow stretch of road and I was pushed to the outside, close to the small metal bollards with the three Xs in relief that were Amsterdam's symbol.

I kept my head down as much as possible whilst still looking ahead, and soon passed the Westerkerk. The garish blue paint on the adornments of the steeple and Amsterdam's symbol in vibrant red and black stood out against the demure grey of the rest of the church. Three skulls above each of the side doors reminded every churchgoer of the brevity of their lives. The postcard shops, currently closed for the winter, would open to hordes of tourists in a few months. People from all over the world would come with their cameras out, eternalising Amsterdam's picturesque historic heart of canals and bridges, as well as its seedier side closer to the station. They would record the slight tilt of the tower of the Westerkerk or the Homo monument to the gay community, situated just behind the seventeenth-century church, and talk about how interestingly mixed the city was.

Now, in January, cleansed of visitors, the city felt empty. I hadn't seen a living soul since the car went past. On this stretch there were only tall houses on one side and frozen water on the other. The signs of life were all indoors, where lights were on to drive away the dark of the snow clouds, even though it was still morning.

Should I call my father? Demand an explanation? Tell him that I knew anyway? Explain that I had to protect myself so that I would have to cover for him, even if that wasn't what he wanted? He still hadn't called me back. He obviously didn't care. Didn't want to talk to me. I could still see him – old, shrunken, standing in front of his house, waving, saying it had been nice to see me. If it had been nice, why hadn't he contacted me?

I rammed my bicycle in an open slot, chained the front wheel to the metal stand and stumped up the stairs to my flat. My cheeks were wet, numb from the snow's embrace. I took my coat, gloves and shoes off, put my slippers on, lay down on the sofa and stared at the light coming through the window. My whole body was heavy; even my fingers

126

resting on top of each other felt as if strings attached to the earth's core were pulling them down. The amber pot of pills called to me from the bedroom. The thoughts from earlier came back.

Ronald had said I looked like my father. I dragged my body upright and looked at my parents' wedding photo, which I kept on the sideboard. They both looked so young. Not all of my features were like his but I recognised his long nose with the flattened end on my face. So I was mentally like him as well: I too could not tell wrong from right. I straightened the photo, my mind made up. I couldn't tell CI Moerdijk about him or about the bribes. I wouldn't get him into trouble. More importantly, I wouldn't get myself in more trouble than I already was. If he wanted to unload the weight on his conscience, someone else could be his confessor.

In my study I took a pen and coloured thickly over my foolishly optimistic faint pencil lines. He'd been on the take, my mother had said, so it was likely he had been bought by Anton Lantinga to destroy the files.

Chapter Twelve

I was reading through files on Otto Petersen at the shelter of my desk, when Hans came in. I hadn't seen my colleague since Friday morning. 'Hans, I'm so sorry,' I said. 'I shouldn't have shouted at you.' This must be what it was like to have a younger brother: you fought, then you apologised.

'It's OK, Lotte. I've been shouted at before. I can cope.' He hung his coat beside mine on the hooks on the inside of the door.

'Still, I was wrong—'

'Let's not talk about it.' He rested his hand on my shoulder as he moved past me to reach his own desk. I tried not to flinch. 'I know how stressed you've been,' he said.

'It's no excuse. Anyway, I spoke to the boss on Friday. Did he talk to you afterwards?'

'Yeah, he told me that you've dug up a new witness . . .'

So the die was cast. There was no turning back now. 'Well, not new exactly,' I said.

'New to him, right?'

I nodded.

'So we're officially reopening it, you and I. And that Stefanie Dekkers—'

'She came round Friday night.' I bent closer to Hans. 'Can you believe it? Made me pour her a drink . . .'

'What I can't believe is that you let her in.'

I smiled and covered my mouth with my hand to cup and hold the unexpected feeling. 'I bet she just wanted to see where I live. How was your weekend?'

'I saw my parents.' Hans pulled his large hands through his potato-peel hair and readjusted his body in the seat, which contained him tightly. 'They're still talking about selling up. They say they're getting too old for farming and have no reason to keep going without any of us wanting to take it over.' He scratched the back of his head. 'I have been thinking about it . . .'

'You wouldn't.'

'If I thought I'd be any good at it, I might.'

'But Irene wouldn't want to give up her job, surely.' Hans and his fiancée were going to get married in April and I couldn't see her as a farmer's wife. I had met her three weeks after I joined the team. We had just started working on the Wendy Leeuwenhoek case and Hans had invited me for dinner at their house. He'd told me that Irene wanted to meet me and I assumed that she wanted to check me out. She had nothing to fear from me because, even though I'm the latest addition to the team, I am a good ten years older than either her or Hans. But I was wrong – that wasn't what she was after at all. She was obsessed with Wendy Leeuwenhoek and wanted to hear from me what the parents were like. I didn't tell her anything she didn't already know from the newspapers' endless speculation and the annual interviews the parents gave to keep their daughter in the public eye.

Hans's house in one of Amsterdam's suburbs was nice, and photos of his parents' farm, the farmhouse, the land and the livestock adorned many of the walls, but I didn't get the impression farming was Irene's thing. She was a doctor at the VU Hospital and had slogged to get to where she was. It must be difficult to fit a life around two people on shifts. I'd been with my previous team for more than five years, but I'd never been to any of their houses. When I'd still been married, I would have had to take Arjen and he never had much interest in mingling with my colleagues and listening to police talk. After those early refusals, I wasn't invited again.

Irene had wanted to cook me another meal last week to thank me for swapping shifts with Hans over Christmas. She'd said I should come over for New Year's, but I'd said I had other plans. I thought she was going to set me up with one of her friends and I couldn't face having to make pleasant chit-chat with a stranger who I was supposed to like but inevitably had no intention of seeing again.

'She says she'd like to give it a go. There's good money to be made in farming.'

'Don't you dare leave me alone with Thomas. If you're leaving, we'd be a two-person team.'

'Hi Lotte. Hi Hans.'

I turned round like a naughty schoolchild. 'Hi, Stefanie. Ready to go?'

'Geert-Jan Goosens, here we come.'

'If there's anything I can do to help.' Hans said.

'You could start getting us some pictures,' I told him and pointed towards the whiteboard. I picked up my gun, fitted the holster around my waist and put on my suit jacket. The problem with suits was that they never fitted properly: the cloth wasn't cut to accommodate the extra lump on your hip. When I'd first started as a plainclothes officer, I was young and cared what I looked like, and wanted to wear clothes that veiled the weapon. I'd stopped trying after a stupid incident in the fitting room of C&A. I was checking if the weapon showed through the cloth of the jacket I was trying on, undoing the buttons, turning round, readjusting where the gun sat on my hip, when a shop assistant saw me, around the edge of the badly closed fitting-room curtain. My eyes caught hers in the mirror. Only showing her my badge had stopped her from screaming and calling the police. Now I simply bought clothes a size too big.

Geert-Jan Goosens worked in the glass and steel dominated business park around Amsterdam's World Trade Center, as Director of Research at the Chicago Bank.

'That must be a step down from running your own firm,' I said to Stefanie. My ears popped halfway up our ride in the lift to the thirtieth floor.

131

'He's fifty-seven,' she said. 'Sold his company to Chicago Bank two years ago.' She had done my homework for me. 'This is more an honorary job than anything else. They've kept him on at a high level, possibly for his contacts. Old boys' network and all that.'

We were taken to Geert-Jan Goosens's large corner office, past row upon row of young men and a few young women, often on the phone but always looking at some screen or other. I felt old walking amongst them. What chance would my father have had of understanding these people? Whatever I might think of her, Stefanie was useful as my guide and interpreter in this financial world.

Geert-Jan Goosens sat behind a large desk, which seemed to have been created this size for intimidation only. There was a pile of papers on one corner, a PC on the other, a blotter in front of him, but otherwise acres of bare wooden surface. He was a large man, almost big enough to do his desk justice. When he stood up, he towered over me, and I estimated that he had to be around 2.10 metres tall. A well-fitting suit made his mass look intentional, as if he was supposed to be this big and had worked hard to achieve it.

I shook his hand, then walked across to the window, looked out and surreptitiously wiped the palm of my hand against my leg. Outside, thirty floors below us, people and cars were so small they seemed made out of Lego. From this distance, their lives looked unreal and unimportant. That was probably why business people liked to be in their high buildings; it made it possible to ignore the normal people, to think they were just toys, whilst they made their decisions. A faint smell of cigars lingered in the fabric of the blinds. I pictured Goosens in the evenings, with the door shut because it was illegal even for a director to enjoy a cigar in his office to celebrate a job well done. Maybe a law to protect those unimportant men and women who worked to clean this office could be broken.

I heard a chair being pulled back and knew Stefanie had taken a place opposite the man. I turned round. She beckoned to me to come over and sit next to her, but I remained standing and watched the pair from where I stood. I could do what I liked as well – I could break rules too. I leaned against the windowsill. The view was perfect: Stefanie and Goosens opposite one another, like a talk-show host and his guest, separated by the barrier of the desk, and me, their audience, just outside that circle.

Goosens opened the exchange. 'Otto Petersen, eh? I hope you know something about finance. Not like that idiot who was investigating it before. What was his name?'

'DI Huizen?' Stefanie said.

'No, that's not right. The guy from Amsterdam Police.'

'Moerdijk?'

'Right, that's it. Complete idiot.' Goosens's voice reached every corner of his office as he called our boss an idiot. I imagined his voice could fill this trading floor or break the window if he really let rip.

'In what way?' Stefanie asked. She crossed her arms. Her left foot pulsed in the empty air.

'He kept going on about the money. Said it had dis- appeared and that I must have it.' The big man laughed. 'Can you imagine? No, if we still had that money, there wouldn't be a problem.'

'So what happened?'

'We lost it in the market, of course.'

Stefanie nodded. She paused for five bounces of her foot, then asked, 'How?'

He picked up a pen and clicked the top. 'Otto made some bad investments.' He got a handful of papers from the pile in the corner and started to read, scribbling with the pen, which looked small between his large fingers, the ends of which were bulbous like upside-down carrots.

'I'd like some more details, please.'

He looked up from his papers for a second, then started to write again. 'I explained it all to that guy last time. He didn't get it. I don't see the point in doing it again.' A small smile played around his fleshy lips. The top one was even thicker than the bottom, but they were still proportionally small in the expanse of flesh in his face.

'Sir, please answer the question.'

He signed the papers he was reading, then put the pen down and looked up at Stefanie. 'How about I write it down and email it to you, then someone who'd understand can take a look.'

Stefanie put both feet on the floor and pulled her shoulders back. 'You tell me now,' she said quietly but with force.

'I already told you that I don't see the point.' He took the next set of papers from the stack. 'You won't comprehend and I'll be wasting my time.'

134

'Or you could come with us to the police station and we'll continue the interview there.'

He picked up his pen again, clicked the top three times and crossed out something on the first page. 'I don't suppose you know what calls are.'

'I do.'

'Not telephone calls.'

'I know what you mean.'

'Gosh.' He turned the page over and scribbled something on page two. 'Well, he sold those at the back end of 1994, as the market was going down. But then the market turned and he lost a lot of money and blew up the fund. That answer your question?'

'Why didn't he close out the position?'

Goosens raised his eyebrows. I didn't understand what she meant, so it must have been financial jargon. 'He said he had. Are we done here? I've got another meeting in five minutes.'

Stefanie didn't budge. 'But you must have known.'

'Known what?'

'What positions he had on. You must have discussed these things.'

'I told him to close them out when he'd lost twenty million on the trade. He told me he had. Only he hadn't.'

'Had you worked with Otto Petersen before?'

Goosens got up, moved his bulk from his chair and would have walked to the window if I hadn't been standing there. He started when he saw me and instead turned to look at the bookshelves behind his desk.

'We were at ABN together for three years when we decided to set up Petersen Capital.'

'Why not Goosens Capital?'

He rested an arm on a bookshelf. It creaked under the weight. His mouth tightened on the words he didn't want to say. 'Otto brought in most of the money.' He put his free hand in his pocket as if he wanted to protect any change he carried there.

'So he made the investment decisions?'

'No, he ran one book – Europe. I ran the US one.' Running a book. Just like real gamblers. Bookmakers but higher on the social ladder. Goosens started tapping fingers on the shelf he was leaning on.

'But he made the decisions for Europe.'

'Yes.'

'So there was nothing unusual about what he did?'

Goosens remained silent.

'When he decided not to close the position,' Stefanie continued. 'It was his book, right, so he could do what he wanted?'

'Yes, but he should have informed the investors and me, not forged the statements.'

'Sure.'

I studied the outside world again. Otto Petersen as more senior, more powerful than this man created a different picture. Not someone who had done what Goosens had told him, but the senior partner, the one with the capital, the money, in an industry where money was all that mattered.

'Is that it? I'm rather busy.'

136

'Was it out of character?' I said to the window.

'What?'

'Otto Petersen. Forging the books, lying to you and the investors.' I turned to face him. 'Was it out of character? Had he done anything like that before?'

Goosens moved away from the bookshelves. 'No,' he said abruptly, 'I don't think he had. In my opinion, I think he just got sucked in. He was losing money, losing the firm he'd set up, all his capital, and didn't know what to do. Maybe his wife told him to lie, that wouldn't surprise me, or maybe he thought his luck would turn. Just one more roll of the dice, one turn of the market, and nobody need ever know. Poor bastard, his luck didn't turn.'

'Thank you for your cooperation.' Stefanie stood up and didn't extend her hand. I avoided the handshake too and just walked out behind Stefanie, along the trading desks, where people rolled the dice.

'That condescending fat toad,' Stefanie said when we were back in the car. 'I'll see if I can find the trade that made the loss. Unfortunately, Goosens doesn't have much of a motive if his story is true.' She snapped her seatbelt closed.

On the streets, vehicles and exhaust fumes had churned the snow into grey mush.

'There are still plenty of reasons for Geert-Jan Goosens to kill Otto Petersen,' I said. 'By the time Otto was released, Goosens had landed on his feet and was running his own company. And it was his own company, right? Nothing to do with Anton Lantinga.'

'Correct. He and Lantinga set up a fund each.'

'So he didn't want his ex-partner out on the street, telling his version of events in the same clubs, on the same golf courses, in the same bars.'

'You see now why I'm so keen on getting one of them?' Stefanie stopped the car at a red light and looked at me. 'One of the high and mighty ones, who think they are above everybody and everything else, including the law.'

'It should all be in the notes on the original fraud case,' I pointed out. 'They must have gone through all these trades then.'

The lights changed and we were moving again. 'True – I'll find them. And what about Lantinga? Shame he's in New York.'

'He'll be back soon enough.'

'I hope he won't do a runner.'

'To run would be to admit guilt. Anton Lantinga will be back when he said he would be.'

Stefanie wanted us to stop for a coffee at a department store in the centre. It wasn't the kind of place I would normally have chosen to get a caffeine fix, but I was in no mood to argue. I drank mine slowly, enjoying the warmth on my tongue, craving its bitterness. The caffeine streamed through my veins and drove some of the tiredness away. The noises all around us in the cafeteria were intrusive, a prickly blanket of sound – but I found I didn't mind.

'Do you want to know what all that financial stuff meant?' Stefanie asked.

Not really. I just wanted to sit here and enjoy my coffee. 'OK,' I lied.

'Do you know what calls are?'

'No.' A waitress walked by, carrying a tray of drinks, some beers, some coffees, a couple of pieces of cake. It looked like apple cake – very appetising. If I'd been on my own, I might have ordered one, but here with Stefanie, she would never have let me eat it in peace.

'They are the rights to buy something at a set price.'

The waitress delivered the drinks to a large group in the corner, a bunch of students, skipping lectures to socialise instead.

'So if you buy a call, you expect the market to rise. Say you buy a call on Shell shares with a strike price of a hundred euros. Now you have the right to buy a share in Shell for a hundred euros. If the price of the share goes past a hundred, your call is worth money, as you have the right to buy it for a hundred but it's worth more. It's "in-the-money" as it's called.'

At the table behind Stefanie, a woman with shopping bags strewn around her chair was trying to get her daughter, a pixie of about four or five, to drink her apple juice. The little girl had two pigtails, held together with elastic bands adorned with fake snowballs.

'So, if you sell a call, as Otto Petersen did, you get money up front, but you have to sell the share at the strike price of the call. If you sell a call with a hundred strike price, you have to accept a hundred for that share, even if the price on the stock exchange has now climbed to two hundred.'

The girl was drinking her apple juice from a red straw – no, she wasn't drinking it, she was blowing bubbles in her glass. Her mother drank her cappuccino and stared out of the window at life outside this department store.

'It was a strategy that worked for a long time, getting paid up front and the calls expiring worthless or close to worthless. But Otto's continued success eventually became his downfall. As he was making money he had to invest larger sums and was doing these trades in larger and larger sizes. Then the shit hit the fan and it all went horribly wrong. Petersen sold that final ASX call – the Amsterdam Stock Exchange call – the price went through the roof and he lost a fortune. And bankrupted his company.'

When the little girl smiled I could see she was missing two of her front teeth.

'Did that make sense?'

I took my eyes off the child and looked at Stefanie. 'Yes, perfect sense, thanks. That helped a lot.'

The mother twisted one of her daughter's pigtails around her finger, twizzling it round and round until all the hair was gone, then let go. The hair had turned into a corkscrew curl. The girl shook her head back and forth, put her finger in her mouth and used the wet finger to straighten out her hair. 'Mummy, I don't like curls,' she said loudly. I smiled. So did her mother. Our eyes met.

'Surely it would have been better for Petersen to just go

bankrupt rather than end up in jail. He must have been certain the market was going to turn,' Stefanie said.

The mother looked at me, then smiled again. 'Drink your juice, poppet,' she said. 'We've got to meet Daddy soon.'

'It's clearly Anton Lantinga,' she concluded. 'Let's put this case in front of the committee and get a proper team working on it. Have Lantinga picked up as soon as he arrives at Schiphol.'

'The CI is happy to let you, me and Hans work on it together for the time being,' I told her.

Stefanie downed her coffee. 'Right.'

I finished my coffee as well, only too ready to leave.

Back at the office, Hans had started the wall. Pictures and black marker pen were filling the whiteboard opposite our desks. The dead man took pride of place in the middle. The drawing looked different from the one in my study, but that was the whole point: two different pairs of eyes, two different drawings. Hans's lines and arrows were curved and dipped in the middle like overlong telephone cables. He had photos of two men at the top.

I recognised Goosens as the second man, but didn't know the first: an elegant middle-aged man in a tuxedo. 'Who's that?' I pointed to the photo.

'Anton Lantinga. The philanthropic financier at the opening night of *Tosca* at the Concertgebouw,' he read from the screen.

Of course. The two men who had started firms out of the ruins of Petersen Capital, Anton Lantinga and Geert-Jan Goosens, were at the head of Hans's drawing; Otto's former business partners took the space I reserved for Otto Petersen's widow, Karin. It was Stefanie who made us focus on the money.

She walked over to the whiteboard and looked at the photo from up close. 'He hasn't changed much,' she said. 'He's less angry than the last time I saw him, of course, but he has that sheen of money.'

Karin was equally stunning in a long, off-the-shoulder night-blue dress. 'Same occasion?' I asked.

'Yes. A charity event for Unicef. She seems to do a lot for them.'

Geert-Jan Goosens, in the photo next to Anton's, looked serious and professional, holding a pen as if he was ready to sign someone's pay-cheque, the faintest hint of a smile around his lips, probably at how small their pay was compared to his. 'Corporate brochure, I bet,' I said. 'He still has the same desk.'

Hans laughed. 'Whatever did we do before Google?'

'It's much easier with people who like publicity.' Stefanie took Thomas's chair and sat down. I perched on his desk and looked at the wall. Hans had the marker pen in his hand and stood by the whiteboard looking like a young, but over-sized, geography teacher with his sleeves slightly too short and the leather patches protecting his upper arm rather than the elbow.

'He doesn't fit in, does he?' I picked up a pen from Thomas's desk and twiddled with it.

'Who?'

'Otto Petersen. He stands out like a sore thumb.'

'Well, he is the only one who's dead.' Stefanie laughed at her own joke.

'That's not what I mean.' I got up. 'Look at him, stubble on his face, rolls of fat . . .'

'The man's just come out of jail.' Hans tapped the back of the marker on his photo. 'Of course he looks different.'

'I want another photo. I want one that shows what he looked like nineteen years ago. When he was still rich and powerful, like the rest of them.' I looked at Stefanie. 'There must be one in the original Petersen Capital file.'

'It's not necessary. It's crystal-clear what happened.'

'Just get the whole file while you're at it.' I sat back on the edge of the desk, my feet off the floor.

'I'll go tomorrow.' She planted herself more firmly in her chair as if she expected I wanted her to go straight away. 'But it's overkill, this wall. It's a straightforward case, isn't it? Otto Petersen arranges to meet with Anton Lantinga on his release, angry that his friend has been sleeping with his wife while he was in jail. He asks Karin to pick him up, so she's out of the way and he and Anton can have a heart-to-heart. Things get out of hand, they argue or something and Lantinga shoots Petersen. He's seen by Wouter Vos. Case closed. All we need to do now is figure out if we can get that old guy, Piet Huizen, on taking bribes or perverting the course of justice.' She got up, grabbed Hans's black pen and wrote my father's name on the board.

'Leave him alone.' It was different seeing his name up there. Contemplating his guilt in the privacy of my own flat was one thing; having him exposed here was quite another.

'We can't.'

'Of course we can.'

'No, we can't. CI Moerdijk looks an idiot if we don't do something about the Alkmaar police.' She drew an arrow between my father's name and Anton Lantinga.

'Why?' I couldn't take my eyes from that arrow and was reminded of what my mother had said about my father's money.

'Simple case, perfectly obvious who did it, but Moerdijk fails to close it. Won't look good for him.'

'What do you care?' I began, but Hans sat down next to me, prodded me in the side with a pen, and I shut up immediately.

'What doesn't look good for him, isn't good for me,' she snapped in reply. 'I'm not risking my career for some old retired policeman. We need to make it clear that the files never got here. Make things difficult for the Alkmaar police.' She put the pen in its holder to the side of the board and wiped her hands on her skirt. 'I'll see you guys tomorrow.'

I waited until I could no longer hear her footsteps, then picked up the eraser and made my father's name disappear.

Hans said, 'She's right. It'll make things easier for the boss.'

I shook my head. 'Tough.'

'You don't think he did anything then?'

'I don't know.' I sat back at my desk. Hans looked at me. 'I don't know,' I said again, louder. 'He was taken off the case because he retired. Was *made* to retire. Maybe he was annoyed, wanted to delay Amsterdam and not just hand them the glory on a silver platter. Then he had a heart attack and couldn't put it right. Who knows? But there's no way Lantinga was involved in that.' There it was: my first lie on my father's behalf. The best type of lie: one with a grain of truth in it, one that I could almost believe myself.

Hans shrugged and turned his chair round. 'If he took those files, he should be on that wall,' he mumbled to his PC.

Unlike Stefanie, I thought grimly, I *was* risking my career for some old retired policeman.

'Oh,' Hans added, without taking his eyes off his PC monitor, 'I almost forgot to tell you, Thomas was here this morning. He's coming back to work tomorrow.'

That evening, at home, the curtains hid the outside world. On my sideboard, the wedding photo of my parents had pride of place. My mother hated looking at it, so when she came round I hid it, as much to protect the photo as to protect her. I understood her feelings. There were no other photos in my flat any more. My own wedding photo had gone up in a bonfire of gleefully destructive flames.

I had obtained my parents' photo on a Saturday more than three decades ago. My mother and I had come back from a walk and she'd decided we were going to have a tidy up. Out came boxes that hadn't seen the light of day in years; out went clothes that hadn't been worn. I was curious about a sea-green square box and wanted to open it, but my mother beat me to it. She knew what was inside. When she opened the box, the dusty smell of family secrets flew into the room. Hidden amongst a pile of photos of boring family members better forgotten was the wedding portrait of my parents in a richly decorated silver frame. She loved that frame, but she hated that photo. She hated the sight of her and my father standing side by side and smiling that youthful smile of hope and happiness that disappointment would tear off her face not so many years later, just as it had removed it from mine. She hated seeing his arm around her waist, her arm around his – proof she had once enjoyed this close physical contact.

As soon as I saw it, I wanted it. It was before the weekend visits had started and I wanted to see what the forbidden figure looked like, the man we never spoke of but whose part in creating me was visually so obvious. It was my first memory of lying to her. I said I wanted the photo because she was like a princess. That she looked lovely. As my lips clumsily formed the words, I waited for her to see through my lie and tear up the photo as punishment. But she slid it over the table. I took it and ran out of the room, not wanting her to see how happy I was. She kept the frame.

Now I picked up the photo and carried it by its new demure black frame to the light. My father was so much taller than my mother. I rubbed the dust off the sharp edges with the sleeve of my jacket. It was clear what I was risking by keeping him out of this. If anybody found out, I'd be suspended immediately. I sat down on the sofa, photo in hand. If I didn't have work, what would I do? Even with work, with the daily contact with my colleagues, it was hard to keep going. Was my father worth putting all that on the line?

In my study, I picked up a pen to finish my drawing. Work was the only thing that provided me with stability, the only thing that kept me sane. When I was working, I was a different person: I thought clearly and I had a purpose. I knew I was doing something that was important and worthwhile. Also, the need to pretend that everything was fine made the days strangely more bearable, as if what I was pretending became reality. I talked only about the case we were working on. Trying to catch another murderer made me forget that I had slept with one.

I erased Karin Petersen's surname with Tippex. I blew over the thick liquid to make it set. If I didn't work, my life would be empty, just like my womb, exactly like my mind would be. My mother would come round and she'd scold me, say I should look for another job, that I was throwing my life away; she'd sit opposite me, her wrinkled face pulled into folds of concern, but she wouldn't get through to me. My entire day would be as dark as currently only my nights were. I'd stare at the ceiling for the whole day, my mistakes floating in front of me like the horses on a merry-go-round.

Until I couldn't take it any longer.

I wrote Karin's new surname in the box. To the side of the box, I wrote, *her husband wanted her away from the house.*

147

I drew a quarter circle between the missing forty million euros and Geert-Jan Goosens, and made a note of his statement that the money was lost in the market.

My mother would also point out that work was responsible for putting me in the state I was in now. She'd only be partially right. With Thomas returning to work, I was more worried than ever that someone would find out what I had done.

Chapter Thirteen

The next day, Stefanie was lecturing us on the vagaries of the stock market and financial investments. I was a reluctant student, but we were all in this together so I pretended to listen. So did Hans – or maybe he was genuinely interested.

'We need to track that money,' Stefanie said. At least she hadn't noticed that I'd wiped my father's name off the whiteboard. 'So, let's go back to it. Forty million euros is lost on a trade, according to Goosens.' She wrote the amount in the centre of the board and drew a circle around it. The circle didn't meet at the top, but I would sort that out when she was gone. 'CI Moerdijk thought Goosens had it.' She wrote his name down. 'Goosens says it's lost on a single trade.' She turned to Hans and pointed with the pen. 'This is perfectly possible. I looked at the prices on the AEX index for the beginning of 1995: there was a sharp correction in the market. If he was on the wrong side, it would have been costly. In order to lose forty million, he had to have a position of . . .' she turned to the board like a good teacher and wrote down the calculation: enormous numbers, multiplication signs, divisions, pluses and minuses. 'These are normal-size trades.' She shrugged. 'Perfectly possible,' she repeated.

As in school, numbers rapidly made me lose interest. 'Did you go back to the Petersen Capital case?' I asked. 'See what evidence they had?'

'I've got the files in my office. Want to join me – go through it?'

'No, you're much better at the financial stuff.'

'So what do we want to know?' She wrote down a number 1 on the board and turned back to me.

'What happened to the money?' I replied obediently and saw Hans grin.

'OK.' She wrote it down, then turned to me again, saying, 'But we saw it could have been a trading loss.' She waited for me to nod, so I nodded. Stefanie drew a messy arrow between the word *money* and her calculation before writing down a 2 and *How much did Goosens know?* without asking us.

I wasn't sure how we were going to find that out. My mind wandered and I started thinking about Thomas's return. In the weeks after I had found Wendy's skeleton, Thomas and I had barely spoken. He'd been pissed off from the start about working on the Leeuwenhoek case. No, that was wrong. He'd understood *why* we were looking at that case again – after all, it was only a month before the fifteenth anniversary of her disappearance and all the papers would be full of her photos again and the police would get a kicking in the press for never having found out what happened to her. We had to be seen to do something. What annoyed him was the way the boss had divided the work. He'd told Hans to look at all the known paedophiles in the area, asked me to focus on the parents, and said that Thomas had to listen to the tapes. It was the job we all hated: checking what the previous team had done, finding mistakes in your colleagues' work. But everybody knew this was what Thomas was good at: detecting nuances in voices, in faces, that others had missed; sniffing out everybody else's mistakes.

'And', Hans now said, 'how we found out about the fraud in the first place.'

'Could Geert-Jan Goosens have gone to the police himself?' I asked, putting the thought of Thomas finding my mistakes to the back of my mind.

'Who knows. If he could frame Petersen and keep his own reputation intact, he might have,' Hans said.

'You're right,' Stefanie said. 'It is important to know how we found out. Fraud cases are like drug busts in one aspect only: you need someone to tell you about it. You need a whistle-blower – a disgruntled employee if we're talking finance, a pissed-off gang member in the case of the drugs.'

My phone rang. It was the front desk to say they had Piet Huizen on the phone for me. I told them to put him through.

'Lotte Meerman,' I said. Hans and Stefanie looked engrossed in the whiteboard, but I was not taking any chances and gave my normal greeting.

'Hi, Lotte,' my father said. 'I've been thinking about my reports.'

'Right.'

151

'I don't understand how they could have gone missing. Two people picked them up. I gave them everything.'

'I see.' I wanted to tell him that I wouldn't help him come clean, that he would have to find somebody else. I wanted to tell him to stop lying to me. The circles on my notepad came closer and closer together, the pen digging deeply into the paper.

'And now you say the boxes of files never arrived in Amsterdam.'

My other line rang. Hand over mouthpiece, I gestured to Stefanie to pick it up from Thomas's desk.

'You should check it with them,' my father was saying.

'Do you remember their names?'

Stefanie tried to get my attention but I ignored her.

'Of course I do. I remember everything about that day.' He laughed. 'I've had a lot of time to think about it.' He managed to sound so sincere.

Stefanie put the phone down and gestured more urgently. When I continued to ignore her, she tore a sheet of paper from my notepad and wrote something down, leaning over my desk.

'So what were their names?' I prompted my father.

Stefanie pushed the paper under my nose. *Lantinga is at the airport*, it said. I turned to her and frowned. 'A day early,' I whispered. She nodded.

'. . . a man and a woman.'

'Hold on, hold on.' I ripped the page of doodles from my notepad and said, 'Shoot.' I wondered who he'd come up with.

'The man's name was Freek Veenstra; the woman was Stefanie Dekkers.'

'Stefanie Dekkers? Are you sure?' I turned round to look at her. How did my father know her name?

She raised her eyebrows at the sound of her own name. 'What?' she mouthed. I shook my head to show I couldn't talk yet.

'Yes, absolutely sure,' my father said.

'I've got her right here.'

'She'll remember.'

I half-covered the mouthpiece of the phone with my hand, making sure he'd hear the refusal that I knew was about to come. In a clear voice, I asked Stefanie, 'Did you pick up the files from Piet Huizen?'

'What?' She looked baffled.

'Twelve years ago. Did you go to Alkmaar to pick up files?'

'No, I didn't.' She tapped her finger on her watch. 'That was Schiphol. The airport has got Anton Lantinga in a holding cell waiting for us.'

I nodded and took my hand off the mouthpiece. 'Stefanie says she didn't.' Of course she didn't! It would have been so much easier if my father stopped being deceitful for a change.

'But—'

'I've got to go. Can we talk about this later?'

'Sure. You've got my number?'

I wrote it down on the same piece of paper, said goodbye and hastily grabbed my coat. Stefanie and I hurried down the hall and took the stairs to the car park. 'Are you sure?' I asked her.

'Of course. We've been talking about these files all along. I would have remembered.'

'What about Freek Veenstra?'

'What does he have to do with this?'

'Piet Huizen told me that you and Freek Veenstra came to the Alkmaar police station and picked up the crates containing the files on the Otto Petersen case.'

Stefanie double-bleeped at a row of cars in the garage. An angry-red car responded with a flash of indicator lights. 'Veenstra? Wasn't he already retired then? It must have been around that time. I'll check the dates.' She looked at me over the roof of her car and said, 'But it's pointless. You know he's lying – for money would be my guess,' before getting in.

Anton Lantinga was held in a small room at the airport. In the background I heard the sound of snow-delayed departures and arrivals announced in three different languages. The Schiphol police officer, who had kept him company for the half an hour it took us to get here, left the room. There was none of the light-green paint of our interrogation room. Estate agents would call the decorating scheme here 'exposed brick'. It didn't work as well when it wasn't just a section, but four entire walls. I shivered and wrapped my arms around my waist against the damp that radiated from the bare stone.

Stefanie walked over to the man seated behind the small

table. Anton looked pale, but he had just come off an overnight flight from New York. His short hair was blond, bleached to the colour of set honey by the intermingled grey, and combed back in a side parting. He got up and shook her hand. 'Amsterdam police, I assume?'

Stefanie nodded, speechless for a change.

'My wife told me to expect you,' he said pleasantly.

I shut the door behind me, which cut off the multi-lingual voice in the middle of an announcement about the 10.54 KLM flight to Istanbul, urging Mr van Dam to hurry up, as he was delaying the flight.

Anton's receding hairline created an impression of a high forehead that wouldn't look amiss on a maths professor. His eyes, nose and mouth were huddled together as if they were worried they'd take up too much space and encroach on the area kept for thinking. Stefanie rustled some papers, re-arranging them into another random order. She looked at me and raised her eyebrows as if she needed permission to start. I wanted to give her a shrug, but nodded instead.

Anton rubbed the face of his large, expensive-looking golden watch with his left hand as if he was hoping he could rub away the time. 'Will this take long?'

'I hope it won't. I'm Inspector Dekkers. This is my colleague Detective Meerman.' Stefanie smiled. He smiled back in an automatic gesture, moving his eyes to include me. His teeth were too straight. His cheeks showed no hint of stubble; he must have shaved either just before he got on the plane last night or even on arrival. 'We are re-investigating the murder of Otto Petersen, your former business partner—'

155

'Not business partner – former employer.'

'Your former employer', Stefanie continued, 'and your wife's former husband.'

'Yes, Karin told me. I'm happy to help even if I can't see why this couldn't have waited until I was home. The man's been dead for over ten years.' I looked for a hint of a smirk around his thin lips, but there was none.

'Where were you on the evening Otto Petersen was murdered?' Stefanie's suit, the colour of a eurocent coin, had large creases around her hips, where the skirt had ridden up over her flesh and she'd sat on it.

'At home.' In contrast, Anton's dark blue suit was crease-free, as was the part of the white shirt I could see and the yellow-and-blue diagonally striped tie. He looked as if he'd just come out of a business meeting instead of an eight-hour flight.

'Can anybody confirm that?'

'I was alone.'

I doodled on my notepad, drew circles with my pen and filled them in. Anton was straining his neck to see what I was writing. I tipped the notepad further towards me and added another circle.

'Your car was seen outside Petersen's house at the time.'

'Oh, please. Not this again.' He leaned forward, folded his hands and put them on the table. 'Karin said you had new information.' He kept his eyes on Stefanie and slowly shook his head. 'You don't, do you?'

'I can't say.'

'This is insane,' he muttered. 'After all these years, we have to go through this again.' He pushed his chair back as if he considered getting up, but then thought better of it. 'The guy's an idiot.'

Stefanie sat up and her shirt fell open revealing the top of her breast trying to push free from a blue lace bra. 'Which guy?'

'The witness.'

'Which witness is that then, Anton?'

He frowned at the use of his first name and rubbed his watch again. 'I wasn't in Alkmaar that evening, so nobody can have seen me there. That means the witness must be the same guy who was lying first time round. Oh for goodness sake, you don't believe him, do you?'

'He seems credible.'

'He claims he saw my car. Well, he certainly didn't see me. There must be more people with that car.'

'But none of them wanted to kill Otto Petersen.'

'Neither did I.'

'You just wanted to talk to him? Things got out of hand?'

Stefanie moved her face into Anton's space, but he didn't flinch or retreat. He looked her squarely in the eye and said forcefully: 'I wasn't there. I didn't do it.'

'So – are you saying someone borrowed your car?'

He sighed heavily and rested his chin in his right hand. 'My car wasn't there. *I* wasn't there.'

'Maybe Otto Petersen wanted to kill *you*. Did he bring a gun to the meeting? Was it self-defence? An accident?'

He sighed again and looked at Stefanie through half-closed eyes. 'I told you: I wasn't there. I didn't meet Otto Petersen that evening.'

'Were you going to leave but Otto got home earlier than you expected? Is that it?'

'No, I left Karin first thing in the morning. I wasn't there.'

'But someone saw your car.'

'Someone *says* they saw my car.'

'Why would that someone lie?'

Anton sat back. 'Why indeed.' A pause, then he repeated, 'Why indeed.'

'You know the witness?' I said. Out of the corner of my eye I saw Stefanie give an imperceptible shake of the head. My gaze dropped. To the side of the table, Anton's brown leather briefcase rested on the floor. It was open at the top, revealing a fat book that he must have been reading on the plane.

Anton looked at the ceiling and took a deep breath in and out before answering me. 'No, I don't know who the witness is.'

'How much did you pay Piet Huizen?' Stefanie said.

He screwed up his forehead. 'Who?'

'Piet Huizen – Alkmaar police. Because you paid him, didn't you, to make those files go away.'

'I didn't pay anybody.' He looked at his watch and moved it on his wrist. 'I came back from New York. I didn't ask for a lawyer. I think that shows my desire to cooperate, to help solve the murder of my wife's first husband. It would have been easy for me to stay in the States.'

'And it would have been equally easy for us to have you extradited. Yes, we appreciate that you came back but we would appreciate it even more if you really did cooperate and tell us what happened that night.'

'I don't know because I wasn't there. I was at home.'

'But no way of proving it.'

'Karin telephoned me, when she came home and found Otto's body.'

'What time was this?'

'Seven o'clock.'

'Plenty of time to have driven from Alkmaar to Amsterdam. Traffic jams are the other way at that time of the evening.'

I understood why my father hadn't arrested Anton. One witness who saw a car wasn't enough to bring a case to court. *We haven't got enough*, I wrote on my notepad. I crossed the last word out and changed the sentence to *We haven't got anything.*

Stefanie looked at what I'd written and cut the interview short. 'Thank you, that'll be all,' she said and scraped her chair back.

'Hold on.' Anton got a moleskin notepad out of his leather briefcase. 'What was the name of the guy you mentioned? The guy I'm supposed to have paid?'

'Piet Huizen.'

'Thank you.' He smiled politely at Stefanie before writing my father's name down. As he put the notepad back in the bag, the fat book slid over and bared its title. Anton Lantinga had been reading the second Harry Potter.

In the car, crossing under the Schiphol runway, on the way back to the police station, Stefanie and I agreed that we needed to talk to Wouter Vos again to take a more formal statement and check some details. I called Wouter from my mobile. He didn't sound surprised to hear from me and was happy to talk to us the next afternoon.

Chapter Fourteen

When I came back to our office after the interview with Anton Lantinga, I saw that Hans had been right: Thomas was back. His pretty-boy face grinned at me from the desk opposite Hans's. His hair was ruffled up and he wore a blue shirt as he did every day, ever since I'd known him. He'd once told me that his wife thought it brought out the colour of his eyes. I'd been surprised he was married.

'Hi, Thomas. How was your holiday?' I said, pretending I wasn't concerned about his return.

'Very nice, thanks. Went skiing for two weeks with the kids. Verbier.'

'Well, it's good to have you back.'

'I talked to Hans about your new case. He said you've got it all under control.'

'I guess. There isn't much for us to go on. Missing money, a twelve-year-old unsolved murder and a reappeared witness.'

'And a kid holding up a petrol station.'

I didn't say anything.

'Not proud of what you've done?' Thomas said the words in a deliberately sarcastic tone of voice.

'Not really, no.'

'But he threatened to shoot you. There was a security camera. I've seen the tapes.'

'You have? I thought you'd only just got back.'

'You know how much I love watching those tapes. Or listening to tapes. Either one. Especially if you're on it.' He grinned at me. I knew better than to react. That's what he wanted; that's what he was like. 'The guys from Internal Investigations told me it's all just a formality. They did say they weren't too sure of your tactics going in there, but that it was all pretty obvious from there on in: you'd identified yourself as a police officer, had given him warning: he shot first.'

'Why would they tell you before me?'

'Who knows.' He smiled his pretty-boy grin again. His teeth were white against the wintersport tan. 'Anyway, seeing you on that tape made a nice change from just listening to you talk. How many hours of interviews were there?'

I didn't even pretend I didn't know that he was talking about the Wendy Leeuwenhoek tapes. 'A lot.'

'Yeah, a lot. But not every conversation was taped, was it, Lotte? I might have to tell the prosecutor about that. We wouldn't want him to be blindsided by that, now would we? And if *I* know, I'm sure the defence team can find out as well.'

'Yes, it's a shame the confession isn't—'

'I'm not talking about that final meeting. I'm talking about ones in between. Conversations that must have taken place but were never recorded. Or, if they were recorded, the tapes were never handed in.'

'Every conversation was recorded,' I objected.

'No, they weren't. I know they weren't. I'm not sure how many unrecorded meetings or conversations you and that murderer had, but I know for a fact that there was more than one. Maybe you should come clean to the prosecutor about that, make sure he knows.'

'Everything was recorded,' I repeated.

'Nice try, Lotte.' He pushed himself out of his chair and took his jacket from the back. 'If you won't tell him, I will. I'm not going to let the trial fall apart just because of you. The prosecutor needs to know.'

'Without me the trial *will* fall apart. But tell the prosecutor whatever you want.'

'I will.' He put his hand on my shoulder on the way out. I flinched from the physical contact. 'I came back yesterday and am going to work with André Kamp's team,' he said. 'Just popped in here to check you were OK. But you guys don't seem to need me here.'

'And what is Kamp's team working on?'

'A spate of petrol-station robberies.'

I relaxed. Of course – that was why André Kamp had interrogated Ben the morning after I'd shot the kid. 'So you watched the surveillance tape.' It was good to know that Thomas actually had a work reason rather than just a personal one.

'He doesn't quite fit in though, your kid. All the others were done by two or three people, all heavily armed.'

'The kid had a gun.'

'Different type. Not in the same league. Anyway, those robberies haven't stopped even though we've got the kid here. I'll talk to you about it later. Gotta hop. New team meeting.' He paused with his hand on the doorframe. 'Talk to the prosecutor, Lotte. Whatever meetings you had with Paul Leeuwenhoek, the defence will find someone who witnessed it. They will use it.' He didn't wait for an answer but turned around and left.

The first time I'd met Wendy's father without the tape recorder had been by accident. The investigation had been going on for over a month and the stack of tapes that documented the conversations I'd had with both Paul and Monique had grown rapidly. The parents hadn't been our allies over the years – they felt we hadn't done a good job and did not hold back from sharing their feelings with the press. The boss had asked me to start over with them, bond with them and become their friend, so I had spent a lot of time with each of them. I'd see Monique Leeuwenhoek a couple of times a week. I'd pop in after work, just to have a cup of tea with her, just to chat, me on my own, unthreatening and low-key. I didn't feel bad about searching through the files with a fine-tooth comb all day to find something that would prove her guilt and just chit-chatting with her in the evening. I had to believe the talking would lead somewhere and that eventually she would tell me something I needed to hear. I did the same with Paul. I was recording all the conversations.

Then I bumped into Paul in a bar on the Leidseplein. I was there with a friend; he was alone. He joined us. We talked. My friend fancied him. I wasn't sure if she knew who he was and I had no way of telling her. She wouldn't leave; she hung around, bought him drinks and it was obvious she wanted me to go home. I didn't. I drank too much, but I didn't embarrass myself. I watched him, I listened, I smiled at his jokes but I mainly stayed silent. I was in control. I saw his green eyes rest on hers; I saw his flirtatious attitude towards her. I saw it all and observed.

When my friend needed to leave, Paul walked out with us.

When I said goodbye he put his hand on my arm. 'Will I see you tomorrow?' he said. 'I like talking to you.' He smiled and I could feel the intensity of his eyes in mine all the way through to my stomach. All the people milling around on the Leidseplein, going from bar to bar, the tram coming past, the awful band playing on the pavement . . . all disappeared. 'I enjoy being interviewed by you,' he said, 'your attention on every word I say.' The wind had picked up and blew my hair into my eyes. He tucked it behind my ear. His fingers felt electric where they touched the skin of my neck.

When I got home I took a photo of Paul, Monique, his ex-wife, and their little girl Wendy and looked at it for a long time. I wanted to insert myself into that photograph, take the place in that family that Monique had given up when she divorced Paul. I could picture myself in her position with Paul's arm protectively around my shoulder. I lay in bed, open-eyed, and knew it was impossible. I didn't tell anybody I'd seen him.

The second time I'd met Paul without the recorder, a large number of properly taped interviews later, it had felt surprisingly private. The knowledge that the things we said would not be listened to by Thomas and the rest of the team afterwards had given that meeting an intimacy that had made me happy at the time and later sickened me.

But now, in the bright light of the police station, what worried me was that first time: would my friend remember? She had called me the next day to ask if I'd thought he liked her. I hadn't answered her. Surely by now she must know who he was; there was no way she could have missed all the newspaper coverage. Maybe she had even put two and two together. Would she be a witness for the defence? What could she say? Should I call her to . . . to do what? To warn her or to plead with her to keep quiet? That would surely make things worse. I couldn't do it.

What was the gap on the tapes that Thomas had found? I assumed that Paul had referred to something we'd talked about on the night out. I would have to listen to all the tapes myself, to all the conversations, to find out when and where we had slipped up — *I* had slipped up. But I really didn't want to listen to all those tapes again, listen to hours of his voice. I reminded myself that this was what Thomas was good at. This was what Thomas had done all the way through the investigation: listen to the tapes, take note of nuances and of any gaps. There was no way he would say anything to the defence, since he would do nothing to jeopardise this trial

166

– but he might go to the prosecutor's office. I would just have to sit tight and wait for the call.

That night, my dreams and thoughts got the better of me again and I had to go for another drive across the country. But I didn't stop at a petrol station.

Chapter Fifteen

The files had told me that Otto Petersen's mother was in her eighties, but her eyes looked into mine without a sign of confusion. Her long white hair was tied on the top of her head in a series of loose, intertwined knots. No thin-looking perm. She wore a night-black roll-neck pullover and trousers that hugged her tall thin body around the hips then flared out.

'Good morning, Mrs Petersen,' I said. 'I'm Detective Lotte Meerman from Amsterdam CID. We're re-investigating the murder of your son. Could I have a word?' I waited for her response. Maybe I should have started with some introductory chit-chat.

'Can we go for a walk?' she said. Her smile pulled the champagne-coloured crepe-de-chine of her cheeks into a series of pleats.

'Sorry?'

'If you have the time, it would be nice to go for a walk.' She looked at my boots. 'They're thick enough for the snow.'

It was better to go outside than be indoors in an old lady's small sitting room with, inevitably, the heating turned up too

168

high. 'Fine,' I said. It was a good thing Stefanie was still in Amsterdam, as she would never have agreed to a walk, but she had other work to get on with and we'd arranged to meet at Wouter Vos's place later.

I kept my coat on and waited in the little hallway until she was ready. Large pieces of furniture, the remnants of a previous life, cluttered the small flat. This was sheltered accommodation, under the protective shadow of a nursing home, on the edge of a park.

'Have you been here long?' I asked when she came back, wearing a warm black coat, a bright pink scarf and sturdy boots.

'I'm too good for this place,' she whispered. She gestured at the nursing home with a knotted hand before securing the front door. The swollen knuckles of her fingers locked a double wedding ring in place. 'My son bought the flat for me when my husband died. A lot of my friends are here, so I thought: why not.' She set out at a brisk pace along the lane through the park. The bare branches of trees touched each other high above our heads like the vaulted beams of an outdoor cathedral in which we'd worship winter. The sun slipped its rays through the gaps, so weak the light needed the help of the pull of gravity to reach the path.

Mrs Petersen's steps were sure and her arms swung by her side with the energy of a child kept inside for too long and finally allowed out to play. 'I don't regret it. In the beginning I travelled a lot.'

I had to make an effort to keep up as we moved deeper

into the park. 'Are your friends still here?' I asked, slightly out of breath.

'Yes, there's five of us. We used to go to school together. Ada isn't too well any more, but the rest of us, we go on holidays, walks, to lectures, exhibitions. It's quite a good little set-up. But they're afraid of a tiny bit of snow. Worried they'll fall and break a hip.'

'You're not?'

'I've been inside for a week now. I could do with some fresh air. I'm grateful for your company, for whatever reason you're here.' She looked me in the eye.

'As I said, we're reopening your son's case.'

'I'm not sure I can help you. I don't know much,' Mrs Petersen said.

'Not much, but something?'

She shrugged. 'Probably nothing, but which mother wants to admit that?'

'What was he like?'

'As a child?'

'Or a grown-up.'

'It's dangerous to ask an old lady to reminisce.' She laughed with the sound of the little bell I'd taken from my mother's Christmas tree. 'He was a good child. Always fitted in.'

The sound of our boots on the snow formed the rhythm section accompanying a bird singing in a tree. I looked up to see what it was, but couldn't find it. I could only see two structures, which were partially hidden by the trees on our right. A corner of black wire mesh, the edge of a man-height cage, extruded from between the snow-covered branches. It must be an empty aviary or a monkey house, its inhabitants kept somewhere warm during the winter.

'He fitted in too well,' she added unexpectedly. 'Otto seemed a different person from year to year.'

A sign in front of the aviary would have told us what was normally kept there, if it hadn't rusted to the point where all lettering was illegible. There was a cemented area where children could stand and poke their fingers through the mesh.

We were both silent and just walked. The frost chewed at my cheeks until they felt stiff, as if all the water in my skin had frozen to crystals. I didn't mind. Here, in the cold, in the park with only an old woman for company, time grew elastic. I didn't know how long we'd been walking. By the falling temperature in my upper legs, just at the point where they were no longer covered by my jacket, I guessed fifteen minutes.

'I saw changes in him all the time,' she went on. 'It showed in his clothes, his face.'

'With different fashions?'

'No, it wasn't that.' Another silence fell. Then she said, 'He was what people expected him to be. "Our changeling", we called him.' She laughed again. 'Makes him sound like something out of a fairy tale, doesn't it? But that's how he was.' She looked at me. Her loosely tied knot was coming undone and wisps of hair were flowing around her face where they'd escaped their clips. 'My husband was just a factory worker, you see, just a simple man. And my own parents were small farmers. I was clever enough, I suppose – nothing special. But then Otto – he was different. Highly intelligent, they called him at school, always the top of his class.' A combination of pride and sadness radiated from her eyes. They showed me where her son had got his intelligence from. I wouldn't call her 'nothing special'. She was just from a class and generation where ability had been less noticed and appreciated in a woman.

'The government paid for his education – he was the first in our family to go to university. We couldn't tell him how to behave, how to act, what to do.' She wrapped her scarf tighter around her neck with her bare hands, gnarled and bent like the twigs on the trees by the path. 'He had to fit in from an early age. Going to school with the children of doctors and lawyers, he wanted to be like them, sound like them. And he was so ambitious. He had this hunger for success and money. It burned inside him. It drove him.'

'Did he ever bring any friends home?'

'No, never.' What must it have been like for her to lose her gifted son? Or had she lost him years before, when he went to university and did all he could to remove all traces of his parents from his speech, his appearance and his entire life? Was that when she'd lost him?

'And Karin?'

'That was much, much later. When he married her, she was his secretary; he thought that was what he should do.'

'I didn't know she used to be his secretary.'

'She's different now.'

The trees around us shrank the world to just me and

172

Mrs Petersen. It was a colour-free world, the black of the branches and the white of the snow. We compressed it under our boots and walked for a while without speaking. Deep in the park I could no longer hear the traffic. There were no playing children; they must be back at school now that the Christmas break was over.

'Do you like her?' I said after the pause, my breath adding more white to the world around me.

'She never visits me, but I don't blame her for that. Yes, I liked her when they got married. I'm not sure I like what she turned into.'

'What do you mean?'

The old lady led me down a left turn. 'Like Otto, she changed her voice, her appearance and her manners. They were alike and they wanted the same thing. To fit in.'

My fingers were starting to feel cold inside the gloves and I stuffed them deep in my pockets. 'He must have taken the collapse of his company very hard.'

She didn't respond.

'Mrs Petersen?' I said.

She looked over to me. 'Are you his new girlfriend?'

'Whose?'

'Otto's. All these questions.'

'No, Mrs Petersen, I'm from the police. Remember? Your son's murder?' I said it as gently as I could.

'They stitched him up.' Her voice sounded louder in the frozen park.

'They?'

'Geert-Jan Goosens, Anton Lantinga – they're all old

money. Rich parents, rich children. Clearly, Otto wasn't.' She glanced at me and said more quietly, 'I'm worried it was our fault.'

'You've met them?'

She shook her head from side to side, setting more strands of hair free. 'I never did, but they all went to university together.'

Goosens hadn't mentioned that. 'And then Karin started an affair with Anton.'

Mrs Petersen laughed. 'Otto probably expected that to happen. Isn't it in all the movies and books? When you're in jail, your wife runs off with one of your friends. He would've been disappointed if she'd been waiting, pining for him.' She clasped her arms around her waist, her hands tucked away under her elbows.

'Are you cold? Would you like my gloves?' I took mine off. I reached out and she put her hand in my bare one. It was like a shard of glass under my fingers. 'God, you're freezing!' I exclaimed.

'I'm fine.' She looked down at her hand. It was white with mottled pink around the edges where I was holding it.

I took my other glove off too and wrapped both her hands inside my warm ones, careful not to rub them, until they weren't cold to the touch any more. All the time, she stood still and looked over my shoulder at the trees in the park. 'Here.' I gave her my gloves.

'I'm fine,' she insisted again.

'No, you're not. Put them on.' I pulled them over her hands as you did with a toddler. She held her hands up and wiggled her fingers. The cold bit mine. I pulled my sleeves down so that they covered my hands.

A block of snow fell from a tree branch and landed on the ground with a loud plop. The trees opened out to a pond. Ducks and coots were huddled together in a small area, hemmed in by the ice.

'We should have brought some bread,' Mrs Petersen said. 'Poor creatures.'

'I read somewhere that bread's bad for them.'

'I'm sure they prefer it to nothing, don't you?' A large mallard, his green wing-feathers glistening with water, was clambering up the bank of the pond, sure we'd come to feed him. 'Let's go. We've got nothing to give them. It's cruel to get their hopes up.' She turned around and walked away.

I looked at the waddling ducks and remembered feeding them, with my mother, in the Vondelpark, bags of leftover bread disappearing in their flat beaks. It never did them any harm; there had always been more ducks each Sunday than there'd been the week before. I remembered the feeling of my mother's hand around mine, keeping me secure and safe. I followed Mrs Petersen's footsteps. The compressed snow under my boots whispered with every step. It gave way for a centimetre or so, then supported and carried me.

If Otto had adapted so well to his varying environments, what would seven years in prison have done to him? Made him violent? Made him feel he had to kill his wife's lover?

'Did you visit Otto in prison?' I asked.

She raised her head, probably as deep in thought as I had been. 'Yes, I go once a month.' She took a few more steps then stopped. 'No, not go – went.' She took her hands out of her pockets and swung her arms.

'And he changed.' It wasn't even a question.

'He always changed. This time, he put on weight and his vocabulary got coarser. He started to sound like his father again, back to his regional accent.'

'Aggressive?'

'Not towards me.'

'Did he talk about life after getting out?'

'Yes. He said he wanted to go into politics. A joke, of course. He said there was only one profession where getting caught with your fingers in the till was an advantage.'

I smiled but didn't reply. I let the silence last.

His mother said softly, her voice barely louder than the crunch of the snow, 'He was talking about revenge.'

'Revenge for what?'

'He didn't say.'

It all fitted. Otto arranged to see Anton, his old university friend, who had taken his wife. And hadn't he taken his business also?

We were back on the road her house was on. She slipped on the pavement, a small slide sideways, and I put my arm through hers to make sure she was safe. As I walked her to her door, I remembered what I'd come for. 'Do you have a photo of Otto when he was young?'

'I've got one from university somewhere, with a group of his friends.'

She disappeared through the door and almost immediately came back. The photo must have been close by. She handed it to me, together with my gloves. 'You will give it back to me, won't you?'

'Of course.' It was the friends together, Otto Petersen, Anton Lantinga and a younger, thinner Geert-Jan Goosens with another young man I didn't recognise. But one face was there as well, familiar from television and the financial papers: Ferdinand van Ravensberger, the man whose nephew claimed he'd killed someone.

Stefanie showed no interest in Wouter's art collection and walked straight past the paintings without stopping. She had already been waiting for me outside Wouter's apartment building.

Wouter wore a Ralph Lauren polo-shirt over a pair of jeans. He had tidied up: there were no computer magazines all over the sofa any more and the PC that had been in the process of being built had disappeared. We went through the same questions as before. He described Anton's car and told us his story again.

'Did you see Anton?' Stefanie asked.

Wouter shook his head. The slicked-back hair hardly moved and the curls at the back of his neck stayed in place. 'I only saw the car.' He lit up a cigarette and offered us one too. I was surprised when Stefanie refused. She probably didn't think it was appropriate. 'Then I heard that someone had been shot, and I told Piet about the car.'

'OK. Let's talk about what happened then.' Stefanie got her notepad out to indicate that this was the part that she was actually interested in. 'You gave a statement to DI Huizen?'

'Yes, I came to the police station and signed it.'

'Did you see what DI Huizen did with it?'

I wanted to stop her questions but couldn't interrupt her. I should have known she would turn the questioning to my father again.

'No, I didn't,' Wouter said. 'It was typed up, I signed it and that was it.'

Stefanie took some notes.

'Why do you ask?' Wouter said. 'Did something happen to my statement?'

I looked at her, willed her not to tell him, but she ignored my silent plea. 'It's gone,' she said, 'your witness statement. It's not in any of the files.'

'That bastard.' Wouter grimaced. 'Sorry, didn't mean to swear.'

Stefanie gestured to indicate that she was far from offended.

'So that's how he got away with it,' Wouter said. 'I always wondered why Anton was never arrested.'

'I've got no further questions.' I stood up.

'Sorry to put you through this inconvenience,' Stefanie said, 'but we'll need your statement again. I'll type it up and maybe you can come to Amsterdam to sign it.'

'Fine. Or can I sign it here – in Alkmaar.'

Stefanie shrugged. 'Why not.'

Wouter got up and walked us to the door. Even on the way out Stefanie didn't look at the art. I lingered by

178

the painting of the dream world, admired its vibrant colours for a few seconds before shaking Wouter's hand and following Stefanie down the stairs.

As she opened her car door she paused. 'He's a reliable witness,' she said, 'but there's no way we'd get a conviction purely based on his evidence.'

I got my car keys out of my handbag.

'Why was Anton so concerned about it?' Stefanie mused. 'I don't understand why he paid Piet Huizen to get rid of those files.'

'I don't think he did.'

'You're right. Piet Huizen probably ripped up the witness statement straight away. But there must have been something else as well. Was there another witness, maybe? More evidence?'

'I've no idea.'

'Strange.' She got in her car and slammed the door shut. I waited on the pavement until the engine started and her car moved forward. Then it stopped and the window was wound down. 'Are you sure they told you everything?' she called. 'I bet they're still holding something back. Anyway, I'll see you at the office.' She closed the window again before I could even respond.

Alkmaar's police station was becoming a familiar sight, as was the milkmaid on Reception. 'I've come to see Ronald de Boer again,' I told her.

As last time, she dialled his number by heart. 'Hi, Ronald,

that Amsterdam detective woman is here again for you.' She turned away and spoke quietly into the phone, so that I couldn't hear. She laughed softly, then, turning back, she informed me, 'He'll be right down.'

'Of course. Thank you.'

Ronald was waiting for me at the lifts. 'She's nice, your receptionist,' I said, and then wished I hadn't.

'Hi, Lotte. What's up?'

I looked around to see if anybody could hear us. The corridor was empty. 'Can I talk to you about the Petersen files?'

'Let's have a coffee.'

I followed him to the canteen. We sat at a table in the furthest corner, closest to the window, and drank coffee from brown plastic cups with white plastic stirrers. Over Ronald's shoulder I saw the broad canal that linked Alkmaar to Amsterdam. A few boats kept the ice open. Seagulls followed them, hoping the movement of the engines would bring fish to the surface. Even the seagulls were more relaxed here than at home in Amsterdam, floating on the wind for longer, diving less often. The water, wider than a motorway, was a reminder that we were below sea-level.

I leaned closer to Ronald and lowered my voice. 'When these files went missing, was there ever any . . . any mention of money?' I wouldn't admit the possibility of bribes to my Amsterdam colleagues, but I wasn't telling Ronald anything new.

He frowned. 'He never offered me money.'

180

'No, that's not what I mean. I mean . . . do you think *he* took money? My father?'

'Took it? What – you mean stole it?'

I sighed, frustrated that he wanted me to spell it out, was making sure he didn't tell me anything I didn't already know. It was apparent that he still didn't trust me. 'A pay-off,' I explained. 'One of my colleagues, she thought that maybe he took a pay-off – from Anton Lantinga. To get rid of those files.'

'I don't think so,' he said slowly, looking at me closely for a few seconds. He took a sip of coffee, grimaced and fished a sachet of sugar from the table next to us. As he stirred, the light showed up the scratches in the otherwise smooth surface of his gold wedding ring.

I understood his hesitation and sat back in my chair. 'I'll cover for him, if that's what you're worried about. But I'd like to know.' I had a right to know.

He nodded. 'There were rumours. You've been to his house . . . Questions were asked.'

Yes. It was exactly as I thought.

'Have you asked him? Outright?' Ronald enquired.

'No.'

'Maybe you should keep it like that – you know, don't upset him too much. Think about his heart. And let me know if I can help. You can call me any time.'

'Thanks, Ronald. I need all the help I can get.' I held the brown cup between both hands. The plastic did nothing to stop the heat of the coffee hitting my skin, making my fingers tingle in delicious pain. 'I saw Otto's mother this morning.'

Ronald laughed. One of his incisors was at an angle and overlapped the front tooth. 'If you'd called me beforehand, I could have saved you the trip. Did she talk at all?'

I took the photo she'd given me out of my bag and slid it to him over the table, past a small pile of spilled sugar.

'She was rarely lucid when her son got killed,' Ronald said. 'We talked to her a few times, but there wasn't any point.' He bent his head over the photo and rubbed one greying eyebrow, making the hairs in the corner, longer than the others, stand on end. 'Petersen, Goosens, Lantinga and this one.' He moved his finger to the last figure. 'Is that Van Ravensberger?'

'Yes. Don't know who the other guy is.'

'Me neither.'

'I took her for a walk.'

'What for?'

'She wanted to get out. She seemed perfectly compos mentis.' I took a sip of coffee. 'I had no idea she wasn't quite with it. Then I noticed how cold her hands were. I felt so guilty. Can you imagine, bringing an old lady back with frostbite after a stroll in the park with a police officer?'

'I'm sure she's fine.'

'I hope so. It was minus five and I let her walk around without gloves.' I remembered reaching out to those fingers, the touch of her hand in mine, feeling the protrusion of her joints, swollen like catkins on a thin willow branch, and holding them as life returned to them. The first physical contact I'd sought in weeks.

Ronald fished a packet of chewing gum from his pocket and took a piece out. As he chewed I could see it move from right to left, collecting all traces of food from between his teeth with each movement of the jaw. I drank the last of my coffee, said goodbye and set off back to Amsterdam.

I felt safe again when I was in my green car and en route for the police station. Was it by chance that I took a wrong turn and drove past my father's house? A Freudian slip of the steering wheel? Now that I was here, I thought, I might as well go in, I might as well see him. Mum need never know.

I rang the doorbell but no footsteps came to the door. Nobody appeared to be at home.

Chapter Sixteen

It said 13.57 on the clock on my desk when I walked back into our office. There was too much space around my desk, even though it was days ago that CI Moerdijk had taken my files, papers and photos away. The paperwork on the Petersen case hadn't taken its place yet. The two white cardboard boxes behind me, pushed up against the wall, were packed again, all the papers that I'd thrown on the floor returned to their green folders. But they were CI Moerdijk's papers. There wasn't much filled with my writing. My notepad was covered with circles and squares, not with any evidence of original thought. I'd wasted too many pages, then torn them off, leaving the thin edges stuck to the spiral binding as evidence of my failure. Somehow my brain didn't want to kick into gear.

'How was Otto Petersen's mother?' Hans said.

'I'm really not sure. I thought she had some useful info, but then someone at the Alkmaar police told me she's not with it any more. I'd like to know what the boss thought at the time of the murder.'

I straightened the files up, opened the top one and soon

found the transcript of the interview. The chief inspector
had met up with Otto's mother in September 2002. She'd
been in hospital at the time, having been found in her house
two weeks before, undernourished and seriously neglected.
How thin her fingers must have been. I rested my forehead
in my hand and hid my face behind a curtain of short dark
hair while I read. CI Moerdijk had spoken to her but, as
with Ronald, she hadn't made much sense. She must have
been placed in the sheltered accommodation when she got
out of hospital, I thought. The flat clearly wasn't bought by
her son if she'd still been living in a house, a few months
after his death. How much of what she told me had been
true?

'They had a whistle-blower. I always said you need a
whistle-blower, didn't I?' It was Stefanie, marching into the
office with a handful of printed pages. She jiggled them at
me to celebrate the fact that she'd been right.

How come she always knew exactly when I was at my
desk? I thought irritably. I should check with Hans if she
popped in and out every half an hour to see if I was here.
Or maybe her office overlooked the Marnixstraat and she
could see when I got in.

'I don't know who it was, though. It doesn't say.' She stood
opposite me, leaning against the side of Thomas's empty
desk. I didn't know if he had joined André Kamp's team
permanently or if he was temporarily helping out. The boss
would tell us at some point.

'Here.' She read from one page like an actress learning her
lines. 'This is the mention of an anonymous tip-off.' She

185

pushed the pages across the desk to me. 'He or she provided evidence. I haven't found out yet what it was. Must have been conclusive though. They didn't testify in court.'

I glanced over the papers but went back to thumbing through the CI's notes.

'Not even behind closed doors?' Hans said.

'No.'

He motioned that he'd like to see the papers and I handed them over to him. 'It must have been something in writing,' he said thoughtfully, 'something the whistle-blower had access to. Maybe he was a risk manager, or another one of the traders.'

Stefanie shrugged. 'Risk manager is a possibility. They have to sign off on those things. Any illegal trading would be their responsibility.'

'And if', Hans continued, 'Otto wouldn't listen . . . Wouldn't they have gone to Goosens? Get him to talk to Otto first?'

'Goosens said he didn't know anything about it,' Stefanie told him.

'Maybe he lied,' Hans said.

'He definitely lied,' she agreed. 'There's no way he didn't know. Anyway, I haven't yet found the particular trade they lost the money on.'

I fished the photo of the young men who'd been together at university out of my bag. Whatever Otto's mother might or might not have remembered, this photo *was* real. 'He also forgot to tell us about—'

Behind me someone knocked on the doorframe. 'Excuse me,' said a familiar voice.

I turned round to see my father, his nose red from the cold. He took out a handkerchief and gave the nose that was so much like mine a rub. His hair was dotted with flakes of snow.

'What are you doing here?' It came out harshly in my surprise.

'I came to see Stefanie Dekkers.' He took his glasses off and wiped the condensation on the arm of his coat.

'That's me,' Stefanie said.

I kept looking at my father, watching his reaction at the sound of Stefanie's voice.

'No, you're not.' His eyes narrowed and his face went pale.

'Give me your coat,' I said and got up to take it. As I lifted the garment from his shoulders, I saw that his hair was sticking up at the back and I wanted to smooth it down, because he clearly wanted to look smart. He was dressed carefully for the occasion in a pair of sharply creased dark blue trousers and a grey-checked jacket over a shirt and tie. His shoes had thick soles that still carried a trace of snow, but they were the same colour grey as his jacket.

'Thank you,' he said.

'Well,' Stefanie said stiffly. 'Who are *you*?'

'Sorry, I should have introduced you,' I said from behind my father's back. 'This is Piet Huizen.'

'Ah, the famous Piet Huizen.' Stefanie jerked her thumb at the wall with the photos, her face still carrying a frown. 'You were on there for a while.'

My father walked over and looked at the diagrams. 'You're exactly as far as I got. Funny.'

'This is Hans Kraai,' I said.

My father reached over to shake his hand. 'Nice to meet you.'

'And you. Have a seat.' Hans gestured to the empty desk next to Stefanie. 'The more the merrier.'

My father went past her and sat down at the fourth desk. He turned to her. 'You're not the right Stefanie Dekkers.'

She raised her eyebrows. She would have raised just one if she'd been able to.

'You didn't come to Alkmaar, I mean,' he said.

'I know. That's what I've been telling Lotte.'

'Is there another police officer with that name?'

'No, I think I'm the only one.'

'And Freek Veenstra?'

'Dead now, retired ages ago.'

My father slumped in his chair. He gazed out of the window where the swirling snowflakes slid down the glass like small white snails, leaving trails of wet behind.

Stefanie looked at him, a small smile around her lips. 'What did you do with those files?' she said.

He turned his head away from the window. 'Two people picked them up. Police – Stefanie Dekkers and Freek Veenstra.'

'But I didn't go, and Freek Veenstra had already retired.'

My father let several seconds tick by in silence. 'That's what they said their names were.' He sounded tired.

'Did they identify themselves?'

188

He shrugged. 'I expected two people from Amsterdam to collect these files and so they did.'

'Where did you get our names from?'

'*They* gave me those names.'

She sat up straighter in her chair, raised herself to her full height. 'Where did *you* get our names from? Because nobody turned up to collect those files, did they? You got rid of them.'

'No, two—'

'I don't believe you.'

'Stefanie, shut up,' I said, more forcefully than I meant to. 'Lotte—'

'Lotte—' My father and Stefanie said my name at the same time. I flinched at his use of my first name but nobody else seemed to have noticed. Stefanie's voice was louder than my father's and probably covered up what he'd said.

I wanted to go up to him, stand behind him and put my hands protectively on his shoulders. It was a stupid impulse. I remembered the other time I'd wanted to hug him but didn't, on the first of those excruciating weekend visits.

I'd seen him as soon as I'd got off the train. He'd been watching the stream of people move past. I'd liked the way he checked every face. I'd wanted to raise my hand, I'd wanted to jump up and shout: 'I'm here, I'm here!' but I didn't: at thirteen I was hypersensitive about how to behave in public. Taking three deep breaths, I walked up to him. 'Hi, Dad,' I said. He said something about it being lovely to see me. I wanted to give him a hug or a kiss on his cheek, but

189

stopped: doubts had already started to creep in. If it was so lovely, then why hadn't he wanted to see me before?

My father frowned, looked over my head and asked where my mother was. I had to admit that she'd got off at the stop before Alkmaar. He was getting annoyed, was starting to have a go at her for letting me come here by myself. The impulse to hug him left me in the need to defend my mother. I explained that she had had to go back to Amsterdam, but he didn't listen, only called her irresponsible, unsuited to take care of me – well, there was nobody else willing to do it, I answered silently – and that I was only twelve and shouldn't be travelling on my own. He had got my age wrong: I was thirteen. I stuffed my hands back in my pockets and told him she had a doctor's appointment. That she had to get home or she would have been late. He said it wasn't safe for me to travel by myself, but of course it was. This was provincial Alkmaar, and I was used to cycling around Amsterdam on my own. 'You wouldn't know how dangerous it is,' he said.

We walked down the stairs, me in silence by his side. And then, as if nothing had happened, he asked me what I wanted to do that day. I shrugged. By now, I just wanted to go home.

Hans moved his eyes from me to my father and back again. Ronald had said he could see the family resemblance, but then he had known we were daughter and father.

'Let's keep this civil, Stefanie,' Hans said. 'The man is a colleague of ours, after all.'

'Ex-colleague.' She swivelled her chair towards him and crossed her legs, looking him up and down.

'Two people came to pick up the files?' Hans resumed.

'Yes.'

'You said you were expecting them?'

'Yes. Our commander told me Amsterdam were coming in to take the case over. I asked Ronald de Boer, my colleague, to help me pack the crates. We had a couple of hours, the commander said.'

'And then they turned up.'

'Yes. Our receptionist called to say they were there. A little early, if I remember right.'

'How early?'

'I don't know, an hour or so. But I remember thinking you were clearly keen to get your hands on my case.'

'And then?'

'Then I took the stuff down. Both crates. They picked them up, carried them to their car and drove off.'

'Uniformed?'

'No. No, plainclothed.'

Hans addressed me. 'Could have been anybody.'

I nodded but didn't say anything. I didn't understand why my father was here, talking about this, putting himself in the middle of everybody's attention, blatantly lying.

'Why didn't you ask for ID?' Stefanie said.

'I expected two people; two people turned up. I suppose I didn't want to make it more awkward than it needed to be.'

'Awkward?'

'Well, I didn't want to hand them my case on a silver plate. You can understand that, surely. There was some pride involved.'

'Hardly a silver plate.'

191

'We had the witness. We traced the same path you're tracking now.' He pointed at the wall behind him. 'You got no further than we did. If I hadn't told you about our witness, you wouldn't even have come this far.'

'We are equally stuck,' Stefanie said. 'We followed your red herring so we land up in your dead end.'

'The chief inspector didn't get anywhere either,' I said, immediately biting my tongue.

She directed her attention at me. 'And *you* keep dragging us off at a tangent to look at the Petersen Capital case.'

'All I'm saying is that the boss—'

'Let's do a Photofit,' Hans interrupted. 'Do you remember what the two Amsterdam policemen looked like?'

'Hans, there is no point; those two people don't exist,' Stefanie said heavily.

'I remember,' my father said.

'Am I the only one here who sees he's lying? For goodness' sake!'

'Stefanie . . .'

'Don't Stefanie me, Lotte,' she snapped. 'You've got me running around, checking all the finance part, and when I find something, you ignore me and listen to what a lying, conniving old man's got to say instead.' She stood up and dropped the files she'd brought in on top of the CI's reports on Otto Petersen. 'Don't count on me to do any more of your legwork.' She stomped out and slammed the door shut. We could hear her footsteps all the way down the corridor.

'Let's spark up that computer.' Hans crossed the office to

the desk my father was sitting at. 'It has the Identifit soft-
ware on it. Do you know how to use it?'

'If it's made for policemen, how hard can it be?'

'I'll give you a hand,' Hans said.

'Would you both like a coffee?' I wanted to leave the
room. I couldn't sit here and watch while my father made
up some faces. He looked and sounded so sincere. He was
so good at hiding what had really happened. I was reminded
of my own thoughts in Alkmaar's police station a few days
ago, when I realised that I could lie easily about what had
happened in the Wendy Leeuwenhoek investigation because
I'd told the same untruths so often. Maybe my father
believed what he was telling us because he had managed to
convince himself in the intervening years that he hadn't
done anything wrong, that the two people he'd invented had
really existed.

'Milk and sugar?' I asked my father. He nodded.

When I came back, they'd created perfect Photofits of a
man and a woman I'd never seen before.

After he'd finished his coffee I walked my father to the
tram stop. It wouldn't take too long to get back to the station for the train to Alkmaar. It had stopped snowing and
patches of blue were unveiled between the clouds. He slid
on the snow-covered pavement and I hooked my arm
through his to stabilise him, just like I'd done with Otto
Petersen's mother, just like I'd do with any stranger who
needed help.

'How's your mother?' he asked.

'She's fine. I told her I'd been to see you.'

'Ah.'

'Yes. She was pissed off that you saw my new car before she did.'

He laughed, a rumbling sound that started in his stomach and that I could feel through my skin. I pulled my arm back. We looked at each other.

The smile died on his lips. 'Sorry,' he said. 'It's not funny.'

'It's OK, it is really.'

The tram stop was at the Leidseplein. The bars' outside tables looked empty and cold, and the lights that tried to tempt drinkers inside were gaudy and desperate in the broad daylight. I turned my back on the bar where I'd had drinks with Paul Leeuwenhoek and where I'd first realised how attracted I was to him.

The tram came screeching around the corner, sounding its bell to grab the attention of anybody who hadn't heard the contact of the iron wheels on the iron rails.

The doors opened and my father went up the steps at the back. On a sudden impulse, I jumped on and followed behind him. He looked over his shoulder and smiled. We forced our way through a group of Japanese tourists, who'd probably got on the tram at the Rijksmuseum, a couple of stops earlier. They were wrapped up in scarves and hats and must have had a cheap deal to come to Amsterdam at this time of year. He put the card against the reader to pay for the trip to Centraal Station. We took a seat behind a young girl talking in English on her mobile. She finished her call and started another one, speaking German this time.

The doors opened again and the sweet floral smell of marijuana drifted in with a group of young students.

'Ronald told me about your heart attack.' I turned to look at my father. 'I'm really sorry. I didn't know, otherwise I would have given you a call. Before coming to Alkmaar last week, I mean.'

He gave a sigh and rested his arms on the back of the seat in front of him. The slight hunch in his upper back became more pronounced. 'Not a problem. I'm perfectly fine now. It was twelve years ago.'

'Just after your retirement?'

'Had a heart attack the day I was told my retirement date. How sad is that? I was so attached to my job.'

'I understand.' Wasn't this what I too had been afraid of for the last month? 'It would be the same for me. Work's all I have.' *And now I'm risking it for you.* I didn't say the words out loud.

'What about. . .' He gestured at my hand.

'He went off with another woman.' The tram started again. *He left me for someone younger and I looked in the wrong direction for a replacement.*

'I'm sorry.'

'It's been a year now. Plus you didn't like him anyway.'

'I didn't know him. Not the same thing.' He coughed. 'Work is a good way of forgetting.'

'How did you cope when work wasn't there any more?' I asked him quietly, my voice barely rising above the rattling sound of the tram. If the CI ever found out this old man sitting next to me was my father, I would soon have to find out for myself.

'I had medication – that helped,' he said.

Maybe I should use the little blue pills in that pot on my bedside table. The thought of losing my work safety net was so frightening I had to push it out of my mind. My father coughed again.

'Are you OK?' I asked.

'Just a tickly throat.' He took one glove off, got a sweet out of his pocket and peeled off the wrapper. He held another one out to me. I shook my head. 'Honestly,' he said, 'it was hard. There was nothing. A black hole.'

'You should have told me . . . you should have said. Did Mum know?'

He nodded. He didn't say anything for a while. Then he went on, 'But the work is hard as well. It's no picnic. You know that yourself, don't you, Lotte?'

'Yes.' I wasn't sure my response was audible.

'If you ever want to talk, I'm here,' he said. 'I've seen most things – nothing would surprise or shock me.'

He would be surprised if I told him the truth about sleeping with a murderer. Not just sleeping with him, but being in love with him. I'd been so infatuated with Paul, and for the first time in a long while I had been hopeful that I could start a new family, could replace my ex-husband with someone who'd love me more, with this man who'd gone through the same things as I had: the loss of a child and the subsequent break-up of his marriage.

I couldn't risk talking to my father about this. I needed

196

to change the subject. The question that had been on my mind ever since the Photofit, ever since my father had told Hans and Stefanie about the two people who picked up the files, reasserted itself and came out into the open. 'What you said back in the office – was any of that true?'

His face pulled into deep wrinkles. 'Of course it was. All of it. Why?'

I bit my lip. I didn't want to tell him what my mother had revealed to me. When he'd said that nothing would surprise him, that he'd seen most things, was that what he meant? That he'd taken cash, therefore he wouldn't be shocked by anything I could have done?

The tram took a sweeping left corner past the university building and passed the Grand Café Luxembourg, where Stefanie had first met her husband Patrick. The bell rang to warn a group of students who were crossing without looking. They dashed like cats back onto the pavement, laughing but indignant.

'Why are you asking, Lotte?' he repeated. 'I was careless not to check their IDs, but my mind was on something else.'

I wanted to ask about the money that my mother had told me about, that Stefanie was so fixated with, but decided not to. 'Just checking how much . . . how much you exactly remembered and how much you were filling in the gaps.'

'Oh, I clearly remember it all. Don't you have some of those moments – deciding moments in a case, or in your life – that are so burned in your memory, you won't ever forget them? This is one of those for me.'

I nodded. For me that was the first time I'd met Paul. I

didn't want to remember, but it was as my father said: the moment was burned in my memory. The first thing I had noticed about Paul was his age. I could see the damage that the years and the pressure had done to him. When I'd made the appointment over the phone, I'd heard the voice I'd recognised from the tapes. But voices didn't change much. I'd watched him so often on television or seen his photo in the newspapers that I'd felt I knew him. I'd forgotten he was now fifteen years older than in those initial TV interviews where he and his wife asked the public for help to find their daughter. When I'd met him, his dark hair had faded to grey, his green-grey eyes had spoken of years of hurt. He hadn't needed to tell me he'd suffered from the disappearance of his daughter; I thought I read it in the lines of his face, that it was all there, clear for everybody to see.

'Do you mind if I record our conversation?' I had asked. This all had to be done by some semblance of rules.

'Of course not. Whatever it takes to find her,' he'd said. 'Whatever it takes.'

How did that memory make me feel now? Dirty? Stupid? Gullible? Did my father's memory of his last case make him feel awful too?

'How do you feel about the Petersen case?' I asked.

'It was my last case and I never closed it. It's unfinished business. However, I had never given it much thought until you turned up, Lotte. I'd wondered why it was never resolved, but I assumed that Wouter Vos's witness statement had probably turned out to be a dead end. Now I feel guilty because it seems that I should have checked who I was giving those files to. It seems it was my mistake.'

I thought I could understand why he was doing what he was doing: he was trying to steer us in a certain direction. Maybe he wanted to make up for what he'd done twelve years ago. I was tempted to follow my father's lead and see where it took us.

The tram took a last, final sweep and my father and I arrived at Centraal Station. In the mass of people swarming outside like ants from a disturbed nest, we said a quick goodbye. He hugged me. I didn't hug him back, but nor did I resist it. I just stood still and let him hold me. He walked off towards platform 13 and I remained in the forecourt of the station, like a rock in the middle of a river, people streaming past me on both sides. From the right I heard a street organ playing 'Tulips from Amsterdam' and from the left the sound of panpipes. He didn't turn round. At least this time I didn't cry.

I walked home to get some fresh cold air, past the building site for the new metro line that covered Centraal Station's front, along the tourist restaurants of the Damrak and the shops of the Nieuwmarkt. A cloud of angry sound drifted from a group of Moroccan youths who walked past a shop that sold fashionable jeans and T-shirts. Their voices intermingled with the swearwords of the rap music pumping from the shop. The noise made me look at them as I walked past, a reflex born out of patrolling these streets on the lookout for trouble for over a decade now, but the vowels and consonants of their foreign language missed the aggressive edge that pointed to oncoming violence. They were just teenagers asserting themselves in a group.

In the summer, groups of youths would congregate outside the shops but now it was so cold that nobody was standing still. Everybody kept on the move, walking up and down the street, throwing quick glances into the shop windows but nobody paused to admire anything. A wine merchant was offering a free woollen hat – a white affair with orange pompoms – to anyone spending 25 euros or more, and the souvenir stalls were doing a brisk trade in ear-muffs to those tourists who hadn't counted on the frost. Every now and then, an elderly couple ambled past but the average age of the people on the Nieuwmarkt was under twenty. The shops knew their target audience: loud music created a sound barrier outside every shop, making sure that older people, such as myself, didn't drift in by accident and waste the time of shop assistants busy talking to each other. Only the young, with permanent ear damage caused by listening to their iPods too loudly, felt comfortable trying on clothes in changing rooms where you had to shout to be heard.

I was relieved when the Kalverstraat ended. I turned right past the floating flower market, left the stink of fries and McDonald's behind me and swapped it for the scentless rows of hothouse tulips and crates of bulbs. Two more turns, ten more minutes of walking along slush- and snow-covered pavements, and I was at my canal. I could see the carriage-clock shape of the gabled roof of my house. I knew I was lucky to live here. I was lucky to have a job I was good at. I even felt lucky to have met my father again.

Chapter Seventeen

'He's home,' Stefanie said. 'Van Ravensberger — he's at home today.'

I didn't look up from my PC screen. I was surprised it had taken her this long. Ever since his nephew had told us what he'd overheard and Stefanie had said she wanted to get the uncle on something, I had expected this meeting. Stefanie had stayed away from our office since she'd walked out in a huff yesterday and I hadn't minded at all. Feeling that I had to protect my father against her, without being seen to do so, was tiring. This was her first visit since then.

'I spoke to his secretary,' she said. 'He can see us at ten.'

The clock at the bottom right of my computer screen said 08:47. 'Where does he work?'

'We're meeting him at his home. Blaricum.'

'That's less than an hour's drive. I'll pop round to your office in fifteen minutes then.'

I knew how long it would take to get to Blaricum because I'd been there a few times. My ex-husband had wanted to buy a house in that small town after he'd made his first million. It was where a number of his golf buddies had a house and he'd thought it was more in keeping with our new financial status because it was where the rich lived: in lovely countryside but still within easy commuting distance from Amsterdam. It was where the women played tennis and the men played away. But the price of houses there was well out of our reach, and owning a small flat in an expensive part of the country was not what he'd had in mind. So we'd stayed where we were, in our house in Zaandam, north of Amsterdam, the house we'd moved into just before we got married. I hadn't minded. I didn't think Blaricum was the kind of place where I'd fit in.

Instead of leaving, Stefanie walked over to the whiteboard, bumping against my chair as she passed.

'Who's that?' She pointed at the Photofit of the woman who'd borrowed her name when she'd collected the crates from my father.

'Why?' I said.

'Looks familiar.'

'What about the guy?'

'Not sure. Maybe.' She peered closer.

'Those were the two people who went to Alkmaar.'

'Ah, OK.' Stefanie stepped away from the wall. 'Is it some actress? Sportswoman?'

'If you've met her . . .' Hans said.

'He made the whole thing up,' Stefanie interrupted him.

'But the woman who used your name looks familiar to you,' I said.

'I'm not interested in this guessing game. I'll see you in fifteen minutes.' She drifted her fingers over my desk as she

202

walked past. They rested for a second on the stack of files from CI Moerdijk that were still on my desk from yesterday. 'Was he . . . any good?'

'Sorry?'

'Moerdijk's work. Up to the standard you'd expect?'

I took some time to respond, trying to figure out why she wanted to know. The boss was difficult to judge. On the one hand, he hadn't understood the financial intricacies of the Petersen fraud and had assigned a motive to Goosens that hadn't been there. I didn't blame him for not understanding, but surely he could have had help from the Financial Fraud department, similar to the assistance that Stefanie was giving me. But on the other hand, he had completely backed me over the Wendy Leeuwenhoek case, given me a large part in the inquiry in my first case in his group, after my move from André Kamp's squad. What came to mind were the pencil scribblings in the margins and the clean-up of my files. 'Very diligent,' I said.

She laughed with her mouth only. 'Diligent. Yes, he's definitely that. Very thorough.' She put a hand on my shoulder. I swivelled my chair until it fell off. She laughed again. 'See you in fifteen.' The swell of her hips made them bounce even more than they normally did. The flesh bulged out at either end of the line of underwear like a pillow tightly bound in the middle with a single piece of string.

When we could no longer hear her footsteps, Hans opened his mouth but I raised my hand to stop him. 'Don't say it; I don't want to hear it. You were going to say something about her joining our team. I dread to think of it: she

203

already hangs around here enough.' I opened the report again and looked at the spidery writing.

'She recognised that woman, was all I was going to say.'

'Yes, she did.' But the woman looked completely unfamiliar to me.

'They must have met,' Hans said. 'The person who used her name must have known that Stefanie Dekkers worked for the police. Or she'd been told to use that name by somebody who did.' He got up and gave his whole body a long stretch. 'And of course Freek Veenstra too.' He walked up to the whiteboard and drew a beautifully straight arrow between the Photofits and Anton Lantinga. 'They both worked the Petersen Capital case.' He turned back to me with an enormous grin. 'Freek Veenstra and Stefanie Dekkers. It was one of her first cases, did you know that?'

'Fits very nicely,' I said. I didn't tell Hans the truth: that my father had got rid of those files and that nobody had come to collect them. 'She confiscated Anton Lantinga's PC. She told me he was absolutely livid. Her best day at work ever, she said.'

'He'd have remembered her name.'

Hans's smirk seemed to follow me as I walked down the corridor to where the Financial Fraud team sat. Stefanie would have interpreted the use of her name completely differently: she would no doubt say that my father had picked the name from the police directory and had chosen two people from the Financial Fraud department exactly to sow this plausible seed. She would say that it had backfired on him, now that she was working on this case herself.

204

She would say that, now, his lie had finally been found out. Seeing as I knew that he'd been taking bribes, she was most likely right.

Van Ravensberger's house in the green heart of Blaricum was as I'd imagined it: imposing. Stefanie rang the doorbell. I hadn't expected the man himself to open the door, but here he was: Ferdinand van Ravensberger – the man whose nephew Ben started it all by trying to shoot me in the petrol station. He wasn't as tall as I thought he'd be, but was the same height as me, wiry and trim and with a haircut that spoke of money; you imagined some girl spending hours cutting it hair by hair. Of the three men who went to university together – Van Ravensberger, Lantinga and Goosens – Ferdinand van Ravensberger looked by far the youngest. He was attractive and I found it hard to imagine the man I saw in front of me as the bad-tempered tyrant his nephew had described.

'Inspector Stefanie Dekkers, Financial Fraud department.' She smiled widely as she said it. Maybe this was what she dreamed of at night, picturing in her mind the moment she could finally arrest Van Ravensberger. Or just anybody famous. She showed her badge.

I showed mine. 'Detective Lotte Meerman, CID.'

'CID?' The muscles around his jaw tensed up. His eyes narrowed and he squinted at the badge. He looked from me to my badge and back.

I nodded.

'I see. You'd better come in. Does this have anything to do with Ben?' He stepped back into the hallway and opened a door to the right. 'We'll go in here: the office away from the office.' As he let us pass I got the smell of soap but no aftershave. He closed the front door behind us.

His home office was made up of two rooms. The smallest seemed to be a meeting room with a glass and stainless-steel table and eight chairs. It was connected to the second room by a glass door. This second room was about six times the size of our office, which seated four. At one end was Ferdinand's desk with three computer monitors; at the other his plasma TV was tuned to CNN and the screen showed a woman talking about the situation in Afghanistan. Opposite the door to the meeting room were French windows that in summer must extend his office into the garden.

'CID and Financial Fraud.' He silenced the woman on TV with a remote control and sat down. 'That must mean this isn't about Ben, right? Financial Fraud wouldn't be here for him.' He said it to himself more than to us and neither Stefanie nor I reacted. 'Here,' he said, 'take a seat.' His voice was deep, not gruff or rumbling, but clear and full of sound like a large church bell. If he ever wanted to change careers, he'd make a perfect newsreader: when he talked, you'd automatically listen.

I sat in one of the Le Corbusier chairs opposite his desk, a surprisingly comfortable contraption of steel and black leather. The chair had that typical male smell: leather mixed with cigars. Stefanie sat down beside me, but I didn't look at her. I kept focused on his face as I said, 'We're investigating a murder.'

He crossed his arms and sat forward. 'Is this where you are going to ask me where I was on this-and-this day in 1973?'

'Not quite that long ago,' Stefanie said coolly. 'We're re-investigating the murder of Otto Petersen and we're pretty sure it's linked to the Petersen Capital fraud.'

He nodded. 'Petersen – of course. How long ago was that?' He seemed to relax, scratched the back of his head and smiled a rueful smile. 'I lost a lot of money in that fund.'

'It was twelve years ago that he was shot, nineteen years since the fraud. We're currently talking to investors to find out how the fund worked. What can you tell us about Otto Petersen, Geert-Jan Goosens and Anton Lantinga?' Stefanie asked.

'I didn't know Petersen well. I mainly dealt with Geert-Jan.'

I didn't interrupt him even though I knew from the photo that Otto Petersen's mother had given me that he was lying. I wanted to hear where he was going with this, give him just enough rope to hang himself with.

'Did you talk to him after the fraud?'

'The next day, after it became public, he called to apologise.'

The shrill sound of my mobile suddenly interrupted Ferdinand with its old-fashioned ring. I had tried a number of ringtones, but experience had taught me that if my mobile didn't sound like a normal telephone, I didn't pick it up. Stefanie turned to me, looking annoyed. 'Excuse me,'

I said, and opened my handbag. The first thing my hand connected with as I rummaged for my mobile was the frame of the photo Mrs Petersen had given me. I couldn't believe I hadn't got round to putting it on the whiteboard. I'd gone to Alkmaar especially to get this photo and then had forgotten all about it. Come to think of it, I hadn't even told Stefanie I had it. I had been going to when my father turned up yesterday afternoon. Another mistake caused by my father. The curly edge of the ornate silver frame felt like cold waves under my fingers. My mobile kept ringing and I opened the bag further.

'Do you remember how he sounded?' Stefanie continued the interview.

'Embarrassed, I think. As if he couldn't believe this had happened . . .' Ferdinand's eyes moved down towards my bag. He stopped talking and frowned. I wasn't sure if it was at the interruption or if he'd seen the photo. I took my phone out of its pocket.

The display told me it was Hans. I gestured an apology to Stefanie and Ferdinand, mimed 'sorry', then got up and answered the call. 'Hi Hans. What's up?' I walked past shelves laden with a large number of DVDs and turned to keep Stefanie and Van Ravensberger in my sight as they continued the interview.

'Hi, Lotte. Sorry, but I had a call from Anton Lantinga and thought I should let you know.' I took a DVD from the shelf. It was in a white cover. In square handwriting in black ink it said: *Nova interview, 23 Dec 2012*.

'What did he want?' I talked softly. I read the spines of

the other DVDs. *NOS Journaal* interview, 15 June 2012, CNN interview, 3 March 2013. Ferdinand van Ravensberger had a long row of these, all recordings of his own television appearances. What kind of a man would keep such a collection of his own image?

Hans said, 'He wants to talk to you.'

'What about?' I put the DVD back and looked out through the window, where two small children dressed in thick skisuits and identical red wellington boots were building a snowman on a large lawn in front of a rhododendron. They had two balls of snow stuck on top of each other. The girl took her scarf off and tied it around the snowman to indicate where its neck was supposed to be. They looked too young to be Ferdinand van Ravensberger's children – unless there was a younger wife, of course. But his nephew had said he was still married to his first wife.

'Don't know, wouldn't say. Just wants you to go to his house tonight at eight,' Hans said.

'Thanks, Hans. Look, I've got to go. We're in the middle of an interview. Thanks for the call.' I clicked the mobile closed and rejoined the others.

'. . . Geert-Jan looked up to Petersen', Ferdinand was saying, 'and found him wanting. It was the making of him really.'

'In what way?' Stefanie asked.

'He moved out of Petersen's shadow, set up his own firm,' Ferdinand explained.

'Only you didn't invest with him any more.' Stefanie smiled.

'Oh, but I did. I gave him five million euros to run and he quadrupled it by the time Petersen came out of jail. Made me all my money back and more.' He waved at the office around him as if to indicate what that money had bought. 'And he has kept on going. He has done well by me. The best revenge I could have had.'

'And Anton?' Stefanie asked.

'Never spoke to him,' Ferdinand said.

'You never spoke to him?' I said and sat back in the Le Corbusier chair.

Ferdinand went slightly pale underneath what must be a fake winter tan.

'You don't think Geert-Jan Goosens had anything to do with the fraud?' Stefanie tried to come back to the original line of questioning.

He moved his eyes from me to Stefanie and forced his shoulders down and back in a more relaxed posture. 'I wouldn't have invested with him again if I had. I wanted to make that gesture, so that other investors would follow. Actions speak louder than words.'

Of course. Ferdinand van Ravensberger voted with his money – the only thing that mattered in these circles. He'd given a vote of confidence in Goosens. I was sure other investors had watched that and followed his lead. What had he got in return? Was all his current wealth based on the money that Goosens had made him?

'In your opinion, what happened? How did Petersen Capital lose that money?'

'It was all Petersen's doing. He never thought he could be

210

wrong . . . In his eyes, he was always right. It was the market that was wrong. The market would recognise the error of its ways and come over to his views.' His eyes stayed on me and Stefanie. Not once did he glance over our shoulders at the playing children outside. The windows must be well insulated as I couldn't hear them at all.

'So why hide the losses?'

Ferdinand van Ravensberger shrugged. 'I'm not sure he did. I think he didn't feel he had to tell us. We were only the investors, you see. He was the brain. He made the decisions without any need to justify himself.'

And Ferdinand van Ravensberger wouldn't have liked that. The collection of DVDs of his interviews showed how important Ferdinand thought he was. For someone with such an amount of self-worth to be seen as not being worthy of information would have been a real insult. But being insulted was not a reason for killing someone seven years later. Also, the money that Goosens had made him would have taken the edge off any bad feelings. It was clear like never before that Ferdinand van Ravensberger didn't have anything to do with Petersen's murder, at least not with money or insults as a reason. I was still intrigued by the early connection between the men that the photo revealed – a connection to which Ferdinand so far had not referred.

'Was he already like that at university?' I asked.

'Sorry?'

'You said that Otto saw himself as the brain, not telling you anything. You knew him from university, didn't you?'

'I didn't know him well.'

211

'Not as well as Geert-Jan Goosens and Anton Lantinga, you mean?'

'Yes, I knew them much better.'

'But you said you never spoke to Anton.'

'Not about the fraud, not at Petersen Capital, I meant.'

'But you talked to him about other things.'

'Yes, but much more social, not work-related.'

'And Otto wasn't a friend.'

'No.'

'Because he thought he was better than you?'

'It wasn't that.' Ferdinand waited for a bit and looked at the ceiling, seemingly for inspiration. 'He hung around us all the time. Didn't really join in, didn't do anything, just followed us around like a kid brother. He watched us all the time and then did whatever it was we were doing. Always imitating us, never with any ideas of his own.'

'Annoying?'

'Yes, sometimes.' The phone on Ferdinand's desk rang. He let it ring for a few seconds, looking to see who it was, then said, 'Sorry, I have to take this.' He seemed happy to be interrupted. Ferdinand van Ravensberger turned away and talked in such a low voice that I couldn't make out any of the words although I was trying hard. Apart from his obvious lies, he was too open with us, too willing to answer our questions. But the obvious lies made me doubt every answer he gave.

'What did Hans want?' Stefanie whispered.

'He had a call from Anton Lantinga. Anton wants to talk to us.'

212

'Did he say why?'

'No.'

'So we'll go after this?'

'No. Anton said to be at his house at eight o'clock tonight.'

'I'm not on lates, but I can come along,' Stefanie said.

I nodded. I shouldn't go by myself anyway and there was no way she'd let me leave her behind.

Her large face glowed a deep pink. 'He's going to confess,' she hissed. 'This is it.'

I disagreed but didn't contradict her. I didn't have an alternative suggestion, but confession seemed unlikely.

Ferdinand finished his call and apologised.

Stefanie continued my line of questioning. 'Otto Petersen might have been annoying, but when he set up his investment firm, you gave him money.'

'I gave Geert-Jan money. He told me of this company he was starting with Petersen.'

'You thought it was a good idea?'

'I never trusted Petersen, but Geert-Jan was my friend. He asked me for the money, had some good ideas and I was willing to invest with them.'

'So you lost all your money in your friend's firm.'

'As I said: he made it up to me. Made me a fortune.'

'Do you think he knew about the fraud?'

'I don't think anybody did.'

'Otto's wife might have known . . .'

'Maybe. But only if he thought she needed to know. He probably decided it was better to keep her in the dark.'

'So she couldn't tell the investors?'

'Or anybody else. When more than two people know something,' Ferdinand said with a smile, 'it's no longer a secret.'

Stefanie drove us back to the office. During the journey, I thought about the things that more than two people knew. I stared out of the window for a long time and watched the landscape go by, past the faint reflection of my own face. I'd thought that Paul had loved my face, had desired my body. I wondered if he'd told his lawyer, and whether the lawyer would try to use it. Did more than two people know what happened between Paul and me? I would never talk about it, of that I was certain. I would never want anybody else to know this about me.

What Ferdinand van Ravensberger had told us about Otto Petersen – that he had watched his fellow students and tried to ape the way they were acting – fitted in with what his mother had said: that he was her changeling. What had he changed into in prison?

Chapter Eighteen

The A9 north to Alkmaar was starting to look familiar on my third trip in a week. Music bounced off the inside of the windows and around the car seats. The engine hummed an additional little one-note tune in the dark. Softly, under my breath, I sang along with Massive Attack's 'Safe from Harm', and glanced sideways to check that Stefanie was still asleep. She was leaning with her head against the door, snoring softly; only her seatbelt kept her upright. Under the sound of the radio I also heard the whirr of the heating, which was gallantly fighting the severe frost in an attempt to keep us warm. As in my other nightly drives, I felt that my car protected me from the outside world where the snow-covered fields were eerily luminescent under the glow of the full moon, and villages and houses twinkled at scattered irregular intervals like decaying Christmas lights. On the other side of the road, every now and then, cars enveloped by vague haloes of light hurtled towards me on a collision course until they bent to my left, steered there by the central crash barrier.

The road surface shone for one breath in the headlights of the car, then got run over by the wheels. They consumed the kilometres until the football stadium at Alkmaar's round-about outshone the moon. Come match day it would swallow up thousands of supporters, attracted by its light like moths to a flame. They would come on foot or by bicycle, wearing their club's red and white team colours in scarves and T-shirts, come in the hope of victory, not even consider-ing the possibility of defeat and crushed dreams.

We left the motorway and passed some cyclists, dressed like Michelin men in order to protect themselves against the freezing temperatures. The cry of a siren rose then fell and a blue light tore through the darkness.

'What's that?' Stefanie had woken up.

'Just a police car. We're nearly there.' Ice flowers started brave attempts to establish themselves on the corners of the windscreen, but the car heating destroyed them as quickly as they bloomed.

Nerves marched around in my stomach. When people wanted to talk, it was not always a good thing. Being told the truth could be a painful experience.

Eight o'clock, Anton had said. The green clock on the dashboard showed 19.23. We had plenty of time to get to Bergen. Before she'd fallen asleep, all Stefanie had talked about was how Anton obviously wanted to confess that he'd killed Otto Petersen and would claim it was in self-defence. I bet she'd already picked out what she was going to wear at the press conference. She was wrong. It was probably about those blasted files. Why else would he have written down my father's name?

I wanted to speed up, get to our destination more quickly, but needed to slow down to make sure we weren't early.

In the village of Bergen, curtains were closed against the cold and the dark. I imagined a whole multitude of sins hidden behind those pieces of cloth: rowing couples, people eating in a resentful silence, screaming children. Or worse. Somebody hitting somebody, hurting them with fists or with words, a thief coming in through the window at the back. My mother had been right. A side-effect of this job was that you always expected the worst of people. It was because we always saw the worst. It altered your view of the world.

A second police car overtook us.

I took the same turning as the blue light. This was the road where Anton and Karin Lantinga lived. Giant houses on both sides proclaimed the wealth of their owners.

A group of police cars and an ambulance were parked at the end of the street. I took my foot off the accelerator and slowed the car down to walking speed.

'Oh shit,' Stefanie said.

I switched the radio off. We crawled along and I hoped to see number 32 on one of the houses before we got to the swirling sirens. However, as I counted the numbers, I already knew that these emergency vehicles were parked where Anton lived. I knew it deep down inside. I had been right to expect the worst.

'Now he's not going to talk any more, is he? Do you think Karin shot a second husband?' Stefanie almost sounded as if she was laughing.

217

'Shut up!' This was our fault. If we hadn't pressurised him, if we hadn't pushed him . . . I knew this wouldn't have happened if he hadn't wanted to talk. I hoped he hadn't killed himself. Maybe he'd had a heart attack or maybe Karin had. I parked the car behind the ambulance, pushed the door open, flashed my badge to the paramedic with one hand and grabbed my coat with the other.

'What happened?' I heard Stefanie ask. But I didn't stop. I didn't want to hear an explanation. I wanted to see it. I was putting my coat on as I moved, no time to stop. A flash lit up the dark sky. A photographer. No need for that ambulance then. Who was it, Karin or Anton?

I hurried along the path towards the garden where the snow was being trampled by myriad feet. As I added my footsteps to those of my local colleagues, the snow underneath my boots whispered of death. Tall trees stood like black-dressed undertakers at the edge of the white lawn. Making for the flashing lights of the photographer, I passed an orderly row of box shrubs. As I turned the corner at the end of the row I saw the feet of a forensic scientist clad in what could be camouflage gear, the white of the plastic identical to the colour of the snow. Between the footsteps, between the marks of the people who photographed, examined and investigated the dead body, was the trail of a bird, the small tracks leading over the ground from the box hedge to the shed. I followed the bird's trail with my eyes to avoid looking at the body lying in a pool of coral-red snow. My chest felt tight and there was a large lump in the place where the two underwires of my bra met. I held out my badge to nobody in particular and forced myself to have a closer look. The tears in my eyes froze to small sharp icicles. Frost bit my face and the cold air burned my lungs when I inhaled.

I looked at my watch. It was eight o'clock, exactly the time we were supposed to meet. The body was wearing a pair of jeans, brown loafers and a dark blue V-neck jumper over a T-shirt. Why wasn't he wearing a coat? It was well below zero. He must have thought he'd only be outside for a short time. Had he heard something? Seen somebody?

A hand gripped my arm and I pulled free without taking my eyes off the dead man. He was lying on his right-hand side and there was a hole in his left temple. Maybe shot from close range. There might be traces of powder on the skin.

'Lotte, what are you doing here?' The hand was on my arm again, more insistent this time. I didn't like the physical restraint and I tried to shake it off, but the hand wasn't budging. I looked up and saw Ronald de Boer. His hair had escaped its severe control and rioted over his forehead. Another flash of the photographer drew his face out of the darkness. It looked criss-crossed with wrinkles like dark pencil lines on his skin, which had a pallor that made it almost as grey as his eyes.

'I . . . we were supposed to meet up with Anton tonight.'

'We?'

'Yes, I'm here with Stefanie Dekkers.'

Ronald cursed softly. He looked over my shoulder to check who was nearby and tugged me off to a darker and more secluded corner of the garden. 'We've got to be careful,' he said. He took one glove off, cupped my jaw with his palm, then ran his thumb along my cheekbone. His skin felt warm and alive to the cold of my face, and on my arms goose bumps rose. Nerve-endings on the skin of my face came alive and contracted in my stomach.

He brought his face close. 'Your father was here tonight,' he whispered. His breath tickled my eardrum and ran a shiver down my spine. I could see the white cloud of his exhalation more clearly than I could hear the words. The rasp of his stubble grated my cheek. I stumbled and put my hand on his shoulder. I could smell cigarette smoke in his hair. I closed my eyes.

'Not everybody here has his best interests at heart.'

I took a step back and looked at him. His grey eyes weren't on me but on the group of people around Anton's body. 'I know,' I said.

'I knew you would. Leave it to me, Lotte. I'll deal with everything.' He traced my cheek again with his thumb; the skin felt rough like grains of sand. 'I'll protect him, just like I did before.'

'But—'

'I'll talk to you later.' He moved his hand to the back of my neck, to that vulnerable place that used to be protected by hair, and gave it a squeeze before he walked off to join the group.

I stood and watched him.

He approached Stefanie and shook her hand. She offered him a cigarette out of the packet she always had in her pocket. Two small lights glowed side by side. He gestured at me with the cigarette between his fingers. Stefanie nodded, her mouth sucking nicotine into her lungs. She breathed out a white cloud of cancer-causing smoke.

I left the garden and walked up the drive to the cavernous house. The front door was ajar and I pushed it further open, running my fingers over the knocker that was in the shape of a bronze lion, his teeth exposed in an eternal growl. I paused on the doorstep. Parquet floors and high ceilings, a chandelier in the hallway and mirrors on either side were meant to give an even greater impression of space. Dirty footprints covered the hallway where people had traipsed a mixture of mud and snow into the otherwise clean house, and now the mirrors reflected how it had been soiled. I tried to scrub my boots as clean as possible, reluctant to add to the mess on the floor. From behind a door to the left I heard voices. Female voices. Crying. I followed the sound and pushed the door open.

Karin sat huddled on the floor in a corner of the sitting room. She was hiding behind the dining-room furniture like a frightened wild animal, the striped wallpaper behind her like bars. Her hair was still in its Grace Kelly chignon but unravelled strands hung about her face. Black mascara was smudged around her eyes like a large bruise, and her wrinkles were red as if they'd been recently cut in her skin with a razor. 'What the fuck are you doing here?' she burst out. 'You know this is your fault. I told him not to—'

'Not to what?'

She caught hold of her necklace, a single long strand, and pulled it round her neck, pearl by pearl, as if it was a rosary.

'I've got nothing left. Nothing.' Her other hand clutched her BlackBerry.

I crouched down beside her. 'Mrs Lantinga, I'm so sorry. Have you got any idea who did this?'

Karin stared from the policewoman who was keeping her company, back to the open door. I glanced over my shoulder to see what she was looking at, but didn't see anything. I only heard the footsteps of my colleagues walking up and down the hallway. 'I'm not talking to you. I'm not suicidal yet,' she said, her eyes not leaving the door.

'Shall I close it?'

She shook her head and wiped the tears away with her left hand. Her BlackBerry whirred as her thumb continuously scrolled the trackball in a compulsive gesture. She didn't look at the device; her eyes were riveted to the open door.

'Did you hear anything?'

'A shot. I told him not to talk to you. And not to that old guy either.'

'Which old guy?'

'The retired policeman – Huizen?' There was tension in each of her muscles. She looked scared to death, ready to jump up to attack anybody coming through that doorway. At that moment, she looked the same age as Otto Petersen's mother.

I sat down on the floor next to her and we both looked at the open door. A hint of her jasmine and apple perfume was a reminder from a happier, less frightening time. A couple of forensic scientists walked by in their plastic outfits. I waited until they'd gone.

'He came here?' I said it quietly.

'Yes, around six. Wasn't here for long. Didn't come in.'

'What time . . .' I looked at the policewoman for answers, wanting to spare Karin the entire question.

But Karin replied. 'I heard the shot at just after seven,' she said. 'And I called the police immediately.'

An hour before we'd been due to meet. I remembered the blue police sirens overtaking us on the road from Alkmaar to Bergen. 'You know who did this,' I said. 'Tell me what happened.'

She hid her face. 'Please don't ask. Leave it.' She sounded exhausted.

'I can't leave it. Your husband is dead — you say it's my fault, and it feels as if it *is* my fault. I need to know.'

'First Otto, then Anton.' She spat out the words.

'Did you hear anything? See anything? Anybody?'

The BlackBerry flashed a red light but Karin didn't look at it. She kept staring at the door and remained silent.

I wanted to talk to my father but I couldn't as I had to drive Stefanie back to Amsterdam. If I'd been here with Hans I could have taken him along, but with Stefanie I couldn't take the risk. Her conviction that he was involved and her quest to nail him for something to get our boss off the hook were too strong. The inside of the car was cold but I had to take my coat off; it was too bulky to drive with it on. I switched the heating on full. The odour of warmth filled the car, which would have to do before the actual sensation materialised.

'I saw you,' Stefanie said. She smelled of the cigarettes she'd had with Ronald.

'Saw me when?'

'With that Alkmaar detective, Ronald de Boer. I saw the two of you together.'

I didn't say anything.

'I don't care,' she said. 'You can do what you like. I won't tell anybody.'

I switched the radio on. A female voice was telling us the weather forecast: more frost for the next three days, but a lower chance of snow. Stefanie reached out and changed the channel, pressing the button to change it again every time she heard a talking voice. In the end a radio station playing Abba satisfied her and she sat back. The road was practically empty. Without the snow of last week, this drive was a whole lot easier. It shouldn't take us more than forty-five minutes to get back to Amsterdam.

'So Anton Lantinga didn't kill Petersen then,' she said.

'We'll wait for forensics, but it seems the same modus operandi.'

'Will Alkmaar take the case?'

'I'm not sure. Those files . . .'

'Forget about those files, for goodness sake!'

'They're important.'

'Yeah yeah. Anyway, Goosens then? Or do you think Karin killed both men?'

'She was distraught and scared.' I turned the sound of

the radio up and whispered along with Agnetha that the winner takes it all.

'I talked to Ronald,' Stefanie said.

I tapped my fingers on the steering wheel in time with the music.

'He didn't have many ideas on who could have killed Anton. He worked the original Petersen case, didn't he?' she wanted to know.

We entered the tunnel under the Noordzeekanaal and the radio cut out. 'Yes, he did.'

'He's very good-looking. You're a lucky girl. I'll be pissed off if they take the case after all the work we've done.'

'The two weeks of work we've done.'

'You know what I mean.'

I did. I thought of Ronald's words, that he'd protect my father. Like me, Ronald must think he needed protecting from himself.

Chapter Nineteen

It was still dark when I cycled to work. The dynamo on my bike whirred like the trackball on Karin's BlackBerry when her thumb had turned it compulsively last night. The sight of Anton's head with the gunshot wound at the temple and Karin's tears had haunted me until the early hours. The only reason I hadn't taken my car out for another restless nocturnal drive was because I worked instead. I'd spent a long time in my study.

It had only taken seven seconds to change my drawing and cross out Anton Lantinga's name in its box, but then I'd been left with nothing that made sense – unless the witness, Wouter Vos, had seen Karin drive Anton's car. I stared at the piece of paper for ten minutes or so, then got the Tippex out and removed the cross through Anton's name with white. My drawing was about who killed Otto Petersen. Unless we had evidence that the same murderer killed both men, Anton was still in the picture for the first shooting.

Petersen's mother told me her son was talking about revenge. But what if that wasn't revenge for Anton's affair with Karin, but revenge for the collapse of Otto's company?

I drew a new box and wrote in the anonymous whistle-blower that Stefanie had unearthed. Van Ravensberger admitted to getting most of his losses back from the investments that Goosens made for him. Was that what happened to the money? I drew another dotted quarter circle, concentric to the first one, connecting Goosens to the missing forty million euros, to show this second alternative.

I'd paused my pen on the line connecting my father to Anton. So far it only said *Did he pay him?* above it. With an unwilling hand I wrote *He was seen at Anton's house* below the arrow.

After another half an hour of looking at the partially empty sheet with a totally empty brain, I gave up. In my bedroom I shook a number of the small blue pills into the palm of my hand. They looked like blueberry jelly beans. I raised my hand to my mouth, then lowered it again and tipped the pills back in their amber pharmacy pot.

Now as I moved my legs in a steady rhythm, the effort of cycling brought some warmth into my cold calf muscles. Anton's murder had to give us new information. He'd wanted to talk to us – and that had clearly forced the killer to act. Had he told anybody he'd set up the meeting? And we weren't the only ones Anton wanted to meet. He had also arranged to meet my father and, who knows, maybe even somebody else.

A car's headlights threw a ghostly glow over my shoulder before it overtook me, forcing me sideways, off the cleared and salted part of the road. I made new tracks in a layer of mushy grey snow that had been shovelled to the side and all thoughts of Anton momentarily disappeared from my mind. The frost and wind made my eyes tear up and I pulled the furry collar of my coat high up my face to protect my skin. The scarf that covered my mouth was dotted with white where the condensation of my breath had frozen into tiny ice particles. At least no new snow had fallen overnight. I cycled past the flower stall where they'd sell their frozen-looking tulips later today and stared at the relief that adorns the police station's wall. The figures symbolise the role of the police force to help and protect. We certainly hadn't managed to protect Anton Lantinga. I would find his murderer, I vowed, even if his wife didn't want me to. I locked my bicycle and entered the police station.

I was at my desk, my first mug of coffee in my hand, when Hans came in.

He sat down and turned on his computer. 'I asked for a list of everybody who worked for Petersen Capital in 1995. I'm pretty sure those people', he gestured at the Photofits on the wall, 'worked there. The list should get here today or tomorrow.'

'Did you hear about Anton?' I said.

'What happened?'

'What happened?' I put my mug down and started writing on my notepad, writing and saying the same words simultaneously. 'Anton was shot dead before we got there. He couldn't tell us anything.'

'Any clues? Did his wife see anything?'

I knew she had seen my father. I should tell Hans about that. Instead I shook my head. I saw Karin's face in front of

228

me. Her fear, the look in her eyes that wouldn't leave the door, the hand scrolling the BlackBerry. 'Or at least, I think she saw something but she won't tell us.'

'And what did the lawyer say?'

'What lawyer?' I said.

'There wasn't one?'

I frowned.

'Last night, Anton didn't have a lawyer there?'

'I didn't see one. But there were so many people milling about: police, forensics, the ambulance crew. So there could have been.'

'Did you search Anton's house for the files?'

I shook my head again. 'No, the Alkmaar police were taking care of all of that.'

'Shame. Oh well. Apart from getting that list, I've gone through your notes from yesterday's interview with Ferdinand van Ravensberger again. Especially the great returns he got on his money with Goosens – that is very interesting. We've got: two employees from Petersen Capital – yes,' he said when I raised a finger, 'I know that's not certain, but it's likely if Stefanie's met them. They intercepted the files from Alkmaar. DI Huizen knew how long beforehand?'

'He said two hours.' Why had my father put me in this position, where I had to lie to Hans? I felt bad that I couldn't make him aware of the possibility that my father had destroyed the files in return for money, and that I hadn't even bothered to look for them.

Hans sucked some air in between his teeth. 'That's not long. Not long to contact somebody, I mean.'

'Somebody knew before he did?'

'Maybe . . . I don't know. Anyway, they could have been protecting either Anton Lantinga or Goosens.'

'Or Karin.'

'I checked her alibi yesterday, met with that prison warden. He's still there, still at the same place, and he remembered things very clearly. He said she was there until about half past five, then drove off to Alkmaar.' Hans chuckled. 'He said he remembered her because she was so pissed off. She was swearing at her husband for making her sit out in the rain, and now she had to drive all the way back. He even remembers that the traffic had been horrendous. He listened to the radio and had a laugh with his colleague because Karin would now be even more pissed off. But her alibi stands: there was no way she could have been back in Alkmaar in time to kill Otto Petersen.'

I was disappointed and pleased at the same time.

'Could she have killed Anton?' Hans asked.

'I don't know.' Clear in my memory was that thumb scrolling her BlackBerry. Had she just been scared of being found out? 'If he had been shot in the house then maybe. But I can't imagine she got him to go outside, followed and shot him there.'

'Then we have missing money, or maybe not, and stellar returns, as Ferdinand van Ravensberger said, for any of the investors who put cash in Goosens's new fund,' Hans said.

230

'Stefanie seemed quite convinced that there was no missing money,' I responded. 'But you think that maybe Goosens paid previous investors out of the funds Petersen embezzled?' He was thinking along the same lines as I had been, last night.

'It's a possibility, isn't it?'

'Are you sure there were good returns for all the investors in Goosens's fund?' I dug the photo out of my bag. 'Maybe it was just money for Goosens, Lantinga and Van Ravensberger. And what about that whistle-blower?'

'But surely Van Ravensberger wouldn't have told you about the great returns if there was something dodgy going on.'

'I don't know. He was a bit too happy to talk to us. If Goosens dripped the money back into Van Ravensberger's account, he might not even have realised. CI Moerdijk always thought it was Geert-Jan Goosens, or at least that he had kept the money. What if', I tipped my chair back and speculated towards the ceiling, 'Goosens takes the cash, stitches up Petersen for the fraud, promising him a share when he comes out, but then shoots him instead. Anton knows and is worried that Goosens is trying to stitch him up as well, so he wants to talk to us.'

'But there was Alkmaar's witness . . .'

'OK, so Goosens and Anton split the money. Anton was still at Karin's house, is seen by Wouter Vos, kills Petersen . . . Then what? He wants to confess?'

'Doesn't seem right.'

231

The phone rang and disrupted our speculation. 'Will they never leave us alone?' I grumbled to Hans. I enjoyed bouncing ideas off him, throwing them across the office to see which ones stuck, even if this time my ideas were ones that I knew were wrong. I picked up the phone. 'Lotte Meerman.'

'Hey, Lotte, it's Ronald de Boer.'

As if I hadn't recognised his voice. I leaned back on my chair and looked up at the ceiling. A spider had found refuge against the cold outside and now lived in the corner. 'Hey, Ronald. Any news?'

'It was a different weapon.'

I was close to swearing but stopped myself. A man had died, after all. 'Interesting,' I said instead.

'Yes. It was from a further distance this time. No traces of gunpowder on Anton's head.'

'But it could still be the same perp. There are twelve years between both murders . . .'

'I don't think so. Leave it to us.'

'Sure – your patch. You didn't find your lost files at Anton's house, by chance?'

'Lotte, leave it to me, OK? I'll take care of this.'

'But we're actually getting somewhere—'

'Don't drag your father any further into this than he needs to be.' He sighed.

The sounds of the exhalation in my ear reminded me of last night. It reminded me of what he'd said about covering for my father. 'DI Huizen was here on Wednesday.'

'DI Huizen? Right, you've got some other people in your

232

office with you. I understand. Well, he's been busy then.' He laughed.

'He was here,' I repeated, 'and we did a Photofit of the people who picked up the files.'

'Lotte, think about it. He got rid of—'

'Stefanie recognised them. Did she tell you?'

'She told me she doesn't trust him.'

'Yes, well, she's got other motives for that. She recognised them. I think that's important.'

'Lotte, leave it. Your father . . . well, I think he might be more deeply involved in this than we thought.'

There was no way my father would have killed anybody. 'I don't think so.'

'You don't *want* to think so.' His voice sounded louder and more determined.

'No, Ronald, I seriously think—'

'For the last time, leave it, Lotte. Honestly, you don't want to drag him any deeper into this.'

'You've said that already. I heard you first time round.' I wanted to tell him that I wasn't dragging my father into this but that I was dragging him *out*. I understood that my father had got rid of those files and that he'd taken bribes, but there was no way I would believe he'd done anything else. However, I had to be careful what I said with Hans around.

'I know him better than you do – I worked with him,' Ronald said harshly. 'Trust me, I know what he's . . . well, capable of, I suppose. Sorry, Lotte, I've got to go. I'll call you when I've got news.' The line went dead.

★   ★   ★

233

I sat at my favourite table in the canteen with my usual lunch of a cheese sandwich, an apple and a glass of milk. My lack of progress was, I decided, because I'd let my emotions rule me. I had to let my brain take over and do the work. Like I used to. Forget that DI Huizen was my father, lose my preconceptions of him, negative or positive, and look at the facts.

From my handbag I took out the photo Mrs Petersen had given me, the Photofit of the two police impersonators who met with my father and took the files, and my notepad. I glanced at the leftmost Photofit then took a glug of milk and stared out over the canal.

A couple of kids in their mid-teens were throwing bricks on the ice. On other canals people had started to skate. The temperature had got down to minus ten last night, caused by the snowless clear skies, but I wasn't sure the ice would hold. The Singelgracht, however, was being kept open by the tour boats that broke through every day, but the boats didn't start running until midday and the frozen night's ice must seem an enticing short cut.

I looked back down at the pictures and aligned them with the edge of the canteen table: one photo given to me by a demented old woman; two drawings created by an old man. I smiled ruefully. They didn't make particularly convincing evidence.

The kids had come back, carrying a large piece of building rubble between them. It looked like the piece that held a park bench tethered to the ground. They swayed it backwards and forwards. I could almost hear them count:

'and-a-one-and-a-two' before letting go. I leaned over to the window to get a good view of what happened next. The rubble bounced and slid along the ice. But it didn't go through.

I drew a circle on my notepad and filled it in. Wouter Vos had seen Anton Lantinga at Otto Petersen's house, but that didn't mean Anton killed Otto. With Anton dead it seemed less likely. Karin had a watertight alibi. That pretty much left Geert-Jan Goosens. CI Moerdijk would be pleased that he'd been right all along – and maybe that would be enough to move the searchlight of Stefanie's investigation to a more rewarding subject and away from my father's past. However, Ronald thought Anton and Otto had been shot by different people. Anton must have wanted to come clean; that's why he contacted us. But someone else wanted to stop him from talking. Talking about what? Confessing to a murder – or to a financial fraud?

One of the two kids stepped out on the ice. He took a couple of small slides closer towards the weaker middle. I got my mobile out of my bag and put it on the table. His friend stepped out on the ice as well, but stayed close to the side where the ice would be thicker. The kid in the middle of the canal started jumping up and down. I picked up my mobile. Then he stopped jumping and went across in one easy slide. I put my phone back on the table and took a bite of my sandwich.

Anton could have shot Otto Petersen, and Karin could have shot Anton. It wasn't the same gun, but a gun could have been in the house. He wanted to confess, she didn't, they argued, the gun went off. Karin was distraught because she'd killed him. It could have happened but the problem was that Anton was shot outside, not in the house. Anyway, it didn't seem right.

What had my father been doing at their house last night?

I took one last bite of sandwich, put my apple in my bag and went back to our office.

A couple of hours later I got the call from Ferdinand van Ravensberger saying that he wanted to see me and that he would come to the police station later that afternoon. I didn't tell Stefanie – the excitement would be just too much for her, but instead checked with Hans that he was available. I was reminded of Ferdinand's words yesterday morning that if two people knew something, it wasn't a secret any more, and I was curious to find out what he wanted to make more widely known.

It took Ferdinand and his lawyer just under an hour to arrive at the police station. Hans and I met them in a downstairs room that was not as severe as the interrogation room but still fully hooked up with recording equipment.

Ferdinand looked more businesslike than he'd done before: the charcoal-grey suit, white shirt and blue tie all looked more formal than his casual outfit yesterday. Maybe that was because he had other meetings to got to after our little chat, or maybe he wanted to make a different impression. He also looked tired and jaded, his skin still coloured by the fake tan but ashen underneath. His lawyer shook my hand and introduced herself as Ellis. Her outfit was colour-coordinated with Ferdinand's but under her short-cropped curly white hair her face was neither as tanned nor as tired. She had that sharp attention that good lawyers have and that allows them to jump in whenever their clients are about to say anything useful.

Ferdinand came straight to the point. 'I want to tell you something that I think is important,' he said. 'Maybe it's something you already know. Yesterday, I saw you had a photo. This photo.' He opened his briefcase and took out the same photograph that Otto Petersen's mother had given me. His version wasn't in a frame. 'I don't know who gave you the photo but I guess my nephew had something to do with it.'

'I can't tell you that,' I said.

'It doesn't matter; either way you've got it. I want to tell you the truth about what happened to this person in the photo.' He pointed to the unknown young man standing between Anton Lantinga and Geert-Jan Goosens. 'His name is Carl Beerd, but I assume you already know this.'

I realised I'd missed something and that the man we had been referring to as 'that other one' was actually important.

'Could you tell us your version of what happened to Carl Beerd?' Hans phrased the question carefully. I was grateful to him as I was too annoyed with myself to ask it.

'I don't know what Ben has told you, but Carl died in an accident – a car accident. I was driving. It was 1987 – another harsh winter just like this one.' He exchanged a glance with his lawyer. She nodded and he continued. 'We'd

237

come back late from some lectures and I was driving us back in Carl's new car. There were four of us in the car – we rented a house together.'

'Who else was in the car?'

'Anton Lantinga. And Ellis.'

'You were in the car?' I felt foolish for having thought Ellis was Ferdinand's lawyer, even if she did look like one.

'I sat directly behind Ferdi, Anton sat next to me on the back seat and Carl was in the front, next to Ferdi,' Ellis said.

'When I lost control of the car, it spun, swerved and the front right crashed into a lamp post. Nobody was wearing their seatbelts and Carl took most of the impact. We were all taken to hospital with various injuries but only Carl never came out. He never woke from his coma.' Ferdinand fell silent and Ellis took his hand.

'Would you like some water?' I asked.

'No, I'm fine. I'd like to get this over with.'

'Of course.'

'We hadn't been drinking; we were breathalysed and the tests were clean. The ice on the road and the marks were clear to see, and the verdict was accidental death.'

That's why I hadn't been able to find it when I looked for Ferdinand's criminal record.

'Ben somehow heard about this story some years ago and always thought there had to be more to it than that. His imagination is far too active. When I saw the photo in your bag yesterday, I realised he must have told you this story too.'

'What made you think that?'

He sighed. 'Ben has been trying to get money out of me for the last six months. He, of course, has a good allowance but unfortunately all the money seems to have disappeared up his nose.'

Ellis gave him a sharp look.

'Just a manner of speaking, of course. I didn't want to imply . . .' He coughed, waited for a second to gather his thoughts, then said, 'He wanted more money. He said he'd tell everybody about this man I'd killed. I refused to give him anything and he started to threaten me. Last week, his father – my brother – called me about the hold-up of the petrol station. Of course, now part of me wished I'd given him the cash, so that he hadn't set up this charade with his university pal that went so badly wrong. But part of me knows that if he's capable of shooting a police officer, I was right to stop funding him.'

'Why do you say "charade"?'

Ellis answered for him. 'We know the boy who mans the petrol station at night. He goes to university with Ben. That's all.'

'So you think . . .'

'I don't think anything. It was just stupid, ridiculous, that's all. A disaster.'

'Where were you last night?' Hans asked.

'At what time?'

'Between six and eight.'

'We were home, having dinner.' He exchanged a look with Ellis. 'Weren't we?'

239

'I got home from the office just after six, six fifteen probably. You were already there. We spent the whole evening at home.'

'I see. Was anybody else at home with you?' I asked next.

'Well, our daughter came to pick up the grandkids,' Ferdinand said.

That at least explained who the young children were. 'What time did she arrive?'

'She collected the children just after seven.'

Nobody questioned why we wanted to know. 'Who told you about Anton?' asked Hans.

'Geert-Jan phoned us this morning, right after he got the call from Karin.' Ferdinand and Ellis exchanged a glance. 'It's why we're here,' he said, 'to make sure you don't look in our direction, but concentrate on finding whoever killed Anton.'

The phrase sounded rehearsed. The couple must have weighed up the consequences of coming here after Geert-Jan's phone call and discussed what it was that Ben could possibly have told us about Carl Beerd and the car crash. It was a smart move, to come forward and set the record straight. I believed what they'd told us and also thought that the insight into Ben's habits was interesting.

'If that's all,' Ferdinand said, 'we'd like to leave now. Please feel free to call us at any time.'

Hans explained about needing a statement about Ben's threats of blackmail and said that this would help our investigation into the spate of petrol-station robberies. Ferdinand nodded his agreement. 'My wife and I are happy to help, aren't we, Ellis?'

As Hans left with the couple to deal with the formalities, I stayed behind in the interview room and wondered if I was completely losing my touch. Or my mind. When had I last had a decent meal, a proper night's sleep? Was that why I was finding it so hard to think?

My hands were shaking. My mind was what I'd always relied on. I'd always thought that my ability to think and observe was what made me good at my job. Now I didn't seem capable of doing either: I had initially misinterpreted the looks exchanged between Ferdinand and Ellis as those of businessman and lawyer whereas they were those between husband and wife. I was seeing what I was expecting to see rather than what was actually there.

On my notepad I wrote down all the things I now knew I'd missed. I had thought all along that Ben's story that his uncle had once killed someone was a complete lie, but it turned out to have been a lie like so many of mine: based on a grain of truth. I should have recognised it. Secondly, I'd had the photo for a while but had focused solely on the fact that it showed that Ferdinand van Ravensberger had known Otto Petersen as well as Anton Lantinga. I had never bothered to check who 'the one that we don't know' actually was. And I had automatically assumed that Ferdinand would bring a lawyer – but he hadn't; he was here with his wife as she had been in the car during the car crash and formed his alibi for yesterday. Or maybe she was here to provide him with emotional support.

Was I still capable of doing this job? Should I take some time off? I was clearly in no state to work: too absorbed in

241

my previous mistakes to do a proper job. In fact, I had been so absorbed in my previous mistakes that I kept making new ones, layering faults on top of errors.

Where did that leave all my other conclusions? That my father had been taking bribes, that he or Anton Lantinga had destroyed those stupid files, that Anton had been killed because he'd wanted to come clean about something. Which of those were lies, maybe based on grains of truth, and which ones were actual truths, maybe with a veneer of lies?

I stared at my notepad of mistakes and saw only one route out of the mess: tell the boss that Piet Huizen was my father, accept the suspension and let Hans take over the case. It was the only possible route and one that I couldn't possibly take without putting my father in danger. If only Stefanie wasn't so keen to nail something on him to protect the boss's reputation.

Chapter Twenty

My mind was still in a whirl when I left the interview room to inform my colleagues of what Ferdinand van Ravensberger had told us about his nephew. Hans would give them the official statements later, but I just wanted to fill them in.

The team working on the robberies at the petrol stations seemed busy and I paused on the threshold of their shared office. Thomas and André Kamp were looking through piles of photos. I hadn't seen André since I watched him interview the kid I'd shot and I still hadn't heard if Thomas was joining this team permanently.

'Hi, guys. Sorry to interrupt,' I said.

'Hi, Lotte. What's up?' André said.

'I've just come out of an interview with Ferdinand van Ravensberger. He told us that Ben had tried to blackmail him. Ben had spent all his money on cocaine, and probably staged the hold-up at the petrol station with a friend from university.'

Thomas's eyes blazed. 'Well, thank you, Lotte! What do you think we have been doing here?' His voice was getting

243

louder. 'Do you think we're doing sod all, just waiting for *you* to tell us what happened? That we need your brilliant input to figure out the one hold-up that didn't match the pattern?'

'I was only trying to—'

'Trying to interfere and take all the glory. We know what you're trying to do. Get your photo in the paper, talk about how you "solved the case". And it's all lies, isn't it, Lotte?'

'What are you talking about?' André interrupted him, but I knew full well what he meant.

'Sorry, Thomas.'

'And now you prance in here, telling us about this kid you shot. Well, maybe you could have asked André over the last few days what he'd found out, but we haven't seen you here, Lotte.' He got up from his chair and walked over to me, stopped just a metre in front of me. 'We haven't seen hide nor hair of you until now, when you think you've got some information to get one up on us. We've had the other kid, the one manning the petrol station, in custody since yesterday. We did blood tests when Ben was arrested, of course, so we knew he was a coke fiend. His friend was pretty pissed off: said that Ben took a shot at you because he was off his face. We already knew all this precious information you lowered yourself to share with us. Thank you very much, Lotte. Much appreciated.'

He stared in my eyes for two breaths, then turned round and walked back to his desk. 'So, where were we?' he said deliberately calmly to André and turned over another page in the book with photos. Even André wouldn't meet my eyes. I left.

As I stepped out of the police station, I shivered and shrunk in my large coat, pulling the thick collar as high around my face as I could to keep the wind from peeling the skin off my nose and cheeks. The canals were deserted. Parked cars and blocks of stalled bicycles with their dimmed red back lights and white fenders close together were the only signs of life. People who didn't have to be out were staying indoors by the fire. They said that if you laid down in the snow, you'd get the most wonderful dreams and visions as you slowly froze to death. It sounded good. Not that I wanted to touch the grey heaps at the side of the road where the snow had mixed with the dirt of the street. The stress of today was catching up on me, as were the many nights when I hadn't slept. I kept walking.

In the dark the houses on both sides started to look unfamiliar. I took this route every day, but now I didn't know if I should go left or right. I stood still. Looked left and right, but both sides appeared identical. There was nothing to choose between them. So how did I choose? That seemed funny to me somehow. I turned. And turned again. And again and again until I wasn't sure what direction I'd come from. Had the canal been on my right or my left? My brain refused to function. My knees were trying to give way. There was a bench overlooking the canal. I wiped the snow off with my gloved hand and sat down. Just a little rest for my exhausted body and my tired brain that was playing tricks on me. The cold of the seat crept up through the back of my legs. I was so close to the edge of the canal that I could rest my feet on the cloth-covered roof of a moored boat if I'd been half a metre taller. My eyes closed; I couldn't keep them open any more. I heard a car pass behind me, then all was silence and I was embraced by the generous darkness . . .

Something was pulling my arm, someone was talking in my ear: 'Wake up, wake up,' and my body obeyed the voice. I wanted to go back to sleep now that I'd finally got some rest without dreams, but the hand on my arm wouldn't let me. 'No, no, stay with me. Open your eyes.' My head fell forward and the jolt jerked me fully awake. A uniformed policeman stood next to me. His colleague, a woman, was talking on her radio. 'It's OK,' he said to her, 'she's conscious. She's awake.' He helped me to my feet. 'Can you stand? Are you OK?' Yes and no. I took a step forward but my legs were numb and hesitant to obey my brain's commands.

'It's dangerous to fall asleep in this cold,' he said.

'Sorry, I was . . .' My lips had difficulty forming the w and I slurred the word into a hiss of breath.

'What did you take? Are you on drugs?'

'No, no.' I wanted to laugh. If I had been taking my pills I wouldn't have been so tired. Feeling was coming back to my legs and I stamped my feet to the ground.

'You're lucky we found you,' he said. 'Where do you live?'

I took my glove off and put my bare hand against my lips to get some warmth into them. When I could talk again, I gave him my address. The policewoman, off the radio, looked at me. 'I know you,' she said.

I nodded. She looked familiar to me too. 'Lotte Meerman.' My fingers felt twice their size and I had problems getting my ID card out.

'Don't bother,' she said, putting her hand on mine. 'I know who you are.'

'I'm exhausted,' I said.

She smiled a fleeting smile that sparked her eyes before being hidden again. 'We've all been following it,' she said.

Her colleague looked at me again. 'Sorry I didn't recognise you. The hair . . .'

I gestured that it wasn't important. He took me by the arm and we started to walk towards my flat. 'Let's get you home and we'll get you warm.' Their kindness made my eyes sting.

My fingers fumbled the front door open and as we went up to my flat I was followed by sound, first the soft whistle of one of my companions when I opened the main door to the marble-floored hallway with the chandelier, then the surprising clamour of multiple sets of boots on the wooden stairs. On the first-floor landing I unlocked the right-hand door. The wood on my personal flight of stairs was darker; fewer feet had walked and scuffed it over the centuries, and it had a certain smell, that of carpentry and sawmills, that the lower stairs lacked.

The policewoman introduced herself as Ingrid and sat with me, while her colleague, Erik, put the kettle on to make me a cup of tea. 'We'll get you all warmed up,' she said. And so it was that I had one more person in my apartment than ever before. It felt so empty, after they left.

Chapter Twenty-one

I walked to the office the next morning through frozen sunshine. I had searched for my bike for half an hour and become convinced that it had been stolen again before finally remembering that I'd cycled in yesterday morning and stumbled home on foot. Last night I'd been tempted to take one of the small blue pills but had not succumbed: I'd felt I could still do this without medication. I hadn't slept much but at least I'd thought about Anton Lantinga, Otto Petersen and my father. The advantage of making new mistakes had been that I'd had other things to fret and worry about.

The snow on the houses along the canal made it look like a picture postcard, a city scene by any one of our famous seventeenth-century painters. On my canal people were skating, holes in the ice were marked out and gaps under bridges signposted. The next canal along was still partially open, cut through by the tour boats every hour. There were requests to stop the sightseeing tours, in order to improve the ice and make a larger tour on skates possible. As long as there was some sort of compensation, I was sure the tour

249

operators would agree to it. Their boats were largely empty in January anyway.

As soon as I stepped into our office, Hans held up two pages. 'I've got the list', he said, 'of all the people who worked for Petersen Capital in 1995.'

'Any photos?'

'No, none.'

'That's going to make it tricky. You know what we could do? We should also get the employee list of Omega Capital in 2004 or so. If someone from Omega took the files, then that would automatically point us to Karin and Anton. Those two would have asked someone they trusted. Someone they took with them from Petersen Capital to Omega. Someone who had worked with Anton for a long time.'

'Maybe.'

'You don't sound convinced.'

'It's too convoluted. Let's stick with the Petersen Capital list, find out if it's one of them, then see if they are linked to the Lantingas or to Goosens. I'll google the names, see if I can come up with any photos.'

I had only wanted to make the list of names longer, so that it would take more time before anybody realised that both faces came out of my father's imagination. 'And use Facebook as well.'

He grinned. 'Of course. Our new favourite.' He turned to his computer.

My phone rang and I reached across my desk to answer it. It was Ronald again.

'Hi, Ronald,' I said. Hans looked at me. I shrugged – I didn't know what he was calling for either. 'Any news?'

'I just wanted to make sure you were . . .' he was silent for a few seconds, 'following my advice.'

'Your advice to do what?'

He sighed. 'I didn't get through to you yesterday, did I?'

'No, you didn't. And no, I'm not going to drop it.'

'You're wrong, Lotte. Don't do this. Leave it.'

'Ronald, I can't possibly leave it. One more man has been murdered. What happened to that paperwork is crucial, I just know it.'

'Lotte, please.'

'*No*, Ronald. We're making real progress here.'

'You know we didn't find those files at Anton's house.'

'I know. I'm sure—'

'Your father said he saw them in the shed at around six p.m.'

'He did?' I signalled to Hans. This was interesting. Did that mean that it had been Anton's people who'd picked up the files, after all? That my father hadn't destroyed them, but sold them? That made the case different. I wasn't sure what it meant but I knew it was important.

'We were there shortly after seven,' Ronald went on. 'We didn't find anything. There was no large pile of shredding or any evidence of burnt paper. He's now lying to me too, Lotte. He's much more involved than I originally thought.'

I heard Ronald's warning but I ignored it. Only partially covering the mouthpiece of the phone with my hand so that

Ronald could still hear what I had to say, I told Hans: 'DI Huizen saw the files at Anton's house.'

Hans gave me a thumbs up and went over to our whiteboard with a marker pen in hand.

'You're not objective.' Ronald's voice sounded angry.

'Yes, I am.'

'I'm not sure you should be involved at all.'

'And you should? After what you told me in Alkmaar the first time?' The click of our office door opening behind me, followed by the smell of cigarettes, warned that Stefanie was close and I had to watch my words carefully.

'I never thought he was better than he really was. I can see him far more clearly than you can. I always saw his faults and decided I didn't mind. You, on the other hand . . .'

How dared he talk about my father like that? Ronald might have known my father for longer, but I knew him better, deeper, as he was so much like me. 'Great that DI Huizen saw those files,' I said loudly, my mouth close to the phone.

'Lotte, please—'

'Bye, Ronald. Talk to you later.' I put the phone down.

'Lovers' tiff?' Stefanie said.

'Why don't you just shut up.'

'Rude and unnecessary.' She walked over to Thomas's old desk and sat down. 'I saw them together the other evening, Hans. When we found Anton dead.' There was a small smile around her thick red lips. 'Very intimate they seemed for people who'd just met. Or who'd only seen each other

252

twice. And a very odd place to behave like that as well, with Anton's dead body still lying there.'

'There was nothing intimate going on. It's all in your mind,' I said.

'Anyway,' she went on, 'what I came to tell you is that I've got it. It's a disk.'

'What is?'

'The evidence.' At my blank look she said, 'Remember the whistle-blower? His evidence? Well, I found it − in the archives. It was a computer disk with two files. One is the official fund performance − the one Otto Petersen gave to investors − the other is the real performance. His shadow accounts.'

'And the shadow accounts show . . .'

'All the losses Otto Petersen made in his investments.'

'Who sent the disk?'

'I don't know. We'll have to go through—'

'Through this?' I held up the list of the names of people who'd worked for Petersen Capital.

'Yes.' When I looked at her across our desks, she was smiling with an odd little smile, a crook in the corners of her mouth. 'You're ahead of me again, I see.'

'He was.' I pointed at Hans.

'Well, anyway, with this shadow account it was easy to figure out what happened. Geert-Jan Goosens told the truth. There was never any embezzled money. Petersen made mistakes, he blew up the fund and tried to hide it.' She shrugged. 'Wipes out a whole list of suspects.' She walked over to the whiteboard and stared at what Hans was writing. 'Did you know what Ronald de Boer told me?'

'I've got no idea,' I said.

'He told me that all these years, he's been covering for DI Huizen. He thinks DI Huizen destroyed those files.'

I sank in my chair and felt faint but kept a straight face as Stefanie was watching me for my reaction. Why had he told her that, when he'd said he would protect my father? Why had he told her when I'd had to drag every word out of him when we'd talked about those bribes? Why had he told her when he'd warned me we had to be careful, that other people didn't have my father's best interests at heart? Was this some bizarre double-bluff? Why was he making things so difficult for us, discrediting my father's testimony further in Stefanie's eyes? My head spun; I couldn't make sense of this. That was it though: it didn't make any sense. So he probably hadn't said it at all. She was lying, making it up to make it sound as if Ronald agreed with her. That was why. Conniving fat cow. My heart-rate slowed down.

'Had he forgotten to tell you? Too busy talking about other things? That's a shame. Anyway, we can take these', Stefanie reached over Hans's shoulder and pulled the two Photofits off the board, 'and chuck them in the bin.'

I dashed over and snatched the two bits of paper out of her hand before she could make her threat reality.

'No we don't.' I turned to Hans. 'We keep looking for those two people – and find out who they are. This is important. I'm not letting it go.' I carefully folded up the Photofits, put them in my bag and sat down. 'I think

Ronald de Boer is losing it. There may be too much pressure on him.'

'He wants us to stop doing what we're doing,' Hans stated. It wasn't a question.

'But we're not. We're going on.' I picked up my pencil and traced down the list of the employees of Petersen Capital, ignoring Stefanie as she came round to look at what I was reading.

Her hand on the back tipped my chair and she whispered in my ear, 'Why does it matter so much, Lotte?'

I sat up with a jolt and cursed under my breath. A long scratch of my pencil now ran all the way down the page.

Chapter Twenty-two

I had been expecting the summons ever since yesterday's run-in with Thomas. He was the vengeful type and I should have known he'd call the prosecutor as soon as he'd finished shouting at me. If I hadn't annoyed Thomas, I wouldn't be having this meeting that I'd done so much to avoid. When the phone call from Prosecutor Kraan himself had come, with a request to join him in his office, I knew that there was no avoiding it any longer.

Amsterdam Zuid, where the prosecutors were based, always seemed a different place from the centre, where I lived and worked. As I cycled south, the city changed from seventeenth to nineteenth century, from narrow roads along canals to wide pavements, from flats to houses. Then, when I got closer to the place of the appointment, it changed again to new build and main roads. It was like time-travelling four centuries in an easy fifteen-minute cycle journey.

Prosecutor Kraan, or Michael as he asked me to call him, was sitting behind a desk strewn with files – files that I recognised because they were my files. He was looking at my little girl's photos, the ones in the green cardboard folder.

He was reading through my notes. He was touching my photos.

I was so busy looking at those photos and checking which files he had, or didn't have, open on his desk, that I missed his outstretched hand until he made a movement to retract it. I managed to apologise and shake it just in time to avoid embarrassment.

'Detective Meerman, thanks for coming in and my apologies that I haven't had time to arrange a meeting with you sooner. I thought you would deliver the files to me yourself and that this would be the time to discuss the investigation.'

'I was working on a new case.'

'Yes, so the chief inspector told me. He was a bit over-zealous with what he dropped off.' Michael Kraan picked up some pages and dropped them back again on the desk.

I recognised which bits of paper they were: they weren't important. But I wasn't sure what I'd do if he treated Wendy's photo with the same contempt. My reports were one thing, my little girl quite another.

'I've also been working with Thomas, who has helped me find my way through the hours and days of recordings. He has pointed me to the places that the defence are likely to question. But clearly, what I need to talk to you about is the missing tape.'

Tape. Not tapes. That was a good sign.

'You didn't record the final meeting with Paul Leeuwenhoek.'

'Correct. The investigation was officially over. You yourself had called it over, I understand.'

'Yes, we thought we had our murderer.'

'Exactly. So I met with Paul in order to give him the news.' I was getting good at this. How often had I told this new version of events? It almost felt as if this was actually what had happened.

Hans had called me that afternoon, ecstatic, because they had arrested someone for Wendy's murder. It had been a paedophile after all, the one that he'd been investigating. Hans said he'd been to the guy's house and found a cellar full of photos of Wendy. The paedo had confessed to Hans that he'd killed Wendy, after he'd found her alone in the park, and had burned the body. The prosecutor had called the investigation closed and I stopped recording. I went to Wendy's mother and told her. She reacted strangely, almost as if this was an anti-climax for her and that she found it hard to believe. Afterwards I went to Paul's house, and we had a few glasses of wine. I thought we'd arrested the killer so I dropped my defences and did what my feelings had urged me to do. Now that I thought I knew for certain that he was innocent, I was relieved. I was sad too, because my dream of an immediate family was gone with Wendy's death, but I thought that at least I'd started a new relationship. I thought this would give Paul closure, and that he could move on with me.

'And then he just came out with it?' the prosecutor asked.

'Yes, out of the blue he told me that Wendy's body was buried in his garden.' We had been naked and in bed; he had been playing with my hair when he began to speak.

'After all these years.'

258

'He said he wanted to come clean, that he needed to confess.' And he had thought he'd put me in such a position that I could never tell what had happened. That I would have no option than to keep quiet.

I had woken up and his green eyes were staring into mine. I hadn't slept long, maybe dozed for half an hour or so. The afternoon sun was creeping around the corner of the curtains. He looked at me with an intensity I hadn't seen before, not even an hour ago. I smiled at the memory of his body in and on mine. He took a strand of my blonde hair and raised it to his lips. I felt the tug as he pulled it closer. He wound it around his fingers. My face followed my hair and I enjoyed the feeling of his mouth on mine.

'We shouldn't be doing this,' he said. The smell of his breath wasn't off-putting, as it would have been with anybody else, anywhere else.

'It's OK, you're no longer a suspect,' I said, the first time I'd admitted to myself that he ever was. 'You're in the clear – case closed.' My voice sounded smug to me, as smug as I felt. His hand was exploring the curve of my stomach and moving slowly down. We could become a perfect family. We could become complete.

'But I'm sure this is against all protocol, isn't it?' he persisted. 'What would your boss say if he found out?'

'I wasn't planning on telling him.'

'I bet nothing I tell you now can be used in court,' he said.

I smiled.

He played with my hair again. 'Such lovely blonde hair,' he murmured, 'just the same colour as hers. I've kept quiet for fifteen years but all the photos will come back, all the press coverage is starting up again, and it hurts. Every year it hurts more – the hurt grows until it will make me burst. I need to tell someone.' He looked at me with his green eyes. 'You know she's here?' he said.

My fingers, on their caressing path, stopped. My breathing stopped. I was sure even my heart stopped. 'Here?' I repeated.

'I buried her here,' he said. 'The man you arrested . . . He didn't do it.'

I moved my hand from his face to the side of the bed. My fingers were feeling for my gun but couldn't find it. Over his shoulder I could see it lying on his bedside table. He must have moved it when I was asleep. I saw something under his pleasant smile, something I hadn't seen there before. How had I managed to miss it? It was so clearly there underneath the layers of attractiveness. Now he allowed me to see his secret coldness. Oh my God, he had planned this.

'Where is she?' I whispered.

'She's in the garden.'

'But we looked . . .'

'I moved her there much later,' he said. 'From the park. When the police had stopped searching the house.' His fingers slid further down and now only created revulsion.

I stopped his hand.

'Monique was right,' he said. 'She told me you're a fool.

That's why I knew you were perfect – recently divorced, needy, easy to manipulate. I had to tell someone. Her photos in the papers again, people talking, I had to find someone to hear my confession. When I first went away,' his fingers continued to run over my hair, 'I found people who couldn't speak English and told them. But it's not the same if they don't understand. You are perfect. You haven't been record-ing our last conversation; you've got no proof. You slept with me – how are you going to explain that in court? Instead you're left with a paedophile in prison. You'll know, but you won't be able to do anything with that knowledge. How does that feel?' He smiled lazily. 'Maybe it's best to keep your innocent suspect in jail.'

'Why did you kill her? Was it an accident?'

He ran the back of his finger over my jaw and said, 'What does it matter? You will never know.'

I tried to judge the angle and the space between the two of us before I struck out at him. My elbow connected with his cheekbone – I heard it crack. His eyes closed and his head fell back on the pillow. I grabbed my pillow between both hands and held it centimetres above his face. I had to use all my willpower to stop my myself from pushing it down. Instead I threw it on the floor, took my gun, checked that he hadn't removed the bullets, pointed it at him and waited until he came round.

The prosecutor's voice cut into my painful reminiscing. 'Afterwards, when you had him in for questioning . . .'

'I didn't interview him,' I said. That time I hadn't been able to watch.

'No, Hans and Thomas did. I know. But he didn't want to talk then.'

'So I heard.'

'He refused to sign a statement; he refused to answer any questions. If it hadn't been for the body . . .'

'I know,' I said.

'He came in with a broken cheekbone.' The prosecutor waited.

I didn't respond.

'You wrote in your report that you hit him out of self-defence,' he prompted.

'It's all in there.'

Prosecutor Kraan picked up his papers. 'This is what I wanted to talk to you about. The defence team are claiming that the case should be thrown out of court because of police brutality.'

It was the best news I'd had all day. I felt jubilant but kept it in, because I knew that Michael Kraan would misread it, would think that I was proud of hitting Paul Leeuwenhoek. He wouldn't understand what I was really happy about.

'I have to say', Prosecutor Kraan continued, 'that I am intrigued by the tapes. From your conversations and the way you talked, it seems that you and Paul were getting on very well.'

'I liked him. I have to admit that I hadn't thought he was guilty. Until he told me and I found the body.'

'But there is no doubt in your mind now?'

'I'm certain he killed her.'

'Any thoughts on motive or method?'

'The mother said in the interview that he must have slapped Wendy. She must have fallen and hit her head on a rock.'

I had watched Hans and Thomas question her. I had wanted to hear what Monique was going to say but even seeing her from the other side of the window had felt too close.

'She said that her daughter always wanted to play outside,' I continued. 'Never wanted to come home for dinner. Paul has a bit of a temper, according to her.' To me he'd seemed rather cold and calculating.

'Yes, I know,' the prosecutor said. 'That's what she's going to testify to.' He paused. 'But what do you think? Did he say anything?'

'He never said why or how.'

I understood why Monique was sticking with this version of events. This was what she could live with. In my dreams, Paul would hit his daughter with a brick. He wasn't angry. He was trying to see if he could do it and if he could get away with it. After a nightmare like that, I would get into my car and drive until I'd calmed down. My dream version and Monique's theory were equally likely according to the forensic evidence. Mine would get him a longer prison sentence but we would never be able to prove it. The defence would ask why Monique hadn't seen blood on Paul when he'd come home.

'I agree with Monique. That's the most likely way it happened,' I said. At least that was backed up by a statement from his ex-wife.

'So cruel, to hide his daughter's body, come back from the little park and claim he can't find her. Then ask Monique to help him look for her. Search anywhere but in the park, as he said he'd combed through that.'

'He kept his wife between hope and fear all those years.'

'A cruel heartless man.' The prosecutor was trying the words out. They sounded fine to me.

When he'd dropped his mask, I'd finally seen the real Paul. I'd seen how calculating he'd been and how hard he had worked to put me in the impossible situation I'd found myself in. Every move, every word, had been worked out beforehand. I was so open to his advances – recently divorced, as he'd said, and very insecure – and I'd fallen for his pretence. But his mistake was that he had shown it to me. That he had gloated. That he was smug about having told someone who could never tell anybody else. Or so he thought.

In the bad times in the middle of the night, I sometimes wondered if I would have reacted differently if he'd continued to show me a loving, caring side. If he'd said that he'd killed his daughter by accident, if he'd asked for my help. In the daylight, I could convince myself that I would always have done what I did. At night, driving along the motorway in the dark, I sometimes worried that I would have kept silent and that I would have covered for him. Luckily for me, that choice hadn't come up.

'Do you think the mother knew?'

'I don't think so. Monique kept talking about Wendy as if she were still alive.' Even though she and Paul had discussed me behind my back, if I believed Paul at least, nothing he'd said had suggested his wife knew anything about Wendy's death.

'You know your role will come under close scrutiny during the trial.'

'I expect so.'

'Is there anything I need to know? Before we go to trial?'

'Nothing I can think of.' I saw the photo of Wendy and for the first time in a while I saw her for what she was: not an older version of my Poppy, but a little girl in her own right. The photo was turned round and Wendy was facing me, holding her watering can and staring at me with eyes full of reproach above her gap-toothed smile. I could imagine how she'd spit the words through the hole of the missing tooth. *'My father killed me, and you didn't realise it. You were too engrossed in your own problems, your own hopes and desires, to worry about me. You only saw me as a replacement for the child you'd lost.'*

I couldn't have saved her, she had already been dead for fifteen years before I first met her father, but that didn't make me feel any the less depressed. I couldn't face that photo any longer and wondered how I could have held it and gazed at it and caressed the place where it showed her pigtails, only last week.

The questions had stopped and I almost ran out of the prosecutor's office. I needed to escape those photos and leave that little girl behind. I dashed into the toilets and made it just in time to be violently sick. I sank to the floor and knelt on the almost-white, almost-clean tiles, my hands together on the toilet and my head bent over it as if in prayer. The smell of urine and vomit mingled and I reached out and pressed the flush. Tears ran down my cheeks, and my stomach and throat burned from bringing up the cheese sandwich and coffee mixture.

As I read the predictably disgusting graffiti on the stall wall from my lowly position on the toilet floor, about the size of so-and-so's privates and what so-and-so had done and with whom, I realised I'd been right to try to avoid this meeting: it had been just as painful as I had known it was going to be.

That evening, I didn't eat anything. I didn't cook anything. I couldn't face food, still nauseous from the onslaught of my memories. I stared at the walls with the lights out as I sat on the sofa and waited for the minutes to creep past. Then I put on my coat and went out.

It was half past ten, still early for a Thursday evening, and the bars were heaving with students on their main going-out night, before they'd all go home to their parents for the weekend, and with people out for a quick drink after their dinner or after having been to the cinema. The Grand Café Luxembourg, which I'd come past in the tram with my father on the way to Centraal Station the other day, was warm and noisy. It felt like being a student again, as if I was twenty years younger and still naively sure that I knew everything and could do anything. The sound created by many people talking surrounded me like a comfortable blanket. I ordered a glass of white wine at the bar. I knew that somebody would talk to me within ten minutes or so, since everybody had had enough to drink to make them more sociable than they'd ever be normally. I would only have to look at someone for long enough to make them come over.

The man I picked was quite attractive, in that slightly fleshy, just past his prime kind of way. He bought me two more glasses of wine in a forty-five-minute period. We chatted about the weather, the news, the Ajax Football Club and work. His work, never mine. He was an accountant for one of the big firms and was out with a group of his colleagues to let off steam after a day's hard work. He gestured towards the other end of the bar, where those colleagues were supposed to be. I couldn't see anybody who was looking at us but there were enough groups who could have been his colleagues. I didn't care if he was lying to me or not.

The inevitable moment came when he said he was going outside for a cigarette and asked if I wanted to keep him company. I said I would. It took me about five minutes of standing outside in the freezing cold to decide that this had been a really stupid idea. I pushed him away as he tried to kiss me. He tried a bit harder and I pushed a lot harder. 'Frigid bitch,' he shouted after me as I jogged for the tram.

It was well after midnight that I emptied the contents of the pot of prescription sleeping tablets in my hand and was surprised by how light the pills were – and how heavy the decision not to swallow them all.

Chapter Twenty-three

The walk to the boss's office never got any easier. He hadn't said what he wanted to see me about, but the tone of his voice was a warning not to take it lightly. It was going to be bad. I had a painful headache directly behind my right eye, probably caused by drinking on an empty stomach, that even three cups of coffee hadn't been able to take away.

The look on his face was one of pure anger. His eyes were narrowed and his mouth looked as if he got a nasty taste in it as soon as he saw me. 'Shut the door.'

My stomach started to flutter. I sat on the chair, back ramrod straight, my body under control.

'Lotte, some information came to me that I hope you will deny.'

The flutters intensified and I started to feel sick.

'What the hell were you thinking? Are you insane?' He hit his desk with the flat of his hand.

I jumped at the sudden sound. My heart thumped in my chest, as much from the shock as from the anticipation of what was to come. I'd known they'd find out sooner or later.

When Thomas had first told me about the meetings he knew I hadn't recorded, I'd known.

All energy left my body and my shoulders sagged. I was exhausted, but in a small part of my mind there was relief, now that the need to pretend was gone. For weeks I'd lied – to the press, to the CI, to my colleagues, and to everybody who congratulated me on finding Wendy Leeuwenhoek's body. Maybe she would stop haunting me in my dreams when I told the truth. This must be why people went to confession. You confessed all your sins and faced the consequences.

Oh my God – the consequences! I'd lose my job. I might even go to jail. I . . .

'It's about DI Piet Huizen. Somebody told me he's your father. Is that right?'

It took me some time to register what he was saying. I just stared at him, speechless.

'Come on, Lotte, it's a simple enough question. Is Piet Huizen your father?'

For a second I considered saying that he wasn't. But that thought left my mind as quickly as it came. There was no way the CI wouldn't be able to find out the truth. There were such things as birth certificates. I knew Moerdijk well enough to know that he would have checked the facts before calling me into his office. He already knew what my reply was going to be.

'Yes, it's true.' The knot that had been unravelling in my chest began to knit up again.

'What were you thinking of?'

I had been thinking of confessing. I had been thinking of telling the truth, of admitting . . . I had been on the brink of telling CI Moerdijk what I had been trying so hard not to remember, but now . . .

'I didn't think there was anything—'

'Anything wrong with what you did?' His face was growing redder and redder, like a stick of dynamite ready to explode.

'No, I wasn't going to say that.' I inhaled deeply. It took time to adjust to this different reason for being shouted at. 'I didn't think there was anything in Ben van Ravensberger's tip-off.'

'But when you found there was?'

'There wasn't, though. We know that Ben made it up. Ferdinand van Ravensberger explained—'

'For fuck sake!' The sudden swearword made me sit up. 'Stop making excuses. I'm sick and tired of covering up for you. You lie to me, you never keep me informed, I need to go to the prosecution with all the evidence in the Wendy Leeuwenhoek case, you work on a case involving your father, who is now the main suspect . . .'

My father the main suspect? Anton Lantinga had been killed because I was poking around in Otto Petersen's murder. Now I'd made my father the main suspect? I spoke before I could consider the wisdom of my words. 'He can't be.'

'That is precisely why we don't get involved in cases concerning members of our family. You can't see straight. You can't be objective. You defend him. Piet Huizen was at Anton Lantinga's house *half an hour* before Anton was shot. How can you still say you were right to stay on this case? To keep me in the dark?' He raked a hand through his hair and took a deep breath. 'Does Hans know?'

'No. No he doesn't. I haven't told anybody.' He didn't ask if Stefanie knew, which was significant.

'That's some good news at least. Means I don't have to suspend him as well.'

'Suspend?'

'For a month. After that we'll talk. See if your position here is tenable at all.'

'But we're so close to solving this case!'

'Don't argue, Lotte. You're lucky I'm not firing you on the spot.'

'But . . .' *But what am I going to do*, was what I wanted to ask. However, it wasn't up to the CI to answer that question. Tears burned in my eyes. This had been such a small mistake. I'd made some really big ones, but now I was suspended for breaking a stupid rule, when I could have made a real contribution. Yes, I knew I should have told Moerdijk, knew the risk I'd been taking. 'Those files,' I began.

'Lotte, just shut up. *Shut up!* You're just making things worse every time you open your mouth.'

I knew that if there was any way to explain my situation, any way I could make him see that I wasn't doing anything wrong, then I could stay at work. Then I wouldn't lose my safe haven. I could of course still confess to the CI – but the words wouldn't come, only tears – and there was no way I would let him see how upset and scared I was. I got up from my chair.

'The main reason I'm *not* firing you', the CI said tightly, 'is that I need you here to testify in Paul Leeuwenhoek's trial.'

I could have laughed at the folly of it all. My job was saved only because I needed to repeat my lies in front of a judge!

'The prosecutor told me the defence team is definitely claiming police brutality. It's such a shame you don't have the tapes of that last meeting, of the confession. I want you back here in time for the trial. We need to make sure you can testify. I'll let you know the date.'

I almost ran down the corridor to my desk, to grab my stuff and head out. I didn't want much, only a handful of pens and my pencil.

Hans watched me from his seat. 'What's going on?'

'I'm suspended.' He wanted to know what had happened but my throat swelled up and I couldn't talk to him. I couldn't talk to him and still keep things together.

'Your gun, please.' CI Moerdijk had followed me to the office.

I picked up my Walther P5 in its holster – I had been going to leave it here anyway – and put it into his out-stretched hand. Through the noisy traffic of my heartbeat, I heard Hans ask the CI what the hell was going on.

Stefanie came and stood in the doorway, in my way, just as I left. She was surely here to watch the outcome of her interference. She must have checked up on Piet Huizen in her attempt to blacken his name, and found out about me instead. I pushed her aside.

She looked shocked, her mouth an O of surprise when my hand connected with the flesh of her arm. 'Lotte, are you OK?'

Of course I wasn't OK. I was not OK because she had grassed me up to the boss. You bitch, I thought, how did you find out? Did Ronald tell you? Did you check my birth certificate? I turned my back on her; I didn't talk to her, scream or shout at her, because, right now, I couldn't stand the sight of her.

Chapter Twenty-four

My mother didn't like going out when the weather was this cold. When I saw how thin and pale she looked, I was glad she was staying indoors.

I followed her to the kitchen. She didn't ask me why I was here but put on a pair of yellow Marigolds and piled dirty dishes in the sink. It worried me that she hadn't done them last night. I briefly hesitated, wondering if I should tell her what had happened, but then came out with it as I thought she'd take it as good news. 'I've been suspended.'

She stopped still, one of her hands holding a plate half-submerged, half above water. 'What did you do?' Her other hand rose to her mouth and she pushed the yellow rubber against her lips as if to keep more questions inside.

I didn't understand why she looked so upset. 'I covered for Dad and they found out.'

'Covered? Why?'

'Because of the money.'

She didn't seem to understand me. 'What money?'

'The money you told me about last time.'

274

'Oh Lotte, I thought we were through with that.' She plunged her hands back in the soapy water.

'I thought you'd be pleased.'

My mother's duck-egg-blue eyes returned to the washing-up bowl where white foam covered the dirty plates underneath. Her hands started scrubbing. 'No, I'm not pleased you've thrown away your career. Especially for your father. Is it permanent?'

I picked up the plate she'd just cleaned and wiped a blue-and-white-checked tea towel in careful circles to remove the water. 'I'm not sure. Not yet.' I put the white plate, without frills, without patterns, in its usual place in the cupboard. 'Just tell me what happened between you and Dad.' She kept trying to avoid my questions, but I needed to hear her say it. I had to know that I'd done the right thing; I wanted her to tell me how she'd found out about the money, the first time she'd realised he was on the take, maybe the first notes she'd found. I wanted to know, because this was what I gave up my job for.

'Lotte, nothing out of the ordinary happened. I don't understand why you are being so . . . so . . .'

I picked up a cup, dried it and didn't fill the silence.

'So official,' she concluded.

As she handed me another dripping cup, our fingers almost touched. The smell of Lux washing-up liquid reached my nostrils.

'Tell me about the money,' I said.

'What money?'

'The money you were talking about last time. Mum, don't make this so hard for me!'

'I'm not making this hard. It's a private matter – I don't see how it can possibly make a difference.'

I put the cup quietly on top of its mate in the cupboard. 'You told me last time that Dad got paid for something he shouldn't have, and that it was wrong of him to take it.'

'Oh, that.'

'Yes, that. How did you find out?'

'I don't want to talk about it.'

'See? You're doing it again.'

'Doing what?'

'Acting as if it's not important. Mum, we lived in relative poverty for years. You still have next to nothing. He has a huge house, a BMW parked outside the door, brochures of expensive holidays . . .'

'And you wish we'd had that too?' Her eyes remained on the plate in her right hand, checked that the stains had disappeared under the brush.

'No, I just want to know why we didn't have some of that.'

'It wasn't my money to take. I told you that. I walked out, so how could I expect him to give some of that money to me?'

'Did he ever offer to pay?'

'Is that what this is about? You want to know if your father cared enough to offer to pay for you?'

I paused with the tea towel limp from my hand. 'No, I—'

276

'Well, he did. He offered. He offered a few times. Especially after you started to visit him, he called to say he wanted to do more for you. But I knew where the money came from so I couldn't accept it.' She picked up another plate and scraped the rest of what looked like mashed potatoes into the kitchen bin with the washing-up brush. There was more leftover food there than I was happy to see. The plate then disappeared under the bubbles in the sink.

'Where *did* the money come from?'

'Ah, so we're back to that, are we?' She handed me the clean plate.

'Yes, we are.'

She picked up a glass, turned it round and round in her hand, the brush firmly inside, until the residue of the orange juice had disappeared before she responded. 'It was hers, OK? It was *her* money.' She put the glass down, took one of the Marigolds off and threw it with force into the foamy water. It splashed in her face and bubbles splattered all over the cabinets and the work surface. The drops mixed with washing-up froth streamed down her face like tears. The muscles around her mouth contorted. The glove filled with dirty water from the round washing-up bowl and went under.

'Her? Who do you mean?'

'That Maaike woman. His new wife. She hired him to do some private security for her real estate business. He did far more for her than that. So much more, I had no choice but to leave when I found out.' My mother wiped her face with her bare hand.

'Oh Mum, why didn't you ever tell me this?'

'Tell you what? That your father left me for a richer woman? That the house he lives in, the BMW you so enviously describe, their holidays, are all paid for by her? That the money he offered me to look after you was hers?' She straightened her back, pulled off the second Marigold and flung it in the sink as well. It floated for a bit, then sank beneath the soapsuds.

'So how is this different?' I muttered, to stop myself from screaming. I was like one of those gloves, drowning gradually in dirty dishwater, bit by bit.

'What do you mean?'

'All along, you told me that my break-up from Arjen was different from your break-up from Dad. I came to you for help. I came to you for advice. And you kept telling me your divorce was different. Well, it doesn't sound so different to me. It sounds exactly the same.' The volume of my voice was rising even though I was trying hard to keep it under control. I wanted to yell at her for making me feel guilty about leaving Arjen. How could she have been all high and mighty with me, making me feel that it had all been my fault, that I'd done something wrong, that I could have saved my marriage, whilst the same thing had happened to her? I remembered the words she had said: '*What did you do?*' But she'd known only too well that sometimes you didn't do anything, that things just happened to you, that the people around you made these decisions to be with somebody else for whatever reason, and that there was nothing you could do.

She pulled the plug out of the sink and the water drained, revealing the dinner debris beneath.

I was fighting back tears. 'Mum, you made me believe that something different happened between you and Dad. You always told me . . . you made me believe it was something important.'

'But it was.'

'That's not what I mean. I told you Arjen had had an affair and got the woman pregnant. You said you couldn't help me, because what had happened between you and Dad was so different.'

'With your father it was all about the money.'

'I thought the money came from somewhere else.' I said it softly, embarrassed now at how easy I'd found it to believe that. 'That he'd been taking bribes.'

'Bribes? What are you talking about?'

'I believed that bribes had paid for his house. That this was why you left him.'

Had I wanted to believe it? Because my own criminal behaviour would be less deplorable if I were the daughter of a corrupt policeman? Then it would have been in my genes, in my make-up: it would not have been my responsibility. I had tried to protect myself as much as protect him, I suddenly realised. It had been so difficult to live with the knowledge that I was the kind of police officer who destroyed evidence, who altered the scene of the crime.

I felt less guilt about shooting a young man in a petrol station than I did over what I'd done at Paul Leeuwenhoek's house. The guilt about the subsequent clean-up operation was maybe even worse than my revulsion over having sex with him. That revulsion was so deep that I couldn't stand the sight of my own skin these days, couldn't endure anybody touching me – but the sex had been an act of my weak flesh whilst the clean-up had been a premeditated act of what I used to think was my strong mind. At least with my father, I'd tried to protect him. The clean-up was purely to protect myself.

My mother took a step back from the sink and said, 'Maybe I would have preferred it if he had been on the take.' She laughed harshly. 'Isn't that awful of me? I would have preferred it if he had been a criminal. Instead he was just sleeping with a rich woman.'

'Mum—'

'No, you wanted me to talk, so let me talk. He was coming home with all these little presents. Presents from her to him: a new suit, a nice jumper, some calfskin-leather gloves. He wasn't even hiding them. He told me she'd given them. He told me! Can you believe it? He told me because he wanted to keep a clear conscience. Didn't want to do anything behind my back.' She sat down on the kitchen floor next to the fridge. 'Instead he was rubbing my face in it. That was the hardest.'

'Mum.' I bent down until I was level with her and wrapped my arms around her. She smelled of the Nivea body lotion she'd used for forty years.

'It wasn't supposed to be like that. Marriage was supposed to be for ever. He was supposed to be faithful to me.' She shook under my embrace. My arms felt her ribs through the skin. There seemed to be no flesh in between. When she spoke, her breath tickled the skin inside my ear. Her whispering voice was so close it seemed she was talking right inside my mind. 'Some days, when you were at school, I'd take the train to Alkmaar. I'd get the bus to their house, stand outside behind a tree, and watch them. He moved in with her – our house wasn't good enough for her, I suppose – and I watched them, when I knew he was on lates, watched their morning routine. And I could see what it was all about. It was about the money. He left me for somebody with a lot of money, so that they could live in their big house, drive her nice car. Have all the things he wanted to have but could never afford. You see, that's why it was different. Arjen just left you for someone younger, someone prettier. Your father left me for someone richer. Don't you see it was totally different?'

'Oh, Mum.' So lying was something I'd inherited from my mother, not my father. I didn't know if I wanted to hit her or hug her. As I was already hugging her, it seemed easier to keep on doing that. Who was I to judge? I'd jumped to conclusions; I'd thought he was on the take. My mother hadn't forced me to cover for him; she hadn't told me he was taking bribes. It had been my misunderstanding, my own stupid fault. My job, my life, my career down the drain over a misunderstanding. How had that happened?

'And then he wanted to see you,' she hissed in my ear, 'but he already had another wife, another house – why should he have his child back?'

'When was this?' I had to work hard to make sure my arms did not crush her but I couldn't stop all my muscles from tightening up. 'When did he want to see me?'

'Oh, immediately. But I didn't want him to see you. I didn't want him and his mistress to tarnish you with all that cash. You would have been unhappy with our flat here; you wouldn't have been satisfied with what I could give you. I couldn't let that happen. I had to protect you from that. So I wouldn't let you visit him until you were old enough to make your own choices. And I think you made the right ones.'

Now it was clear to me that she'd sabotaged those visits from the beginning by refusing to drop me off. And I'd thought she was protecting me. I went to Alkmaar on my own and my father and I got off on the wrong foot because I ended up defending her.

What about me? I wanted to say. *What about my childhood? You always told me he didn't want to see me. How did you think that made me feel?* Unwanted, unimportant, unloved. I had been at the bottom of the pile at school. Not only were my parents divorced, which was uncommon but not unheard of, but I also had no contact with my father. The other girls had called me names, shouted that I was so ugly even my own father couldn't stand the sight of me, was so disappointed in me that he couldn't bear having to talk to me. When I'd told my mother, she'd lectured me to stand up to them, to get angry, to get even. She could have told me the truth: that my father did want to see me, that it was her choice we had no contact.

Instead I said, 'Mum, it doesn't matter.'

'It does matter.' She didn't know what I was referring to. My head juddered. 'He was the adulterer,' she hissed. 'He should have been punished. He shouldn't have a nice life, with his new wife, in her big house. He should have been the one with the hard life, with the two jobs. Not me.' She was talking louder.

I pushed her away from me. She wiped her eyes with the sleeve of her jumper and took a deep breath as if to say, 'Right, that's that. No more crying.' I stood up but didn't give her my hand to pull her to her feet. 'I'm sorry, Mum.'

'I'd like you to go now, Lotte. Thanks for helping me with the dishes.'

I picked up my coat and walked down those stairs again.

Outside the flat I got in my car and stared at the cyclists going past. How the hell had I got it so badly wrong?

Chapter Twenty- five

'I've been suspended,' I said, hanging my head and feeling like a twelve year old who is telling her father that she's been kicked out of school for something she hasn't done – sounding defiant and defensive at the same time.

'What for?' He frowned, his forehead deep ravines of concern, then stepped aside, saying, 'Come in.' He took my coat, hung it up.

I followed him down the hallway. Classical music streamed from hidden speakers. I thought it was Mahler, but couldn't be sure. The smell of lemons was even stronger than last time.

'For this, of course,' I replied. 'For working on this case and not telling them you're my father.' I was angry that he didn't understand.

'You didn't tell them?' He stopped and rested his hand on my arm. I shook it off. 'But why not? Sorry, sit down and you can tell me all about it. Coffee?'

On my nod he walked to the kitchen. I went with him. 'I did think it was strange that they let you work on this case.' He put two mugs under the spout of a stainless-steel coffee machine.

'I was stupid. I should have told them.'

He turned round and looked at me over his shoulder. 'Why didn't you?'

'I didn't think it could do any harm. Coming here, I mean. There was no way Ferdinand van Ravensberger had killed Otto Petersen. I thought I could come and talk to you . . .' The sound of beans being ground drowned out my words. I didn't want to tell him that I'd come here to escape talking to the prosecutor about Wendy Leeuwenhoek. That I had been afraid the prosecutor was going to ask me difficult questions and that I'd hoped I could keep Wendy's photos for a bit longer. I rested against the marble work surface, its sharp edge digging into my hip. I picked up a cleaner, lemon-scented Ajax, and swung it back and forth in my hand.

'Give me that,' my father said. 'Sorry, I was just scrubbing when you turned up.' He opened the cupboard under the sink and put the bottle in beside the other cleaning products. He frothed milk in a stainless steel jug and poured the foam in my cup, then rinsed the jug under the tap and put it in the dishwasher.

I looked around. There were many appliances and gadgets here, compared to my mother's kitchen with the old tins filled with herbs. 'I'm surprised you don't have a cleaner,' I commented.

'Then what would I do all day?' He handed me my mug and filled the other for himself. 'This has been an interesting change. Back to doing a proper job.' The corners of his mouth rose, then he let the smile drop from his face. 'I'm sorry I got you into trouble.'

I took a sip of coffee and bitterness flooded my mouth. 'You didn't get me into trouble. I got myself into it.' Then I corrected myself. 'Actually, I already was in trouble. Don't worry about it. When Ronald told me about your heart attack, your last day at work, those files . . .' Had that only been ten days ago? It seemed like a lifetime. '. . . I don't think I was in my right mind. I should have dropped it there and then, told the chief inspector. But I didn't. I thought it was my duty to protect you.'

'But I didn't need protecting. I told you that.'

'I know. But one of my colleagues kept going on about bribes, money missing.' I pointed a hand around the kitchen. 'And I had seen your house, your car. You had so much. Mum and I, we had so little.' I sighed. 'Those words hit a nerve. It was so easy to believe there might be substance in them.'

'It's all Maaike's. She's very successful and has worked hard all these years.' My father looked tired. 'None of it is mine,' he said.

'Come, Dad, let's sit down.'

'I suppose you could say I've been lucky.' He patted my back. 'And I've been so proud of you over the years. Your career, the cases you worked on . . . I've kept a scrapbook, you know.'

'Doing something for you felt good,' I tried to explain. 'I felt grown-up. Responsible. Making up for earlier mistakes.

For lost time. Even though it was clearly futile, trying to look after you when you didn't need looking after; trying to cover up for you while you were telling the truth all along.'

We sat down on the sofa, side by side on the long leg of the L-shape. He wrapped an arm around my shoulder.

I pulled back and looked at him for a breath or two then I tried out the physical contact and leaned my head on his shoulder. It was uncomfortable but I felt comforted.

'You don't have to explain,' he said gently. 'How are you anyway? You look even more tired than the last time I saw you.'

I moved from under his arm and sat up straight against the back of the sofa. 'I was crying all the way here. But now – I don't know. I just feel exhausted.'

Exhausted and empty. It reminded me of breaking off some early relationship at university. For weeks I had been fretting over whether I wanted to stay with the guy or not, had cried many tears into my patient pillow, and hadn't actually done anything about it. Then Patrick had dumped me. And after I'd recovered from wounded pride, which lasted all of thirty minutes, there had been this real sense of emptiness, the realisation that relationships were meaningless and that they hurt. It had been brutal seeing him in the lecture theatre with his new girlfriend and observing all my friends together with their other halves, but for days immediately after the break-up, I'd felt this awful emptiness. However much of a lonely outcast I was, it was still better than going through that ever again.

Once more I felt barren, without purpose, now that my quest to save my father, my sacrifice, had turned out to be unnecessary. My joints, my very bones ached.

'What are you going to do?' my father asked.

'I'm not sure.' As before, the pot of blue pills by the side of my bed sprang to mind. 'First I'll sleep. The CI said I should take a holiday. I might do that. I'll talk to Hans tomorrow and then I'll leave him to it and come back when I read in the paper that he's done.'

'And Anton's murder?'

'That's Ronald's case now. Hans is going to work with him. At least, I think so; I didn't speak to the boss about that. I'm through thinking I'm the only one who can solve crime. Plus', I laughed, 'I'm not allowed to anyway. I'm suspended. I don't want to get in more trouble than I already am. So, just out of personal curiosity, nothing to do with the investigation, what did Anton Lantinga say to you on the night of his death?'

'It was funny. When I got there, he looked at me and said: "Oh yes, I recognise you. You interrogated me once or twice." Can you believe it? I was ready to lock him up and he only barely remembered me. He took me to the shed and showed me the two yellow crates I'd packed. He must have read some of the reports, but they hardly looked touched. "I think you might have got into some trouble over this," he said, "and I want to make amends. It's been more than ten years and I want the truth to come out. I'm fed up with hiding and lying."'

'You don't think he shot Otto, do you?'

'No, I'm pretty sure he didn't.'

The doorbell rang. My father got up to open the door. I heard voices, him and another man. I sat back against the sofa and thought maybe I would have been a different person if I could have spent more time with my father. I imagined weekend visits that were joyful, pleasurable. Maybe we'd have gone to Alkmaar's cheese market together, where sets of two men would run stretchers with moon-yellow cheeses around the large square. Their white uniforms and summer-coloured straw hats my father had told me so much about would make them seem like ambulancemen, doctors, on a jaunty outing, their red hatbands floating behind them like the streamers from a party. The sun would shine. My father would be holding my hand tight, which was good because I wouldn't want to get lost in the crowd. People would press against me, smell of sweat and cheese, but I wouldn't be afraid, I wouldn't be worried, because my father would hold my hand and I'd be secure.

I rubbed my hand over my eyes. I wasn't that naïve, not even in my own daydreams. It wouldn't have been sunny; it would have rained and bad things would have happened anyway, like in that first visit, which my mother had sabotaged on purpose.

Footsteps came from the hallway.

'Hi, Lotte. Didn't know you were here,' Ronald said. His hair was back under control.

'Is this an official visit?' I asked.

'Is yours?'

'No, I'm off the case. I'm just having a coffee with my father.'

'Mine is not official either.' Ronald sat down on the far side of the sofa. My father sat next to me. 'At least not this time.' He looked at my father. 'I'm sorry, Piet. One of my colleagues has got the idea that you shot Anton – because you were there that night. I know you've got nothing to do with it, so I've come here to warn you. I'll continue to protect you,' he looked at me, 'and I'll protect you too, Lotte.'

'I don't need protecting,' I said.

He ignored me. 'Did Anton say anything? Anything of interest?'

'Not really,' my father said. 'He just showed me the files in the shed.'

'But you said you didn't find anything, Ronald,' I queried.

'True. I checked, and there was nothing. Two sets of foot-prints from the garden to the shed. One is Anton's—'

'The other one is mine,' my father said. He sounded resigned. 'Do you want the shoes I wore that evening?'

'If you don't mind.'

My father nodded and left the room. I could hear his footsteps go up the stairs and walk around above my head.

'How are you, Lotte? Are you OK?' Ronald asked.

'I'm fine.'

'I'm sorry to hear you're suspended. Have dinner with me tonight. Talk about what you knew, how far you got.'

I shook my head. 'Thanks, Ronald, but not tonight. I'm going straight home to bed.' I needed to sleep. I didn't think I could cope with seeing Wendy tonight in my dreams so I'd

take some of the pills I'd managed to leave untouched so far.
My arms felt heavy with fatigue. 'How is Karin holding up?'

'She's hard as nails. We're talking again to her soon. See
what she has to say. She'll tell us who she saw.' It sounded
like a warning.

I didn't understand why he was telling me this. We sat in
silence until my father came back. He held out his shoes.
They looked so innocent, these slate-grey leather shoes with
their dove-grey laces crossing from metal hole to metal hole,
the crepe soles so necessary in the snow, the heels worn
down from walking, the leather marked with a white line
where the salt-mixed melted-snow water had run up the
sides. But they seemed enormous and significant as Ronald
opened a plastic bag and got my father to put them in. He
was careful not to touch them.

'And remember,' Ronald said, 'if anything comes to mind,
anything Anton said, anything you saw, give me a call.'

'Sure.' He walked Ronald out. 'Give my love to Ilse.'

Ronald said he would. He didn't turn round to say goodbye to me.

'Is Ilse his wife?' I asked my father when he returned.

'Yes. She's nice – very caring. But I think you've met her.'

'I have? When?'

'She's the receptionist.' I must have looked at him blankly
because he added, 'At the police station.'

Their smiles together, their glances. I'd missed something
again. 'I had no idea. I thought they were having an affair.'

'No, they've been married for ages. Must be over fifteen years.'

'I had no idea,' I said again.

'Yes, he got her that job. She wanted to join the police force at first, but he thought it wouldn't be right for her, so he got her somewhere safe from where she could see what was involved.'

I remembered that she'd told me about that, the first time I'd come to the Alkmaar police station.

'Another coffee?'

I was thinking, so I'd missed my father holding my empty mug out in front of me. 'I can always do with another,' I told him. 'Thanks.'

He got up, and a few moments later the whine of the coffee grinder streamed from the kitchen.

'Let's talk about something else,' I said when he came back with the coffees. But I said that to stop myself thinking of how easily all the jigsaw pieces would fit together if my father really was guilty. 'You've known Ronald for a long time, haven't you?'

'Yes, we worked together for almost twenty years. Why?'

'Why does he think he needs to protect you?'

'It's funny. I informed him I was going to see Anton and he told me not to. Said I was too old, it was too dangerous. I don't know. Maybe because he sat by the side of my bed with Maaike after my heart attack. It feels as if he's wanted to wrap me in cotton wool ever since.'

'He told me about that. He did still sound upset.'

'After more than ten years. Can you imagine?'

I nodded. I recognised the feeling, but I'd only known about my father's heart attack for a week.

His face creased with his smile. 'I'm glad you're looking out for me. Would you like to stay for dinner?'

I looked at my watch. It was just before five. 'No thanks, Dad. I'm going home. I'm exhausted.'

'You can stay here tonight if you like.'

'Thanks, but I wouldn't be good company tonight.'

'That doesn't matter; that's what family is for.'

'Some other time, maybe.'

'I'm worried about you, Lotte,' he said after a pause and a long stare at me. 'I'm worried that you didn't ask me about the money, that you didn't just come out with it. You know you can talk to me, don't you?'

'I know so now.'

'If there's anything you want to talk to me about . . .'

'No, Dad, I'm fine.'

'You're not, Lotte, and it probably would do you good to get things off your chest. I won't tell anybody, I'd understand – why don't you try it?'

Talk about what I did after I'd hit Paul Leeuwenhoek, talk about distorting evidence? 'Dad, I've done some stuff I'm not proud of.'

'Haven't we all.' He no longer smiled; his face was sombre.

'I'd completely misjudged Paul Leeuwenhoek.' I'd been so in love with him that I hadn't been able to see him for who he really was – not until he had taken his mask off, not until he'd taunted me with it.

'But you found out in the end.'

'Yes, I did.' And I'd hit him in the face, pointed a gun at him, had forced him under the shower, forced him to get dressed in clean clothes.

'There are always suspects we get on with better than others, people we'd like to be innocent, people we'd like to be guilty. But it doesn't always work out the way we want it. Our friends can have committed crimes, even.' My father finished his sentence in a low voice and I realised that this was as much a conversation with himself as it was with me.

'So this happened to you too?'

'Of course. You do this job for long enough, you come to realise that the nicest people can be tax evaders; that members of your own family can drink too much and get behind the wheel. We are not responsible for what they do; we are just responsible for how we react, how we deal with it.'

I closed my eyes and the picture of how I'd dealt with it came flooding in.

It had taken Paul Leeuwenhoek a while after I'd hit him to come round, but finally he'd opened his eyes.

'Get up,' I said.

He refused.

'I have to work very hard not to shoot you right now,' I told him. 'Don't give me an excuse, because I will pull the trigger.'

He smiled.

It made me want to throw up. After I'd made him have a shower and a good wash, the gun pointed at his head at all

294

times, I needed him to get dressed. 'Put some clothes on,' I ordered. 'No, not these ones. Clean ones. Get them out of the cupboard.'

He did as I said. He had been silent throughout, probably correctly reading in my eyes that I would not have hesitated to pull the trigger.

'Now go down the stairs.' He started to say something, but I jabbed the gun in the nape of his neck. My fingers had held him there only an hour ago. I pushed the image out of my mind. 'Down the stairs.' He walked slowly down both flights. I opened the cellar door. He looked at me once before going through. I closed the door behind him, wedged a chair under the doorknob and moved a table against the chair.

'It doesn't matter what you do now,' I heard him shout, the sound muffled by the door.

He was wrong. It mattered a great deal. I went into the kitchen and opened the cupboards until I found a pair of household gloves and cleaning fluids. I grabbed a handful of plastic bags and put them over my hair and shoes. All the time tears were streaming down my face and revulsion was coursing through every nerve, every vein in my body

I went back upstairs, into the bedroom, and stripped the sheets and pillowcases from the bed. I stuffed them in a bin bag. I got clean sheets out of the cupboard and made the bed again. Then I hoovered the carpet thoroughly and wiped all the surfaces. I cleaned the upstairs bathroom. I took his comb, pulled some hairs out and scattered them on the bed and on the floor to make sure it didn't look too clean. I looked under the bed, got the used condom and put that in the bag as well. The upstairs clean, I paused to think where else I had been. Or rather, where else I had been that I shouldn't. Or that I couldn't go to when the team turned up. With an old case like this, they'd be less careful about spreading their own DNA around. I would follow them to as many of the rooms as I could. There were used wine glasses, but I was leaving those. I wasn't going to hide that I'd been here. I just needed to hide what we'd done for about two hours of the time.

What we had done.

What we had done and why he'd done it.

I had never been used like this. I opened the door to the downstairs bathroom and vomited violently. In my mind I said it out loud: it was the thought that I'd been drinking with this murderer. That would be a good enough excuse. I flushed but didn't scrub. I put all the cleaning things back in the cupboard in the kitchen. I went outside and put the bin bag in the boot of the car. I'd burn that later. He wouldn't win.

When I was finally ready, I went out to the garden and started to dig.

I would like to think that I did the right thing, because the case would have never come to court otherwise, but today, sitting on the sofa in my father's house, I couldn't accept that I had.

'I'm not sure I dealt with the situation well,' I said to my father.

'You're not responsible for other people's crimes, but you are responsible for getting them in front of a judge. And you did that, didn't you?'

'Yes, I did.'

'Then you shouldn't feel guilty.'

I wasn't sure I agreed with him. I wasn't yet as jaded as his words suggested he was. But I did feel a glimmer of hope that I could at some point be of the same opinion as my father. Maybe by the time I'd retired, after another twenty years of work, I could look back at this episode and think I'd done well, because I found Wendy's body and got her murderer the punishment he deserved.

'It's not knowing why he murdered her,' I said. 'It haunts me at night.' That and wondering if I hadn't been just as calculating as Paul.

'In some of my cases I thought that even the murderers didn't know why they'd killed. A sudden flash of anger, a punch that was harder than intended. It's possible he never meant to do it.'

I wanted to change the subject and was reminded of something that my father had said earlier on. 'You mentioned that Anton told you he was fed up with lying.' The words had stuck in my mind because they were so similar to what Paul Leeuwenhoek had said to me. I no longer believed that this was the reason why Paul had told me part of the truth.

'Yes – he said that he wanted to come clean.'

'Any idea what he was going to tell us?'

'How he got those files, I think.'

'He couldn't have had much time . . .'

'He wouldn't have needed much time. It doesn't take long to get here from Bergen. He could have called some of his friends.'

'But someone must have told him to come for those files though. That's what puzzles me. We're going to use those Photofits . . .'

'You're not going to use anything. You're not working on it any more,' my father said gently.

'Was it wise to give Ronald your shoes?' I asked after a few silent sips of my coffee.

'What else was I going to do? Refuse? He would have been back tomorrow with a search warrant.'

I nodded because I knew he was right, but I wasn't happy about it. 'You've got to be careful. Get yourself a lawyer.'

'I didn't do anything.'

'Since when does that matter?'

My father pulled a face at my cynicism. 'It'll come out anyway, that I was there. Karin opened the door. She saw me.'

'Yes, she told me that.' Ronald's words about interviewing her seemed more ominous. 'How can there be only two sets of footprints if you saw those files and later they were gone? Somebody must have gone to the shed after you.'

'Anton?'

'Maybe. Was Anton forced to retrieve those crates by his killer?' I said the hypothesis out loud to hear what it sounded like. 'But then there would be three sets of footprints, of which two were Anton's.'

'It's not your case any more, Lotte.'

'Those files . . .' I knew he was right but my brain followed the track it had started on. 'You saw them in the shed. But when Ronald turns up, not that much later, they're gone. Someone keeps moving them in the nick of time. Be careful, Dad.'

On the drive home I put the music on as loud as I could and sang along, purely to keep awake. My eyelids were heavy and my arms were only kept up by the steering wheel. I found it hard to focus on anything other than the traffic ahead of me on the long straight road south. My thoughts tumbled around in my head. Ronald had collected my father's shoes; only two sets of footsteps went out to the shed; Ronald was married to Ilse, the receptionist. I had to trust Ronald and Hans to figure out what had happened now. I was off the case; I should just sleep.

Finally in my study, I looked at the drawing on the architect's table, then got a blue marker pen out and drew in my views. With each line and square I got more despondent. I should not have been suspended. I could have solved this case if only they'd let me. I would not have been suspended if I hadn't tried to cover for my father. I had tried to be a saviour, to sacrifice myself for somebody who didn't need any help — as futile a gesture as that of my colleague who nearly drowned in an Amsterdam canal after jumping in to rescue someone who was practising for a triathlon. Why was

I still working on this, still thinking about it, when the chief inspector didn't want me to?

I wasn't needed any more and I couldn't block the bad thoughts about Paul Leeuwenhoek any longer with the dam that work used to form. Gripping my marker pen tight in my fist, I destroyed my carefully outlined arrows and squares with thick lines. I pressed too hard and tore the paper from one of its bindings. Then I cast my pen into the corner, went to my bedroom, undressed and sat on the edge of my bed. What was I going to do tomorrow, and the day after, and the day after that? I tipped a large number of blue pills into the palm of my hand.

Chapter Twenty-six

The doorbell woke me up at 9.22 a.m. There was pressure on my bladder. I tested the temperature in the flat with a big toe, only to put it hastily right back under the duvet. I held out for ten minutes or so, then the need to pee won out over the need for warmth. I'd forgotten to turn the heating on and started to shiver as soon as I was up. I wrapped my dressing gown around me and protected my cold toes with woollen slippers. The doorbell rang again. The bathroom was freezing; ice flowers covered the glass and a cold draught whistled in from around the window and hit my face. I emptied myself and smelled the sweet strong odour that told me I was dehydrated. The doorbell rang again; this was the third time maybe. Then the phone rang. Ignoring both, I ran back to bed to stuff my frozen feet under the duvet.

Someone banged on my front door. I pulled the duvet over my head to make the world go away but the banging got louder and louder until it sounded like someone bringing a hammer down on the wood. I rolled out of bed and stumbled down to the door, calling out, 'I'm coming.'

'Lotte? Lotte!' a man's voice shouted at the top of his lungs.

When I opened, Hans was waiting on the other side, rubbing his bruised hand, anger showing in his face. 'You're not answering your phone, not answering the doorbell?'

I tried to tidy my hair, which felt as if it was alternately spiked up and flattened like a hedgehog road-kill.

'I was in bed.' The stink of my own morning breath was embarrassing and the odour of sleep lingered around me.

'In bed?' He was shouting again.

I tried to rub away the effects of the last pill I took – this morning? Yesterday? – from the corners of my brain. 'What day is it?' My words sounded croaky, my voice unused to speaking.

'Are you OK? Are you ill?' His anger melted into concern. 'It's Monday morning.'

I coughed and swayed on my feet from the movement. I hadn't eaten in days. 'Not ill, just exhausted. I've slept for a few days.' My body had demanded it, but I had been helped by pills. During the last forty-eight hours I'd only got out of bed to use the loo and to fill up my water glass to quench my thirst and swallow more pills. Four pills, two more pills and then two more pills. Two days had disappeared from my life, turned into shadows.

'Days? So you don't know . . .'

'Know what?' I hugged my arms around my waist to protect myself against what was coming. I was shivering in my night-clothes.

302

'Get dressed.' He said it quietly and it scared me. 'You get dressed, I'll make you some coffee. Do you have any food?'

'There'll be something in the kitchen. I had some bread but it might be stale by now.' In the bedroom, the door shut, I quickly threw on jeans and a jumper plus thick socks. I heard him rummaging around in the kitchen. Then his footsteps came down the hall and stopped outside the door.

'I telephoned. Then I sent you a text. Yesterday. Didn't you get it?'

'I was asleep, Hans.' The telephone had woken me up a couple of times but its shrill voice was in the other room, muffled by closed doors in between, so it had been easy to ignore. I had just pulled the duvet tight around me. When the phone rang again, I'd thought that if it was important enough, they'd leave a message. I'd reached out and taken two more pills, to make more time disappear.

Now I opened the bedroom door.

Hans raised his hands in an apology. 'I'm sorry I shouted. I was just worried.'

I rested against the doorframe.

'What have you been taking?' He pushed past me into my bedroom and picked up the amber bottle of pills.

'Prescription. To make me sleep.'

'How many?' He came up to me, held me by the chin and looked into my eyes, like we did with the druggies we found asleep on park benches. 'How many?' he said again when I didn't reply.

I shrugged. 'A few.'

'Coffee,' he said.

I went to the kitchen to finish making it. The bread was only good enough for toast. No time for that. There had to be a packet of biscuits somewhere. I opened a few cupboards. He followed me and continued talking. 'I know how down you've been, and now with your suspension . . . I was concerned I would find you – well, you know what I mean,' he cleared his throat, 'just a little worse than I actually did find you.'

I poured the coffee and felt tears well up in my eyes. Partly because I was touched by his concern and partly because I hadn't eaten in ages. 'Oh Hans,' I said. And I followed it with, 'I'm OK.' The automatic lie rolled easily off my tongue. 'I'm OK,' I repeated, as much to myself as to him. I found a pack of *speculaas* biscuits and opened them. I hadn't had time to comb my hair. But I didn't fix it. I just sat on my sofa, held my coffee and ate two biscuits in quick succession. My stomach cramped at the sudden food and sugar rush.

Hans looked at me intently, then said, 'Lotte, I've got some bad news.'

I held my mug so tight I was afraid I'd snap the handle. 'What's happened?'

'Piet Huizen. Your father. He's—'

In that second, in that instant, I saw my father dead in the snow, a bullet wound in his left temple, so that when Hans said, 'He's been arrested,' it was almost good news. Of course it wasn't.

'You phoned me?' This time my father had really needed me and I didn't know anything about it. I should have felt it. I should have woken up.

'Of course. Look at your answer machine.' The display said there were twelve messages. He frowned. 'These aren't all from me.'

'What's he been arrested for? When did this happen?'

'Anton Lantinga's murder. Yesterday evening.'

I drained my coffee and poured myself a refill. 'Did Karin ...' My head felt light and airy, as if open to new ideas, devoid of old thoughts, old mental baggage.

'She said she saw him. She said she opened the door.'

'But he never denied that.'

'You've also got to see this.' He showed me the list of the people who'd worked at Petersen Capital, the list I had been going through when I was summoned by the prosecutor. Hans held out the second page of names to me, the one I hadn't seen before. The familiar name was far down the list, only about ten from the bottom, and as soon as I saw it, it hit me in the stomach. Wouter Vos. Alkmaar's witness had worked at Petersen Capital.

'He was the head of IT,' Hans said.

'So that disk, the one that the whistle-blower sent—'

'Could easily have come from him.'

If only I'd known that when I'd seen my father last. 'Anton didn't just call us, he called my father too. Told him he wanted to come clean. My father went, saw the files but Anton told him that I was coming later, so my father left them there for me. But then they disappeared. I told you that. Didn't I tell you that?' I drank the coffee in gulps, I was so thirsty.

'No, you didn't.'

'My father told me after I'd already been suspended. Anyway, I didn't look for the files; the Alkmaar police did. But that could have been much later.' I finished my cup and filled it up again. My heartbeat bounced through the veins in my neck and even without pressing my fingers to the arteries I could measure my pulse.

I beckoned to Hans to follow me to my study. 'Here.' I pointed at Friday night's additions, the changes to my drawing, half-hidden under the destructive thick marker pen cross-outs I'd made before I'd taken the first pills. 'Sorry about the mess – can you still see the writing?' I waited for Hans's nod. I then got my pen out and drew a pleasing arc that connected the whistle-blower box to Wouter Vos. 'What if Otto Petersen wanted to meet the man who had destroyed his company? By saying that he saw Anton Lantinga's car just before Otto's murder, Wouter Vos has admitted he was at the scene of the crime.'

Hans stared at the sheet of paper on the architect's table. 'We thought about that, but what about your father?' he said softly, carefully. 'When I look at this,' he pointed at the paper, 'you knew that he was at Anton's house and you think he was paid by him.'

I walked out of the study. My footsteps sounded surer than I felt. I dropped my body on the sofa and drained the rest of my coffee. 'Not any more. I don't think that any more.'

'Lotte . . .' Hans had followed me.

'What are you going to do next?'

'We've got Karin coming in for questioning this morning.'

306

'Great.' I put my mug on the table and got up again. I paced around the apartment.

'Lotte, slow down. You're hyper from the coffee.'

'Do we have time to slow down? My father is in prison.' I walked to the window and saw a group of children throwing snowballs. 'Can't believe it's still not thawing.'

'Lotte, please sit down. You're making me nervous.'

I did as he told me.

'So what did your father say when you saw him on Friday?'

'As I said, that he saw Anton. Ronald turned up.'

'Yes, at Anton's house, we know.'

'No, I meant at my father's place. He took his shoes.'

'What are you talking about?'

'Ronald took my father's shoes – on Friday when I was there. Said he saw his footsteps going to the shed. The shed with the files.'

'So Ronald knew where the files were?'

'I think so. I think my father told him. I told my father he should be careful. I told him to get a lawyer.'

'I'm sure he's got one now. You should have let me know he was your father.'

'I had to protect him. You know, he and my mother divorced when I was just little.'

'You didn't see him later, when you grew up?'

'Yes, a bit, but Mum always made that difficult. So my father and I never really had a chance to get to know each other; it never seemed worth it, the hassle my mother gave me. I thought he didn't love me, but he did.'

307

The words flowed out of my mouth. It was strange how simple it was to admit this. This morning, everything was crystal clear. A wonderful sense of omniscience had taken over. Thoughts tumbled in my mind like somersaulting acrobats. Sentences toppled off my tongue to keep up.

'Lotte, calm down.'

Hans's words were less important to me than my own thoughts – the realisation that my mother had tried to make things difficult from the beginning – but I stopped talking.

'Stefanie and I talked on Friday, after you left . . .' Hans brought me back to the present.

'That bitch. She got me suspended.'

'No. It wasn't her.'

'So how did he find out?'

'Ronald de Boer. *He* called the boss.'

I gasped. 'Are you sure?'

'Absolutely.'

'But that doesn't make any sense. Why would he—'

'Apparently he thought he had no choice. You were not objective any more. You weren't seeing things clearly. You were hampering his investigation.'

He'd said he would protect me, but instead he'd handed both me and my father over to the police. I remembered how friendly he'd been with Wouter Vos, that first time he'd introduced me to him. I remembered that I'd even mentioned it to Stefanie.

'I don't know what to believe,' Hans said, 'but I owe you one for Wendy Leeuwenhoek. You were right and I was wrong, so this time I'll give you the benefit of the doubt.'

I almost cried at the thought that Hans felt he owed me. In fact, he had no idea what he owed me for.

In the dark of night, when I felt worst about myself, I wanted to believe that I would not have slept with a murderer if we hadn't arrested the wrong man.

Hans said, 'Stefanie and I have gone through the Petersen Capital files over the last couple of days, and his old business partner Geert-Jan Goosens told the truth: all that money *was* lost in the market. Otto was covering up, hiding the enormous losses. Maybe that's why Karin's already back at work: making sure something like that doesn't happen again.'

'She's back? That's quick.'

'Almost immediately. We'll question her about those files and ask if somebody else came after your father. Maybe she saw your father leave.'

'And ask about Wouter Vos. That's key.' I'd love to see Karin's face when Hans mentioned Vos. 'You must let me watch.'

'Don't be stupid. You're suspended, remember? What do you think you can do?'

'I need to get my father out of prison.'

Hans stared at me. The high-pitched screams of the playing children drifted in. He pushed his body out of the chair. 'If you can get in without being seen . . .' he said.

'Thanks, Hans.'

He let himself out.

After the door had slammed shut, I pressed the play button on the voicemail. The first one was from Hans. I deleted it. The second was Hans too. I deleted that as well, I knew what he'd had to say.

Next was a woman's voice. *'Hi, Lotte. This is Maaike.'* I sat down and rested my head in my hands. I knew what my father's wife was calling about. *'Sorry to call but I think you should know – but maybe you know already – do you know already? Piet has been arrested. Please call me back. The number is . . .'* She said the digits so quickly, I would have had to play the tape at least three times before I got it, and I couldn't have listened to that woman's voice that often. Beep. I pressed delete.

The next message came fifteen minutes later. It was Maaike again. *'You haven't called me back yet. I tried at your work but they told me you weren't there. Please phone me. Your father needs your help.'*

Beep.

'Hi, Lotte. Maaike again.' Now her voice sounded less certain, less businesslike. It wobbled and warbled. *'Could you please call me? I've left two messages already and a couple on your mobile too. I can't imagine you haven't been getting these, so I must assume you don't want to speak to me. But please, help me.'*

Beep.

'It's now three hours since your father was arrested.' Her voice broke and I could hear her blow her nose. *'You didn't do that, did you? He is an old man. He has a weak heart. I know you don't like me, I know you blame me, but please, your father needs your help. I know you don't get on, I know you were hurt when he didn't see you as a child, but that's no reason to take revenge on an old man. He said . . . he said that you were getting on better.*

310

That you were talking again. You know he didn't kill Anton, you know he didn't do anything like that, so please let him go.'

Beep.

A couple of audible intakes and exhales of breath. *'Sorry about what I said earlier. I now know you've been suspended, so I know you couldn't have arrested him. But did you say something to Ronald? He wouldn't have done this otherwise. If you could call me back, that would be great. I arranged for a lawyer hours ago, so I'm not calling about that, but the lawyer said it would really help if you could call him. His number is . . .'* she rattled through another eight-digit number. *'If you don't want to talk to me, could you please call him?'*

Beep.

Beep.

Beep.

Beep.

And a last message that was from Hans again.

It was almost ten. I might as well walk to the police station, so I'd be there when Karin turned up. I hoped they hadn't yet cancelled my swipe card. I didn't want to contact Maaike, but I'd do whatever I needed to, to get my father out.

311

Chapter Twenty-seven

My hand trembled as I put my swipe card in the reader. It bleeped green. This had been my sanctuary, the place that had protected me against the harsh outside world. Now the white iron rails of the gate clicked shut behind me like the bars of a prison cell. The courtyard garden was still frozen. Jewelled ice particles glittered on the leaves of a plant in a rare ray of sun; snow covered the roots of shrubs and drips of water fell from melting icicles. I waited in the small white garden for a few visible breaths and enjoyed the feeling of the cold air nibbling at my cheeks. Inside, my ex-colleagues would mill around, chat and look at me. My heartbeat raced in guilty anticipation of detection. I took one more deep breath, then pushed open the door and went in. Nobody stopped me. They probably didn't even know I was suspended. I wanted to run to the interrogation rooms, but forced my footsteps to be slow and deliberate, to appear as if I still belonged here – as if I still had a job to do. It was five past ten when I ducked into the protective half-dark of the observation area.

The interview could have only just started, as Hans was

still shuffling papers around and the lawyer was whispering something to his client. I got my notepad out and my pen, placed my handbag carefully by my feet and pulled my chair close to the wooden shelf. It was the same interrogation room Ben van Ravensberger had been in two weeks ago. This felt so different: gone was my sense of belonging; gone was my belief that I was at home here, regardless of what I'd done. Today I was an outsider, merely acting the part of a police officer.

'The murder of your husband,' Stefanie said. I could see only the back of her head, the reddish-blonde hair a blunt straight line across her grey suit. She must have thought it looked more professional, this subdued colour, than her usual bright ones. I wished I had something to eat, but it wasn't worth the risk to go to the canteen. Instead I sank down on my chair, as low as I could get, picked up my pen and doodled on my notepad.

'Which one?' Karin looked like the woman we had met for the first time at Omega. The scared, defensive creature huddled in the corner of a room had gone and Grace Kelly was back. Her hands rested on the table. She wore a black suit with a round collar and a white blouse with the top two buttons undone. She was with her lawyer, a man about ten years younger than she was.

'That of your first husband. Otto Petersen. Your second husband, Anton, was a suspect in that case.'

'Incorrectly so.'

'So it now seems. There was evidence in that case – paperwork, reports – that went missing.'

313

Karin sneered, 'That was careless of you.'

'And those files were seen in your shed, the night before Anton was killed.'

'So you must have them back then.' Her hand went up to a triple string of pearls. I moved forward, my nose nearly touching the glass, to get a closer look at them. The necklace was the same one she had been touching compulsively after her husband's death. The deep lines around her eyes were no longer as deep as they were on that night, but still red.

'They weren't there any more.'

'You searched the place afterwards. Every centimetre of it, it seemed. If they were there, you must have found them.' She sighed pointedly. 'Are you saying you lost them again?'

Stefanie ignored her needling. 'Do you know what happened to them, after Anton died?' I fidgeted on my chair. Yes, those files were important, but could we get to the more crucial part? I wanted to scream through the glass: *Please, Karin, tell the truth. Tell Stefanie and Hans that Anton was still alive and well after my father left and that somebody else came to the house later.*

'No, I don't.'

'We believe you or Anton were involved in taking those files from the Alkmaar police station under false pretences.'

'I don't know anything about that.'

Stefanie leaned back on her chair. 'Two people, well known to you, went to the Alkmaar police station, impersonating police officers.'

The door clicked open behind me and the sound made me jump. I kept the back of my head turned, hoping they wouldn't recognise me. After three heartbeats the door closed again. I waited for the sound of footsteps. None came. Whoever had come in must be waiting just outside. They must be staring at me. The skin on my neck crawled with goosebumps. I drew some circles on my notepad.

'I don't know anything about that,' Karin repeated. Her voice sounded the same as it did before, full of defiance. She turned the large ring on her left hand around and around with her thumb. Her nails were short, last week's French manicure bitten away. She scratched her skin under the sleeve of the jacket.

'Mrs Lantinga, we need to know what happened to those files. We're not going to prosecute you if you organised it, we just want to know. It's crucial with regard to finding the murderer', Hans paused and gestured with his large hand, 'of both your husbands.' He moved to the right and his bulk blocked my view. I turned round carefully, but there was no one there. The corridor behind the observation rooms was empty. Somebody must have changed their mind, or turned up at the wrong room.

Karin's face went a little paler as if dusted with a lighter colour powder, but she didn't say anything, just blinked three times.

'Mrs Lantinga,' Hans said, 'could you please tell us if you recognise these people.' He pushed the two Photofits across the table. At one stage this had been important, these two bits of paper with strange faces on them. Now they were a delay. I ripped the first page with circles off my notepad and made a tear in the corner.

Karin looked at the photos and her face turned into a mask. The muscles around her jaw tightened. She slowly shook her head. 'No, I don't.'

'Please, have another look. We think they might have worked for you at Omega, or even at Petersen Capital.'

She pretended to look. I couldn't tell exactly where her eyes went, but it seemed slightly above the photos. She sat back and shook her head again.

'It's no use.' Stefanie leaned forward, her arms folded on the table. 'We will go through everybody who worked at either firm, every friend of yours, every relative of you or Anton, and we'll find who those people are. It will just take us longer and that is time we could use in tracking Anton's murderer.'

'But the police from Alkmaar are working on that, aren't they? DI de Boer came to see me yesterday and the day before.'

Stefanie nodded. 'Yes, we're working closely together with them. Now please answer our questions.'

Karin stared at a point over Stefanie's shoulder. Our eyes almost met; she seemed to be looking at my left ear. I was surprised she'd come into work today, her husband only dead five days, but when it was your business, you didn't have much choice. And, as my father had said, work helped you forget. Or took your mind off it at least.

'And DI de Boer is coming to the office again this afternoon, isn't he?' She looked at her lawyer.

'Yes, at two o'clock,' the lawyer said. 'So I would very much like to know why you have my client here now.'

316

The door clicked open again. This time there were foot-steps too. I sank down in my chair, hoping it was an observer for another room.

Hans ignored the lawyer and kept questioning Karin. 'Your husband, Anton, admitted he took those files.'

'Did he?'

'To DI Huizen.'

She rested her chin on her hand, the large square-cut stone of her ring on display, and smiled.

The steps came towards me. I didn't look up but kept staring at the window, hoping whoever it was wouldn't know I'd been suspended.

Her lawyer said, 'I believe she has answered this question a few times now.'

'She hasn't answered it,' Stefanie replied sharply.

'What the hell are *you* doing here?' whispered a soft voice behind me, straight into my ear. I nearly jumped up off my chair. It was CI Moerdijk.

'How did you get in?' he asked.

I showed him my pass. Without a word he took it out of my hand and put it in his pocket. I expected him to throw me out, any minute now. I waited for his hand on my arm, dragging me out of this observation area. I could almost feel it around my elbow. 'Please don't make me leave before I've saved my father,' I breathed, but I didn't say the words out loud.

'Can you tell me about your working relationship with Wouter Vos?' Hans was saying.

The lawyer in the room sat forward. 'My client isn't answering that,' he said.

'Surely she can tell us if she knows him.'

Karin turned the large ring round and around her finger with her thumb before folding her hands in front of her.

'We've got him here as head of IT at Petersen Capital in 1995. He's on the list of the tax office,' Hans went on.

I didn't look away from her defiant face. 'Vos was Alkmaar's witness,' I said aloud. 'He worked for Petersen Capital. Was their head of IT.'

'So I heard. Did your father know that?' The CI spat out the words. It was an accusation.

'They arrested my father last night,' I said. I shouldn't have been asleep.

In the shadowy light of the observation area I turned to look at the CI. His thin preacher's face didn't smile at me. He got a small notepad from his jacket pocket and put it on the ledge in front of us. I moved mine further along, then looked back to the window.

'You've got to leave, Lotte.' Moerdijk's voice sounded weary. 'You can't be in here.'

I couldn't respond.

'Lotte, did you hear me?' Here was the anticipated hand on my arm, the pressure I had been expecting. I nodded and got up, tears in my eyes because I hadn't achieved anything, hadn't heard anything that made a difference. I had failed. Failed my father.

'Yes, he worked for us.' In the room, Karin said it so softly that I only just caught the words over the sound of my chair scraping the floor as I pushed it back. I didn't know why it was different to hear her say it. I'd seen his name on that list, I knew he'd worked there, but to hear it coming from Karin's mouth made it more real. Wouter Vos with a motive to kill Otto Petersen. Ronald's schoolfriend. Concern about my father made my breakfast of biscuits stomp around in my stomach.

The hand on my arm propelled me towards the door, away from the window where all the important things were happening. I had to count on Hans and Stefanie to finish what I'd started.

On the other side of the door, the hand let go of my upper arm. The CI closed the door and removed any view of the observation area from my field of vision. Everything was lost and over, and I felt sick as I walked towards the exit with my boss. I was lost for words until we got to the garden. This was my last chance to ask something before I was evicted through the white gates.

'Who went to collect them?' I asked.

He frowned. 'Collect what?'

'The files on the Otto Petersen case.'

He stayed quiet. A blackbird hopped around the roots of the plants, black against the snow. 'I went by myself,' the CI said. 'I drove to Alkmaar, to the police station, spoke to the receptionist and she gave me one cardboard folder.'

'Gave it?'

'Yes. I asked her if there was more, but she told me that was it.'

'What did the receptionist look like?'

'Lotte, it was more than ten years ago . . .'

The blackbird flew from the ground and landed in a tree, calling out his displeasure at our presence in beautiful tones.

The CI said, 'I think she was young, with blonde hair, creamy skin – looked like a farmer's daughter.'

Ronald's wife had already been on Reception then? Ronald's friend the witness had admitted to us that Ronald had been at Petersen's house just before Petersen was shot. His wife made those files disappear. Two sets of footprints were actually *three* sets of footprints after the investigating police officer had walked to the shed to check on the files. All the important information had been in my boss's hands, the hands that now shoved me through the gates, the hands that closed it with a bang behind me. From the other side of the white bars the CI looked at me, his angry face cut into segments by the vertical bars, waiting until I walked away.

I didn't go far, just turned left and left again, until I was at the other side of the canal at the back of the police station. I texted Hans: *CI caught me, call me*, and waited. The statue on the wall of the new part of the station was Lady Justice, but a vengeful one, leaning her weight on the Sword of Power, ready to wield it when necessary, almost inviting enemies to attack her, so that she could strike and get the sword's edge bloody. She glowered at me for my lack of progress, annoyed by my attitude. *'Don't you dare give up,'* her eyes told me. *'Don't you dare.'* I smiled grimly at her: *'Don't worry, I'll keep going.'* I waited for a few minutes. I knew where Stefanie and Hans had to go next.

Chapter Twenty-eight

There had been discussions before we'd headed north to Alkmaar: all about procedures and rules and regulations, none about where we were going. Stefanie didn't want to use the recording equipment without the proper paperwork, but she agreed when I apologised for shouting at her after I'd been suspended. She in turn apologised for trying to pin something on my father. I was about to thank her when she followed up by saying that I couldn't blame her for thinking as she had. I explained that my father had made all his money from marrying a rich wife, to which she laughed and meanly replied, 'Like father, like daughter then.' It washed away any good feelings I had towards her.

Hans and Stefanie got out of the car at Wouter's apartment block and I moved to the front seat. It looked less suspicious that way. Stefanie's car smelled of stale cigarette smoke, and sweet wrappers littered the floor.

'Can you hear us?' Hans asked.

I raised my thumb to him through the windscreen. It was odd to be without the weight of the gun on my hip. There was an empty packet of cigarettes on the dashboard. I watched Hans and Stefanie as they entered the apartment building. Stefanie reached no higher than his armpit and Hans took small slow steps to make sure she could keep up with him. They went up the stairs Ronald and I had gone up two weeks ago.

What a risk Ronald had taken, I thought now, introducing me to Wouter so early on. If he had played things differently, if he hadn't tried to get me worried about my father, would I have dropped the case? After that first trip to Alkmaar it had been clear that Otto Petersen's murder wasn't committed by Ferdinand van Ravensberger, whatever his nephew might have said. I could imagine a situation where we would have realised early on that Ben van Ravensberger had been using a lot of coke and had tried to blackmail his uncle. We probably would have dropped the case at that point. Otto Petersen's murder would still remain open and Anton Lantinga would still be alive. But because Ronald had tried to frame my father for the stolen files, to get me to abandon this case, I'd stuck with it and he'd achieved the complete opposite.

However, I also remembered the conversation with the CI where I'd told him about Alkmaar's witness and I had to admit to myself that if I hadn't been trying to cover up what had happened in the Wendy Leeuwenhoek investigation, I would probably have done what Ronald had intended. When I'd continued to investigate Otto Petersen's murder, Ronald had upped the ante, got me suspended and my father arrested.

What a shame that this was all speculation and that I didn't have a shred of evidence to support my case. There was nothing to say that Wouter Vos had really been the whistle-blower other than that he would have had the opportunity and that he had kept quiet about working for Petersen Capital. But I would obtain the facts because that would get my father out of jail.

I sat in Stefanie's car, in Stefanie's seat behind the steering wheel and waited. I heard the doorbell ring. I heard the door open. I stayed silent. It felt as if they would be able to hear me if I talked.

'Good morning, Wouter,' Stefanie said. 'Amsterdam police. Can we come in for a minute?' Her voice rang loud in my ear.

'Of course. I haven't got much time, but come in.' Wouter sounded relaxed, just as he'd done when we met. He'd been such a credible witness. As Stefanie had said, we all liked the geek-done-good.

Footsteps down the hallway. I could picture them moving past the art collection into the sitting room.

'Good to see you again. Where is your colleague who was here the other week?' Wouter asked.

'Detective Meerman? She came here with Ronald de Boer as well, didn't she? You know him well?' This was Hans at his least threatening, his this-is-just-a-little-chat tone of voice.

'Yes, we were at school together.'

'Friends?'

'Best friends.' He said it with a hint of laughter in his voice. 'You know what it's like at that age.'

'Some of those friendships are made for life.'

Wouter didn't say anything.

323

'Anyway,' Stefanie went on, 'we're here to check some details on your testimony.'

'Of course. Well, I saw Anton Lantinga's car—'

'No, not that witness statement.' She was silent for five or six seconds, gave him just enough time to realise what she was talking about. 'We want to ask about an earlier case, the one that put Otto Petersen in jail. The Petersen Capital fraud.' The tone of her voice didn't change. It sounded like a throwaway remark, an unimportant question, wanting a quick unimportant answer. 'You were the whistle-blower, weren't you?'

'No.' The response came too quickly after the question. I'd expected him to be more polished, to claim he didn't know anything about it. Without Ronald in the room, he seemed to have lost his cool.

'No? We have the files here.'

I heard the whispering sound of turning pages.

'You were the head of IT at Petersen Capital in 1995, weren't you?'

'No, not the head. I just worked there.'

'It says head of IT in the company's tax records.'

'I suppose . . . I was the only one in that department, so that must have made me the head. It didn't feel like it, and they didn't pay me like one either.' I heard a laugh that turned into a cough. I assumed it was Wouter.

'Someone sent a computer disk to the Financial Fraud department of the Amsterdam police in 1995. It contained two spreadsheets – one, I assume, Otto's official numbers, which he sent out to the investors – and the other, the real numbers, showing the losses he'd made and was so desperately trying to hide.'

'Let me see that disk.' A short pause. The rustle of the padded paper envelope Stefanie had brought with her. 'That's not right.' His voice sounded purposeful, maybe some relief mixed in. 'We didn't use this type of disk in 1995. Whatever evidence you have, this isn't it.'

'No, of course not. This is our copy of the disk. The original is filed away. What happened, Wouter? Did you see that Otto had two spreadsheets? Did he ask you for help, maybe asked you to retrieve one from the back-up? When did you notice he was cheating?'

Still more silence.

Hans said, 'Otto figured out who ratted on him. So when he got out of jail he wanted to meet you, is that it? He asked you to come to the house.'

I was reminded of Otto's mother's words, that this had all been about betrayal and that Otto Petersen had cared more about his company than his wife.

'But you saw Anton's car there. Did he see you too? He might have done. And when things went wrong and you killed Otto – where did you get the gun from, by the way?' She waited for a bit longer but Wouter didn't respond. 'Then you thought up a plan to throw the suspicion on Anton instead. His word against yours. Was that what you thought? And as long as we didn't know you were the whistle-blower, nothing linked you to Otto Petersen. You were just an innocent bystander. And as you were Ronald's friend, the police – Piet Huizen and Ronald de Boer – would always believe you, wouldn't they?'

'I want a lawyer.' I'd known he'd say that; it was only a matter of time.

'Fuck. Sorry.' The sorry was more to me than to Wouter. 'Of course, feel free to make the call.'

I heard Wouter say, 'I think we're in trouble.' His voice was getting softer – he must be walking out of the room.

Condensation drew in from the corners of the car window, turning it opaque. I made no effort to wipe it away. I didn't have to see out anyway and I'd be here for a while. Stefanie and Hans would have to wait for the lawyer to turn up before they could continue their questioning. The snow outside melted on the car. Water ran from the windscreen. I looked at my watch: it was just after midday. We still had two hours before Ronald met with Karin. Ronald, who might have advised Wouter to act as a witness and to use that as a cover. Ronald, who could have arranged for those files to vanish with help from his wife on Reception. He could have called Anton as soon as he'd heard my father was off the case. That must have been a nasty surprise. He must have trusted that he'd take over, but when that didn't happen he'd reacted quickly and got Wouter's name out of the equation. Taking the files made Wouter's witness statement disappear so that CI Moerdijk never even knew that Wouter existed. Ronald had never responded to CI Moerdijk, not to cover for my father, but to cover for his friend. Then he'd tried to manipulate me by throwing suspicion on my father,

326

suspicions I was all too ready to believe. I rested my head against the window. The cold of the glass soothed my mind.

I could check if any of this speculation was fact by talking to Ronald's wife, Ilse, on Reception.

I could talk to her, I calculated, and be back here before Hans and Stefanie would even notice I'd gone.

I switched on the car heater to blow over the windows and demist them, hearing the minutes tick away while I waited for visibility to return. I found the lever at the bottom of the driver's seat and used it to push the chair back until I could reach the pedals without bumping my knees on the steering wheel. I clicked the seatbelt in place, turned the key in the ignition of Stefanie's car and checked the mirrors before adjusting them, so I could put them back in their original position before handing the car back to Stefanie. Then I eased the car into reverse and drove to the Alkmaar police station.

I walked into Reception, tape recorder switched on in my pocket. Did Ilse know I'd been suspended? She was on the phone, neck straight, head straight, headset covering one ear, her butter-blonde hair tucked behind the other, exposing the milk-and-cream skin of her cheek. I pictured her light colouring besides Ronald's darkness. She saw me but didn't interrupt her call. I waited and watched people walk in and out. I hadn't thought of what I'd do if Ronald came in. I looked at my watch; it was half past twelve, one and a half hours before he was due to meet Karin in Amsterdam. Maybe that was him on the phone to Ilse.

She finally finished her call and said, 'Yes, what can I do for you? Ronald isn't here right now.'

327

I smiled, assumed my most relaxed pretend-nice face. 'That's a shame. I just popped in to see if he wanted a coffee.' I gestured at the car outside. 'I'm waiting for my father to get out.'

'Your father?' Her face looked blank. So Ronald hadn't told her.

'Yes, Piet Huizen. He used to work with Ronald. Surely you must remember him.'

'Oh yes, of course. We all liked him a lot.'

I smiled, pretending gratitude this time.

'It doesn't seem that long since his retirement,' she said.

'Twelve years.'

She nodded pensively.

'You must remember his last day here,' I said.

'We were all so concerned, after the heart attack.'

'My father told me you sent him flowers.' He hadn't said anything of the kind, but she would have done; she was the type.

'Yes, I did. Because I felt so guilty. I should have given him a hand.'

'With?' My heart thumped in my chest but I managed to keep my voice steady.

'Carrying those crates. He was dragging them down the stairs as the lift was out of order – I remember it well. He put them over there in the corner.' She pointed, but her arm drooped and her voice petered out at the sight of my too-real, triumphant smile.

'That's not what you told us when we took over. Our chief inspector, who worked the case, said you gave him a

328

cardboard folder with only a few pages in it. Did Ronald help you pick which bits to keep behind?' Ronald should have briefed his wife better, told her what she should and shouldn't tell me. Maybe Ronald hadn't instructed her at all because he was worried she might talk. She seemed a nice enough woman; maybe he hadn't mentioned anything about Wouter, my father, Otto Petersen and Anton Lantinga. I stared at her milk-white skin, the faltering smile on her pink lips.

She blinked a few times and tucked more hair behind her ear.

I leaned on the reception desk, purposefully moving my body into her space. 'It was a perfect selection, enough to make us think the Alkmaar police were incompetent and not to draw any suspicion. Ronald did a good job there.' I took my mobile phone out and slowly took a picture of Ilse, to show the CI. Not that there was any doubt in my mind.

'Well, no,' she said, 'I didn't—'

'Didn't meet with our chief inspector? He says you did. He says you gave him the cardboard folder. Are you saying he's lying?'

'No, no, I did give him that, but—'

'You just told me you saw my father carry crates of files down the stairs. Now you admitted you gave CI Moerdijk just six pages.' I took the tape recorder from my pocket and pressed the stop button in full sight of her. 'Thanks, Ilse. Much appreciated.'

She didn't say anything, just stared at me. A bright red blush crept up from her neck to her cheeks. I knew she'd call Ronald as soon as I'd gone.

As I walked towards the exit, my eyes scanned every person who walked down the steps, every individual who came through a corridor, to see if Ronald was coming back to work. I wasn't sure what I'd do if I saw him, but because of him my father had spent the night in prison. It was easier to blame Ronald than to acknowledge that my father wasn't free because I'd taken my tablets and slept. I needed to make sure he wouldn't spend another night locked up, and for that I had to get Karin to admit that Wouter Vos had turned up on their doorstep *after* my father had left.

I got in Stefanie's car and sped down Alkmaar's streets. The wheels of the car chewed up the kilometres of bendy asphalt road. In the danger-red car, I overtook a couple of dodderers on the road when it straightened out. I had less than an hour and a quarter before Ronald met with Karin, and I needed to talk to her before he did, even though I was suspended. I pushed the accelerator in to press the car forward and Stefanie's car responded with a pleasing increase of sound and speed. I didn't care how angry she'd be when she found out I had left her and Hans behind. I wasn't doing this to arrest Wouter. My mobile rang, but the caller display showed it was Hans, so I didn't pick it up. I didn't want him to stop me.

The villages flew by on either side of the motorway and, where the railway ran parallel to the road, a train was struggling to keep up with me as I hurtled south, accompanied by the flashes of speed cameras, back to Amsterdam.

Chapter Twenty-nine

Twenty minutes before Ronald was due to arrive I walked up the steps leading to Omega's front door.

'Karin, please,' I said to the receptionist. 'It's urgent.' I didn't have to show the badge I didn't have any more as her face said she recognised me. She walked me through to the boardroom where Karin and her lawyer sat side by side. Papers were strewn over the cherrywood table; Karin held a black and gold fountain pen in her hand.

'You need to tell me the truth,' I said before she could even open her mouth. 'We can protect you, but you need to tell me what really happened.' I reached over the chair, put the tape recorder on the table in front of her and switched it on. I stayed standing.

She screwed the golden top back on the pen, put it down on the table and slid some of the papers face-down underneath a copy of *Het Financieele Dagblad*.

I rested my hands on the back of the cherrywood chair. It was the same one I'd sat on last week, only this time I was right opposite Karin. She was sitting at the long side of the table, no longer at the head, as if she'd handed over control.

Under the apple and jasmine perfume there was a whiff of perspiration.

'I know you're scared,' I said quietly, 'but I also know that he needs to be stopped. Only you can help us to do that.'

She collected the rest of the papers in a pile and straightened them.

'Ronald de Boer will be here in', I checked my watch, 'fifteen minutes. You have until then to tell me.' The traffic had been horrendous because of the snow, and the journey to Amsterdam had taken much longer than I'd anticipated. 'Tell me what happened after Otto's death and what happened just before Anton's.'

She took a deep breath in and out. An award naming her Dutch Business Woman of the Year rested against the wall. Her left hand disappeared up the right sleeve of her jacket and the sound of her bitten nails scratching her skin was loud in the quiet room.

'Karin, please.' I turned to her lawyer. 'Please, convince her. This is the only way.' He looked at me in silence, his expression sympathetic and aloof at the same time. My heartbeat was ticking out how many seconds I had left until the ten minutes would be up. I needed to speak, to use words to cover the thumping in my chest.

'OK,' I said, 'I'll tell you what I think happened. You were absolutely right – Otto wanted you out of the way, so he could meet up with someone in private. Only it wasn't Anton. This wasn't about your betrayal and your affair. This was about something else. He was meeting Wouter. Wouter

Vos, whose testimony bankrupted his firm and put him in jail. This was about that betrayal, wasn't it?'

Karin picked up her BlackBerry.

'The loss of his firm probably hit him harder than the loss of his wife.'

Now she gave a short laugh. 'That much is true,' she said under her breath. Her lawyer reached out his hand and put it on her arm, ruffling the material of her peacock-blue jacket.

But I'd been given a response, a reaction, so I kept talking. 'Anton saw Wouter when he left your house.'

She shook her head.

'He drives off. Wouter stays behind to wait for Otto. Something happens, and Wouter shoots Otto. Wouter knows Anton saw him so he comes up with the idea of being a witness. As long as we don't know he was the whistle-blower, and his name isn't on any of our records, Wouter has no motive – but Anton does. Wouter probably figured it out together with his schoolfriend Ronald de Boer.'

Something changed in her face; her mouth twitched at the sound of his name. She lifted her head, and now that she was not at the other side of a pane of glass, I could see that the wrinkles around her eyes were still red and inflamed. I recognised the signs of long periods of crying.

'Maybe Ronald even suggested it,' I went on. 'Ronald stalls the case: as long as he's working on it, it will never go to court. But then it is taken over by Amsterdam. And Ronald contacts you. In order to remove both Anton and Wouter's names, the files need to disappear. Ronald

333

won't respond to Amsterdam's requests and it will all go away. Is that what happened?'

Our eyes seemed glued together.

'Karin, this time it won't go away. Right now, you might think it will, because nothing happened for twelve years after Otto's murder. But this is different. A second person has died. You're a key witness. How safe do you think you are?'

Her eyes slid from mine to something unimportant on the wall behind me. Her hand disappeared up her sleeve again. As she scratched, the cloth rode up over her arm and uncovered the raw-red marks of eczema.

I gazed up at the painted ceiling and the Dutch ships in full sail, and said, 'After Otto's death, there was a balance, don't you see? You and Anton wanted Otto dead just as much as Wouter did.'

Her expression contradicted me.

'OK, maybe you didn't *want* him dead, but it was convenient, wasn't it?'

She rested her hand on her forehead. 'It was,' she whispered. I didn't ask her to repeat it; the tape might pick it up anyway and it was not important.

'Wouter knows Anton won't rock the boat, you won't either, and you're both implicated in the theft of the files. It's a perfect equilibrium. This is different.' I pulled the chair back and sat down. 'Karin, you know this is different, don't you?' I glanced down at my watch: five minutes left. I wished Stefanie was here to give me a financial analogy that would make Karin understand. 'You worked so hard to build this firm, to go from being a secretary to Dutch Business Woman of the Year. That will all vanish. Both your husbands have been murdered. Unless we make an arrest, that suspicion will always hang over you. Your reputation will be in tatters, your investors will run away, your firm will collapse.'

Karin exchanged a glance with her lawyer and that's when I knew she'd talk. I'd finally got through to her. I let a silence fall and allowed it to last. In my head I counted – nine, ten, eleven . . . and didn't fill the gap.

'He came,' she said. Her lawyer put his hand on her arm again. She turned her face to him. 'I've got no choice. Let me talk. Anton would have wanted me to talk.' She looked back to me. 'Twenty minutes after that old man Huizen left.'

'Wouter Vos?' I said.

She nodded. This time I did point to the recorder and she repeated, 'It was Wouter Vos. I hadn't seen him in years, but he hadn't changed a bit. Smarter, better dressed, but otherwise still the same spiteful little creep. Because of Otto's losses we had to lay off a group of people. We thought that if we scaled the firm down, we might weather the storm.'

She closed her eyes and rubbed a finger under her lower lashes. 'Anyway, Wouter Vos was one of the people we chose to let go. He didn't wait long to send that file to the police. We knew there must have been a whistle-blower but I didn't know who it was until after Otto's death. There were plenty of people who wanted to see our downfall, but I never thought it was Wouter. He seemed too . . .' she sighed, 'too nice. Can you believe it?'

She let the weight of her chignon tip her head back and looked at the ceiling. 'So there he was, back on our doorstep.

Anton walked out with him and didn't come back. I heard the shot. I was scared – I stayed indoors. I was such a coward.'

She stopped and took a couple of breaths. 'Then Ronald de Boer turned up, with the rest of the police circus. He said I should under no circumstances reveal to anybody that Wouter Vos had been there. He frightened me.' She stared back at me. 'What was I going to do? He was police. He'd set it up from the start. Even after Otto's death it was Ronald de Boer who made it clear that nobody would take Anton's word over Wouter's, not as long as he was on the case, not while nobody knew Wouter was the whistle-blower. Wouter had shot Otto in self-defence, he said. We had an hour to pick up those files and everything would be over. Without those files, there'd be no witness statement and Ronald promised us he'd keep it that way. So Anton got two of his friends, ex-colleagues, to do it, using names of the police-officers who'd pissed him off.'

Her voice sounded harsh over the sibilance of the swear-word. 'It was fine until you turned up. You and your digging and your bloody colleague. I recognised her but she didn't recognise me. What did you call it? An equilibrium. And that was fine.'

'Karin,' the lawyer said. I could kick him for interrupting her, but I supposed that was his job.

'Anton was fed up with it. We talked it through and decided that giving back those files was the best thing to do. But how did Wouter know that?'

'I don't know,' I said – and then I remembered my father saying that he had told Ronald, who had warned him not to go. I rubbed my forehead with my hand when I realised that of course it had been my father who'd told Ronald de Boer.

The door behind me opened. Karin stared over my shoulder, her expression both frightened and angry. I saw who it was and had only just enough time to take the tape recorder and stuff it in my bag before Ronald grabbed my arm.

'What the hell are *you* doing here?'

'How could you, Ronald?' I wrenched my arm free and spat the words in his face. 'You arrested my father. You arrested him to save your friend! You worked with my father for years. He trusted you. But you gave him up for Wouter. Was friendship more important than doing your job?'

'Your father shot Anton Lantinga. You're the one who can't see straight.'

I tipped my head sideways, surprised that he was continuing to lie and was keeping up this story.

'Wouter left just before six and your father arrived just as he got into his car and drove away. I'm sorry, Lotte.' He reached out a hand.

I jumped out of the way.

He smiled a small smile at me. 'This is why I had to get you suspended. How did you say it? Is family more important than doing your job?'

I pointed at the bag and said clearly: 'You're wrong. It's all on the tape. It was the other way round: Wouter came to the house after my father had long gone.'

From behind me, Karin's lawyer confirmed this.

Ronald paled. He didn't say anything for a few seconds. The silence hung in the room like a poisonous cloud.

Then: 'She's lying.' He swung his grey eyes back to me. 'Your father *was* at Anton's house after Wouter left. And you're suspended.'

Karin made a movement with her hand and started to say something. I interrupted her. 'It doesn't matter. It's all on tape – I have the recording.' I smiled at Ronald. 'Oh, and I spoke to your wife – she was very helpful too. Anyway, as Karin will tell you, Wouter was there last. He came twenty minutes after my father left.' I waved the tape recorder at him. 'It's all on here.'

His mouth contorted as if he'd bitten into an unripe Granny Smith apple. I put my hand on the rough material of his sleeve. 'Thanks, Ronald. I really appreciate the way you tried to protect us.' The taste of sarcasm on my tongue was as addictive as caffeine. 'I—' My mobile rang. I expected him to bar my way but he just stood and stared as I left the boardroom. Out in the hallway, I kept the tape in my hand-bag, securely pressed against my body by my elbow.

The display on my phone told me it was Hans. 'What's up?' I asked.

'Where the fuck are you?'

'Amsterdam. With Karin Lantinga. We're done. Make sure you keep Wouter Vos there.'

'We could have kept him here if only we had a car – if you hadn't taken our car. He went out of a back window almost an hour ago. We couldn't follow him.'

'Why didn't you let me know?' I checked my phone and saw the six missed calls that I'd ignored on purpose. 'Sorry, I didn't hear my phone,' I lied. An hour ago? I knew where he was headed. 'Could you call the boss? Get him to release my father. He's innocent – I've got proof. Karin confirmed that Wouter Vos came to their house *after* my father had left. And please ask my father to call me as soon as he's free.'

In the downstairs reception, I rested my hand on the door handle and took a few moments to collect myself. My stomach fluttered at the thought of stepping outside without a weapon to protect myself. My hesitation only lasted for a couple of seconds, for then I thought of my father in prison and opened the door.

I left the building and waited at the top of the steps. The man I was expecting appeared, walking along the canal, head bent as if to protect the mobile stuck to his ear. I knew he'd come here to tidy up the last loose end or remove the last witness, but he was too late for that. His eyes met mine when he was twenty metres away and he snapped the phone shut.

'That was Ronald,' he said loudly; his voice could carry a much longer distance.

'What did he say?'

'That I should hand myself in.'

'It's over, Wouter.' The words came out in a cloud of breath that disappeared long before the reverberations died away. I imagined the sound leaving my mouth and arriving in his ear.

He stood still on the pavement below and gestured with his chin at the door behind me. 'Did she talk?' His hands didn't leave his pockets.

'She did.'

'Ronald told her not to, but I knew she would. He thought warning her off was a better solution than the one I had in mind.' Behind him, a woman on a bicycle passed along the canal, a small child on the luggage-carrier behind her.

I saw his hand move in his pockets. Snow started to fall and cut through the air between us. I was listening out for the door behind me to open, but so far nothing. The seconds stretched. I thought I should say something, but I didn't know what. Instead I stood there in silence and watched the wind pull at the blond curls at the back of his neck.

'You'll want the gun,' he said.

Actually, I wanted my own gun – so much I could feel the weight of it in my right hand. But it wasn't here. It was in Chief Inspector Moerdijk's drawer. So I waited, waited for what was going to happen next. I didn't say anything. My focus was entirely on his right hand in his pocket. A man on a bicycle pedalled past, followed by a blue car.

He pulled the gun out.

'Give it to me,' I said.

'Ronald told you to drop the case,' he said.

My hair tickled my jawline, but I didn't touch it. I stood still, frozen to the spot. I only allowed my lips to move when I said, 'Otto's death was unavoidable. Wasn't it self-defence?' I remembered the painting on his wall, the vibrant colours of the painter's dreams. I remembered how Wouter had looked when I'd asked if his dreams were vibrant like this. Instead they must have been as guilt-ridden as mine.

'That's what I told Ronald,' he agreed. 'In a way, it was. Just longer term.'

He kept the gun pointed to the ground. I forced myself to look him in the eye or to look at his mouth as he was forming the words. Anything but at the metal in his hands.

'Otto didn't even know how to use a gun,' he went on. 'He stood there in his white clothes like some overweight baker, pulling the trigger without taking the safety off. He looked incredibly surprised when nothing happened, started cursing the guy in prison who got him the weapon. It was so easy to take it off him and use it.' Wouter shook his head sadly. 'He was going to keep coming at me, and maybe next time he wouldn't fail. I had to get to him before he could get to me. That's the only reason I'd agreed to meet him in the first place: to see what he knew.'

I swallowed the sudden saliva in my mouth. That hadn't been an act of self-defence: that had been the act of a calculating killer. He'd come here with a gun to get rid of the only person who knew. Now an additional person knew and he wouldn't hesitate.

My muscles tensed up in a need to act but I was too far away to tackle him. If I'd still had my gun, I'd have stood a chance. Now all possibility of action was taken away by my suspension, and I observed every centimetre of movement as he lifted the gun higher. Some part of me wanted him to do it – the same part that had wanted Ben van Ravensberger to shoot me two weeks ago. The same part that couldn't scrub away the feeling of Paul's fingers on my body and in my hair, however much I wanted to. I knew I wouldn't get my job back, not after today. What did I have to live for?

Unlike Ben, Wouter Vos wouldn't miss. The range was too close and I wouldn't have time to react. My feet were frozen to the spot, on the freshly wiped top of the steps. Out of the corners of my eyes I checked the street, making sure that no innocent bystanders would get hurt, no playing children, no cycling mothers. I didn't look at the weapon in his hand; I kept my eyes on Wouter's face, watched the wind unravel the slicked-back hair, hoped the cold would steam up his glasses. I held my hands out to the side, palms turned towards him.

'I'm not armed,' I told him. 'Put the gun away.' My voice didn't tremble. I kept telling myself that if I kept my eyes on his, he wouldn't shoot – but I knew it was a lie.

He steadied his right hand with his left.

The door behind me opened with a click, which tore the tension like an exploding bomb. I jolted, but kept looking at Wouter. His eyes swerved away from me but then his shoulders relaxed and he smiled. But he didn't put his gun down.

'Put the gun away, Wouter.' From behind me Ronald mumbled a repeat of my words as if he didn't really want to say them.

Wouter didn't react. His gun didn't move.

'Drop your weapon.' Ronald said it louder, more securely. 'We can still get away with this.'

342

'No, we can't. This is where it ends, Wouter. I've covered for you, but it's gone too far. You lied to me.'

Wouter moved his feet wider to stabilise his body against the wind.

'You swore that Anton was still alive when you left. You swore you didn't kill him. *I* took those files from the shed. *I* threatened Karin Petersen. I said not to tell anybody you'd been at their house. God, she thought I knew all along. Put the gun down, Wouter, or I will shoot you.' Ronald's voice croaked. He coughed.

Wouter didn't say anything but clicked the safety off the gun. If I'd still had mine, this was when I'd have had no choice but to shoot him.

'You're my friend, Wouter, and I don't want to do this. But I will.'

'This is your fault, Ronald.' Wouter gestured at me with his gun. 'You told me you had her under control. You told me you got her suspended. But here she is. That's not under control.'

'Stop it, Wouter. You're threatening an unarmed police officer,' Ronald said. '*Put the gun down.* It's over.'

Wouter's lips worked although no words came out. With his eyes blinking behind the glasses, he signalled the thoughts inside his head. Many snowflakes fell in a few seconds as we stood and waited. The wind caressed my face as if to comfort me. Would the wind's glancing touch be the last thing I felt? Would the sound of my heartbeat and the distant rumble of the traffic be the last thing I heard? Exhaust fumes the last thing I smelled? Would the sight of Wouter and the frozen canal behind him be the last thing I saw?

Then there was the sound of sirens, the high and low two-tone getting louder and closer. Wouter moved his finger. I heard the shot. Somebody screamed. A shard of ice crashed in my right shoulder, then radiated out in heat. I dropped to my knees.

In response, a shot roared out from behind me.

I saw Wouter fall. I watched his body until my own pain dragged me further down and I lay on the ground, the stones bringing a chill to my face.

I wasn't going to die. The black railing of the steps hung against the falling snow. I reached out, grabbed hold of the cold metal and pulled myself up until I was sitting. Pain soared on the movement. I pressed my hand against my shoulder and watched the blood stain the skin red from between my fingers down along the tendons like a henna tattoo. I tore my eyes away from the hypnotic stream and looked at Ronald. His eyes were fixed on the broken body at the bottom of the stairs.

The sirens came to a halt.

'I'm so sorry,' Ronald whispered, his voice drowned in the cacophony of police cars. I knew he wasn't talking to me.

Footsteps approached – my colleagues in uniform. I turned my head and saw Ronald hand over his police-standard Walther P5. 'We need to get you to the hospital,' said an officer I'd never seen before. I recognised Erik, who had found me by the side of the canal a few days ago.

My mobile rang: I knew it was the call I'd been waiting for. I kept my left hand pressed against my shoulder. Erik answered the phone and held it to my ear.

'Hi, Lotte, it's me.' It was my father. 'They let me out.'

'That's good, Dad, that's good.'

As I waited for the ambulance, whose tones I could hear in the distance, my father's voice flowed continuously like a stream of comfort in my ear. He chatted and I said little, until the paramedics walked up the stairs. 'I've got to go now, Dad,' I said – I didn't want to worry him too much – 'but can I come and stay with you for a while?'

'Of course, Lotte. You can stay as long as you like. When will you be here?'

My pain subsided a bit and at last became bearable. 'I'll give you a call tomorrow.' They'd want to keep me in hospital at least overnight.

'I look forward to it,' my father said.

'Me too.' I smiled.

Acknowledgements

Many people have given up their time to read all or parts of this novel and I'm grateful to them all, but especially to Alan Buckingham, Caroline Buckingham and Chris Beton. They provided invaluable feedback on the characters and plot, and their positive words kept me going. I'd like to thank my agent Allan Guthrie for all his work on shaping my novel and finding it a good home, and finally Krystyna Green and all at Constable & Robinson for believing in this book.